Railroad
of
Souls

Jen Brunett

DEDICATION

For those of you who say you can't. You can. You will.

Thank you for giving this book a chance.

ACKNOWLEDGMENTS

Thank you to my husband Tommy, who, forever has faith in me when I have little faith in myself. For always pushing me to move forward and not doubting.

Thank you also to Cash and Jagger, for having patience when Mommy needed to work. I love the three of you endlessly.

To my editor, Sarah Liu of Three Fates Editing, for polishing this little piece of my heart.

To the fine folks over at YeahWrite and NaNoWriMo who volunteer their time to help others find their creative voices. This little book started from a writing prompt and a 30-day writing challenge. Five years later, here we are. Thank you.

1 CHELSEA

I can hear the train before I see it and instinct has me searching. There is a track that runs maybe half a mile behind my house, just past the grove of rotten crabapple trees. At night the moonlight hits them in such a way that they look like upright corpses. I say they are rotten, as they don't bloom a single flower in the spring, but somehow there are always a few stray crabapples that make their way into my yard.

Louder now, I can just make out a bit of silver with dabs of red and blue streaking its way behind the trees—a passenger train. Grandpa used to tell me stories about the old wooden cargo trains that rode on these very same rails and how people used to sneak onto them in the wee hours of the morning to start a new life in another place far away. There was always a hint of sadness in his voice, and he'd talk about how sometimes life isn't just so simple for people and they have to get away to find themselves.

A frantic knock on my front door startles me—it sounds like a desperate woodpecker. I'm almost afraid to answer it. My mother's eyebrows shoot up over the pages of the book she's been reading I look at her, shrug, and click the lock. Autumn bursts through the door, almost hitting me square in the face. She's panting, her hair a disheveled mess, her face prickled with pink heat.

"Autumn! What's wrong?" I don't really mean to laugh, but do anyway, until the desperate look in her eyes stops me.

"Billy McKenzie's actually missing!" she blurts out.

"What do you mean, missing?" I ask. "What happened?"

"I don't know for sure. My dad heard it from a friend of his at work who knows one of the deputies who responded to Billy's mom's call." Autumn is talking so fast at this point I feel like I'm only catching every other word, but my mind fills in the blanks.

"You know how you mentioned that Billy wasn't in school this week?" Autumn says.

"Yeah sure, I mean I could actually see the smart board for the first time this year. Why they won't let me sit anywhere else in class is beyond me. It's frustrating, you kn—"

"I guess he wasn't in his bedroom this morning." Autumn cuts through my tangent. "or the day before that or before that even. He wasn't anywhere. It's like he just…disappeared or something!"

"Oh my god. Does Jeff know?" In third grade, Billy talked some bigger neighborhood kids out of beating Jeff senseless. Billy was friends with them and could have easily walked away from the situation, but he didn't. Jeff has always been grateful.

"No, I didn't even let my father finish talking, I just ran over here."

I text Jeff to come over as soon as possible with emphasis on the exclamation points. I feel like the text barely sent before I hear his front door slam closed from down the street. It's only as he arrives that I realize we are still standing in the foyer of my house, with the door wide open.

"What's up ladies? Why the franta-text?"

Autumn looks at Jeff, her cheeks taking on a new shade of red as she struggles with the words. I close the door, take Jeff's hand, and lead him upstairs to my room, Autumn dragging her feet behind us. He's chattering the whole way up the stairs, and I tell him to be quiet when we get to my room.

"Look," I tell him. "I don't know how else I'm going to say this so I'm just going to spit it out… Billy McKenzie wasn't in his room this morning."

He raises his eyebrows, his smile a crescent moon. "And how would you know this, my dear Chelsea? I always thought maybe you had a thing for him, but I never knew you paid him morning visits."

"No not me, Autumn!"

2

"What?" Autumn is stunned. "I do NOT have a thing for Billy, and I do not visit his home in the mornings!"

Jeff looks back and forth between Autumn and me. No one is saying anything. "Uh... hello?" He grabs my hand and taps it like a mic. "Is this thing on?" He drops it, and I tense my fist leaving it where he let go. "You two better start explaining yourselves here, or I'm going to go home and catch the last of *The Bold and the Beautiful.*"

"Jeffrey, no." I free my own hand from its frozen state and take his hand in both of mine. "Billy is *missing*. Like, kidnapped or something."

"What! How? When?"

"We don't know," Autumn says finally.

We both watch Jeff for signs of a reaction, but he remains stoic. Then he does something that surprises me. He gently takes his hands from my own and walks out of my room. I watch him disappear out of sight, and it's only then that I realize that he has no shoes or socks on. I giggle awkwardly. I'm worried for my friend, but also him being barefoot on a cold late afternoon is *so* him.

Autumn and Jeff have been my two best friends since we were crawling on each other's living room floors. Our street was full of elderly couples who eventually passed away. As they did, younger families started moving in. We were among those families to bring life back into the neighborhood.

Autumn tells me that she should probably go home for dinner and apologizes to me for bursting in the way she did. I accept her apology while biting my tongue because of the irony of her spontaneity. She has a knack for doing things without thinking then feeling bad about it later, it's a continuous cycle with her. We both wear confusion in our hearts and aren't sure what to say next. I tell her I'll text her later, as I have to go and visit my grandparents shortly.

As she makes her way back down the stairs, the shallow ache in my chest that I've had over Billy's disappearance is replaced by a fresh feeling of anxiety about seeing my grandparents. "This is all too much right now," I whisper to no one in particular as I survey the backyard through the window in the hall. The train has moved on and those godforsaken trees are the only things staring back at me.

2 EDGAR

"Edgar Benjamin Slate! Get over here right now!"

Edgar winced at the sound of his mother's tone. He hated getting in trouble, especially by his mother, and reluctantly put the stick down that he'd been using to trace circles in the mud. He figured the more time he took, the more Mama might forget that she was so angry but clearly that wasn't the case. He sighed, then creeped into the house, feeling like a dog that had chewed the leg from a chair and forgot he did it.

His mother was standing in the family room holding a large shovel. He hadn't started cleaning up after the horses yet... and it was piling up.

"Aw, Ma, Do I have to?"

"Edgar if your Papa, God rest his soul, knew you were such a terrible farmer, he'd make sure you lived in the barn with those horses until you figured out how to care for them proper. Now go on, get!"

He grabbed the shovel from her hand and trudged through the back door towards the barn, dragging his feet, not bothering to look her in the eyes. It's true, he was a terrible farmer. He loved animals and loved to feed them, but he hated the cleaning up part. He took a resentful stab at the manure and began shoveling pile after pile into bags and lining them up in the carts. This wasn't what he was supposed to do with his life. Grunting and resentful at first he eventually fell into a rhythm He let his mind wander as he worked and a glint of sunshine on the blade of the shovel transported him back to a time when things were much easier, and he lost himself in the memory.

***

He was seven years old, holding Mama's hand as they walked through the city. Papa took out his pocket watch every few minutes as they walked to make sure they were still on time for the circus. He didn't like to be late.

Papa, "the best banker the Flower City has ever had," according to a few news articles that Mama had clipped, slipped his hand under the jacket of his sack suit to pull the watch from his trouser pocket. It caught the sun just so and bounced right back into Edgar's eyes.

"Papa! Can you put that thing away? It's making my eyes hurt!"

"I'm sorry, Eddie," Papa said through a mustache-covered smile, ruffling Edgar's hair. Mama, of course, started to fuss over Edgar's unruly black mop, trying to pat it down, mumbling this and that about "society" and "standards"—she was a stickler for appearances. She was always threatening to shave him with Auntie's sheep shears, but he wouldn't have it, preferring to run and hide for hours until she caved, agreeing that he could have his long hair so long as he pinned it under a hat or slicked it back with oils.

Edgar tried to swat her away—he couldn't stand being coddled like a toddler—and almost knocked off her great flowered hat in the process. Mama hardly noticed; her patience was saintly even in the midsummer heat while nearing the end of her pregnancy.

"Look at this, Edgar! What a sight to behold!" Mr. Slate beamed as he made the family of three fifths stop on the bridge overlooking the Erie Canal. He was overzealous about grand things, and the Erie Canal was certainly one of the grandest, according to Papa. He made them pause in front it of whenever they were in this part of the city.

"This, my dear boy, used to be the most powerful mode of transportation in the civilized world!"

Edgar gazed down upon a depressed-looking boat with a single passenger lugging its way through the dark water toward some unknown destination and wished he shared his father's enthusiasm.

"Not much to look at now, is it son?"

"Not really, Dad," Edgar said in a soft voice, not sure if it would upset his father who had just bent down to his level to look him squarely in the eyes.

"Eddie, let this canal be a lesson to you. This waterway was a hand-built marvel, connecting us to the entire state, opening up commerce, making Rochester a literal boom town, eventually putting me at the center of keeping books for all the profits coming and going. Then the trains came, their thunder overpowering the canal, and I had to close the canal books and open new ones.

"The canal is a symbol of the vision of man to make a greater connection to the entire world! See what happens when you open doors, Eddie? You open one and others open for you. Just like this here canal and the trains that came after."

"Yeah they killed the canal." Edgar was annoyed that his father kept calling him Eddie. It sounded like a baby name. He much preferred his middle name. Benjamin. It sounded grown up and important. But his father wouldn't let him use that name because it reminded him too much of Mama's crazy brother.

"Oh, but it didn't die, did it?" said Papa. "It's still here, beautiful as ever, carrying the essence of the souls of all the hard workers in its mighty waters. Sure, there's talk of expansion and making it great again, but I think it's had its day. The trains are being built too fast, can carry goods farther. But the canal played its part. This, my son, was the catalyst to something even more amazing!" He stood up, sweeping both of his arms out wide, looking like a proud giant with his top hat touching the clouds for all Edgar could see. "And it will always be a reminder of the vision of humanity. Just like people, its soul will never die. It'll change form and become still more beautiful." He patted Edgar's head, gently this time.

Sometimes Papa's grandiose gestures made him a little uneasy as he knew his papa wanted him to walk in his footsteps, to learn the banking trade, to see the magnitude of all things. But Edgar preferred what was in front of him, and right now, that was the circus.

***

Lost in his thoughts, Edgar had bagged and crated over half of the pile without even realizing it. He looked over to Mama, who was hanging clothes on the line as the twins squatted by the house, sewing clothes for their dolls. Mama smiled at him through the space made between the billowing sheets.

They'd had to make many sacrifices over the past two years. The fire in the city had destroyed everything, forcing them out to the country. Papa had traded his tailored suit and gold watches for a pitchfork and livestock. And then he disappeared, leaving the four of them with Edgar as the man of the house, though barely a man himself, at fifteen years old.

Turning back to his work, he hoisted the shovel in a high arc preparing to tackle the remainder of the pile when he heard a tiny screech and let the shovel escape from his hands with a muted thud as it hit the ground. He hadn't seen Maureen and Mellie sneak up behind him and he was thankful he didn't hurt them. Relieved he glared a warning, but he couldn't stay mad at them for long.

Maureen looked stunned, but Mellie's smile was as bright as the day and she held out her doll for him. "Do you like the pretty dress I made for Beth? It looks just like mine, see, see!"

Edgar took the doll and admired her handiwork. "You did a fine job, Miss Mellie." He handed it back to her and playfully tugged on of Maureen's braids. "You two go on and help Mama before you get hurt over here! I love you both!" he called to them as they giggled and skipped off to see their mama.

Edgar walked the few feet over to the old barn and climbed the ladder to the loft with awkward, gangly limbs. The loft was Edgar's own, and Mama or the girls weren't allowed inside. The only person allowed in was his best friend, Josiah.

He bent low in the corner, sifting through the hay until he uncovered a broken piece of mirror and a black top hat. He put the hat on, fixing it in a downward angle so part of his right eye was covered. He remembered the circus ring leader wearing it just like that. The clowns, animals, even the sweets, he didn't care much for. It was the ring leader that took all his attention.

He'd never seen a man so powerful, more powerful than even Papa. The ring leader was different somehow. The red suit made him appear magical, with his booming voice and the way everyone responded to him. He wasn't just larger than life, he was the oxygen of the circus. Even the lions seemed to bow before him. He'd been untouchable, something Edgar wished he could be.

He strutted around the loft, pitchfork in hand, stretching one long leg after the other in slow motion as if his feet were testing the temperature of water, announcing to his audience of horses below about the marvels of the Slate Circus! He strode all the way to the other side of the barn, throwing back the double wooden window doors, casting his pitchfork aside. "Edgar Benjamin Slate! Ringleader Extraordinaire!" he shouted to a great expanse of land in front of him. And though his voice didn't boom, he imagined the land and everything in it responding to him, bending slightly at his command.

Edgar slumped down onto the window ledge, allowing his feet to dangle high above the ground, drying out the sludge on his boots as he looked out at the field which was completely empty and dead, save for the lone crabapple tree way off in the distance, and the incredible forest beyond that.

As he sat there gazing at the tree, a thought came to him. For as such a mess he made of being a farmer, he did have a bit of luck when it came to plants. He had even managed to keep that maple tree in the front yard alive for two years now when it had been struggling. Why couldn't he turn that field into an orchard? If he worked hard enough, in a few years, he could start growing enough fruit to overtake the manure business.

That evening at supper Edgar asked his mother why they had chosen this place. Why did they have to move here?

Mama responded irritably. "Edgar, the fire in the city ruined everything for a lot of people. Most everyone went bankrupt overnight and had to start a new life for themselves. As you know, we had nothing, not a penny, to our names. And this bit of land— well they were practically just giving it away." She looked out the kitchen window and continued in a more hushed tone, "I guess the owners lost someone in the fire, and it was too painful for them. They wanted to get out as fast as possible. Start a new life."

Turning back to Edgar she said while pointing in the general direction of the ceiling, the front yard, and then to the backyard, respectively, "So here is the house. Here is the land, and there is your shovel. After you finish those potatoes, please go out and finish your chores."

"Okay, Mom." He knew that there could be worse things than having to shovel up after horses. He didn't know why he asked his mom about the land. Maybe he just wanted a way to hear about Papa. After he had disappeared the autumn before last, it had not been easy for either one of them, even though no one talked about it, he knew that they all were secretly waiting for Papa to come home. Mama also refused to let Edgar play past the barn on the barren part of their land. She said that if the horses wouldn't play back there then there was no reason he needed to.

Edgar considered this again as he finished the last of his meal and just for the heck of it, decided to tell her of his plan to grow fruit trees in the very field she so despised. Mama scoffed her response. The soil could have mold for all they knew, and she didn't want him traipsing around where he could track something back into the barn or house which really did make sense to Edgar, but he thought it was at least worth looking into. There was certainly *one* thing growing out there—maybe the land just hadn't had the love and attention it needed for a long, long time. He told her so.

"Sweetie, there is only *one* apple tree out there, and it's a squatty old crabapple tree to boot. There has to be a reason there's only one. You can't grow shit out there that's why."

"No but you can grow shit in here," he said as he looked out toward the barn. Mama made to backhand Edgar but he ducked just in time. "Edgar Benjamin, don't you use profanity in this house! It's bad luck: just look at what happened to your Uncle Benjamin. God scorned him for his constant cussing. Now get out there and finish up before it's too dark, please!"

"Uncle Benjamin was as cuckoo as they come, Ma!"

Her burning gaze told him that the conversation had ended, and he succumbed to the inevitable making his way to the back door. His shovel was waiting for him outside like an obedient puppy. He stopped in the doorway, hiding his green eyes between strands of shaggy black hair.

"Mama?"

"What!" Her face was an angry shade of red.

"That was a good joke though, wasn't it…about the… ya know… manure?"

Mama gaped at him for a moment, and he watched the color drain, leaving her cheeks a pale pink. Her eyes brightened and the thin line of her lips curved slightly.

"Yes… I suppose it was." She bit down on her bottom lip. "And your uncle wasn't crazy. He was a decent, honorable man. Quite the piano player, too." Edgar watched as her whole body sunk into itself, like a little girl whose balloon got away from her.

"I'd always admired him, Edgar. That's why I named you after him. Or partly at least." Her jaw clenched, and Edgar seized the opportunity to put to rest a question that had bothering him for ages.

"Why did Papa hate him so much, Mama?"

She tugged at the crucifix that was hidden under her blouse, exposing the thin chain that encircled her neck, and rubbed it between her thumb and finger. She opened her mouth then closed it a few times before finally speaking. "Listen, I never wanted to talk about this because I don't think it fair to judge someone you never met. But you're nearly a man now, so I think you can understand."

Edgar nodded.

"He was special, Edgar. Different than most folks. He could do strange and wonderful things, but he kept it hidden because most folk don't take kindly to sorcery. But I never saw it as sorcery, I thought it was a gift from God himself."

Edgar had stopped breathing and sputtered his next words. "What do you mean, sorcery? Was he a witch or something?"

"No, no, nothing like that. But he did have an unbelievable talent. We used to sit for long hours on the bank of the Genesee River, and he would tell me how the river felt as it dumped over the falls or how it struggled to move upstream because the natural order of things was to flow downward. He got a whipping more times that I could count for refusing to tend to our land. He said it hurt the land and he couldn't handle its sadness."

Her mouth quivered and she cleared her throat. "Benjamin wasn't the type of person that could be caged. He needed to spread

11

his wings and experience the world. I like to say he was larger than life itself. The world just wasn't ready for him, Edgar." She shrugged. "It just wasn't. So after he'd been in that institute for a while, he snuck into the place where they keep all the residents' medications and swallowed down whatever he could find. One of the nurses found him the next day, just a shell of the man that used to be my brother."

"I thought you didn't believe in the hocus-pocus stuff, Ma."

"I never really did, and I still don't. But I believed in my brother."

Edgar looked down at the ground not sure what to say next, and his mother approached him, putting her strong arms around him. "Anyway. Your father didn't believe in his lust for the sins of the night nor his choice to end his life. But both were great men, Edgar. Don't you forget it."

"Of course, Ma, I won't."

"Now go out there and finish up. I love you."

"I love you, too." Edgar took up his shovel again and started working before the light became too dim. He considered their conversation and gained a new respect for his Uncle Benjamin. Edgar wanted to be just as a free spirit as he was, as he didn't like to be caged either, he thought. He looked again to the empty field, knowing that his orchard would pave the way to freedom.

3 CHELSEA

Grandpa and Grandma have been living at Silver Linings, a small retirement community down the street from our home for quite a few years now. Grandpa has lung cancer, something about the dust he breathed in from working in factories when he was younger… I knew he'd been pretty sick over the last week, but I had no idea it had come to this. I walk in, with my father following behind, and there is Grandma sitting at the dining room table, her feeble hands wrapped around a petite teacup. A nurse is sitting across from her, following suit, and I intentionally avoid eye contact with my grandparents' bedroom.

Grandma seems so delicate and exhausted. Her hands tremble around her cup as though her tea is made of lead. sit down next to her, set her cup down on the table, and take her hand in mine. It's only when our hands touch that she seems to realize that we're here. She has the beginning stages of dementia and occasionally drifts off somewhere mentally, like she has someone important to talk to inside of herself—a one-sided conversation we never get to hear. I wonder where she goes. Does she forget that she has another life here with us? Does she know which world is real?

When she does come back, she picks up right where she left off, like she never left. If she remembers where she went, she doesn't talk about it. Grandpa decided that he was going to take care of her as long as he could, saying that he feels like he's

13

already lived two lifetimes and he's not sure how much more time he'll be given. He's been saying that since I was a little girl.

"Hi Grandma." I try to project my voice, making it stronger. I don't want anyone to hear my voice waver. To give away the fact that the fear over this situation is twisting the pit of my stomach into tiny knots. The air in their little townhouse is thick with the confusion of a lost mind, with my grandfather behind a closed door struggling with his breath, and this stranger of a nurse sitting across from us, expressionless…it's hard for me to breathe.

"Oh Chelsea, Darling," Grandma says, patting my hand, her wise eyes melting before me, "Grandpa loves you so much. So, so much."

And then she continues to stare at me—no not at me, *through* me. I gently squeeze her hand, not taken aback by her sudden silences which I have grown accustomed to. I start to call her name, but the nurse pipes in, and this does surprise me because for a few long moments it seemed like she wasn't real. She hadn't moved or said a word since we arrived.

"Oh, so *you* are Chelsea," she says in a creepy, sing-song voice. It reminds me of the part in a horror movie where the nice little old lady takes the axe she was hiding behind her back and whacks the unsuspecting victim who was helping her get her groceries out of the car.

"Uh yeah." I note the little name tag pinned to her white blouse. *Wendy.*

"Your grandmother's dementia is advancing pretty quickly. I think your grandfather didn't want to draw a lot of attention to it just yet."

I twist my head towards my father, and he looks back at me apologetically. "I guess that would explain why he didn't want many visitors lately," I say, miffed, but it's Wendy who answers.

"Perhaps." There's an odd lilt at the latter half of that word. Something about this woman makes me feel panicky and claustrophobic, and I don't want to talk to her anymore.

"Um… well would you mind if my dad and I spend some time alone with our family?"

The nurse raises her eyebrows. They look like they've been painted on, the middle of each arching into a crescendo which disappears into her hairline as if they are meeting inside to touch her brain. Her short blonde hair curls around her ears, the left side curling one way and the right, the other. As a matter of fact, the more I look at her, the more she looks like a funhouse mirror version of a person. It's totally unsettling.

I can't tell if she's disappointed or amused or both as she wears a smile, but her eyes look like they are frowning. "Okay dear. I just happened to be leaving anyway. I checked on Jo, and he is stable. Since you are family, I feel comfortable leaving you alone here before the next shift comes in."

She picks up an old black medical bag that looks like something Dr. Baker would use on *Little House on the Prairie* and heads for the door. I watch reruns of that show after school sometimes. I suppose it's kind of nostalgic to me, of when my mother and I would watch it together when I was little. I used to make her twist my hair into braids just like Laura Ingalls… except mine were never nearly as perfect as hers, and my uneven blonde hair would poke its way out of the braids, making it look more like a nest of straw. I always wanted to be as brave and strong-willed as she was.

Wendy has a fuzzy green knitted shawl wrapped around her white nursing uniform, the likes of which I have never seen before, and her skirt poofs out like a bell that touches her ankles. I half expect a chime to ding from her body when she moves. As she fixes her shawl, pulling the edges down, some dirt or dust swirls in the air. It doesn't surprise me either because at the moment I'm feeling like this lady is some sort of antique.

She stops at the door and turns around like she's having trouble figuring out which way to go, jerking her body in starts and sputters until she finally faces us and sings, "He'll be here soooon," with a false smile.

When she leaves, I can feel the air physically lighten. I feel like I can breathe again. I look at my father who is now standing next to his mother—he's also still staring at the door. "What the…" I start to say, but he just looks at me like he doesn't know what to say either.

Grandma clears her throat. She's also staring at the door, and I wonder how long she's been "back."

"Come here, Chelsea dear!" she says, bright and cheery like it's the first time she's seen me today. I squat down next to her and put my hand on her shoulder. "How are you doing, Grandma?"

Grandma's voice shifts downward like grinding gears of a car, and she sputters. "The dark man under the soil in spring. Mother Nature's spoil she brings. Full of fruits through autumn's first frost, till summer's end and harvest lots."

The first time she did this, it freaked me out. It still does, but not as much. I try to shake her, but she just keeps going like it's some dark cantrip she has to get out.

"Gourds and apples, we do share. Bright and round then well we'll faire, till winter ushers the frosty air. A vibrant year from seed to harvest, cold to warm to hot to darkness. Yet when warm winds overtake the air, 'tis the season to beware: Indian summer giving rise to the dark man in his guise."

Her finger is keeping time on her teacup, and her eyes are fixed on me as if she's a professor delivering the most important lecture. Yet she sways gently, like a child reciting her favorite rhyme. "The land shifts back, the moon is slight; the devil's fruit appears overnight. Lock your horses tuck your children tight; the dark man will come to you at night."

And then she's gone again, her slow blink the only sign of life. I look to my father for help, but I'm shocked to find that he looks thoughtful and amused.

"Dad! Seriously. What the heck? Doesn't it creep you out when she does this?"

"Huh," he says with a little chuckle, taking off his glasses and rubbing them with his tie. "That was an old nursery rhyme we used to sing when we were kids, I'm pretty sure your grandparents used to sing it, too. About a boogey man!" he says while spreading his fingers in mock horror.

"Some nursery rhyme! Sheesh. Why haven't I ever heard it?" I pout, offended.

"Oh come on, Chelsea, in this day and age if you guys were singing about kids taken from their bedrooms by some dark man, they'd probably send us parents to jail. It's not terribly 'P.C.' now, is it," he says while making invisible quotes in the air.

I want to laugh at his silliness, but I can't. I immediately think of Billy, and my inability to keep a poker face concerns him. He stops smiling. "What's with the face?"

"What if Billy was taken from his house?" I'm assuming Dad, along with the rest of Monroe County, has heard about Billy McKenzie.

"No, honey... I wanted to talk to you about that tonight. And for the record I really was trying to figure out a good time to tell you about your grandmother's declining health, but I didn't know how much you can handle at once."

"Well I can't avoid it either!" I say in defeat as I gesture with both arms in the air signifying the present situation we're in.

"I guess you're right. Look... that family has had a lot of trouble with fighting, and the police get called quite frequently. I'm betting Billy ran away and thought long and hard how to do it so no one could find him. Everyone is working on this case, and I guarantee they will find him. It's a classic runaway scenario."

I'm beginning to think Dad spends too much time watching police shows because he knows way more about things like this than a normal person should, but I say nothing about it.

"I guess so," I mumble, irritated that we've spent way too much time dealing with the nurse, Billy, and waiting for Grandma to pull something else random from her childhood. I feel comfortable here in their home and keep trying not to think that in just the other room Grandpa is dying because right now it feels just completely normal. A little weird. But normal.

Dad breaks the silence by saying, "Are you ready to go and visit your grandfather? There's nothing scary in there or anything. He's in a coma, so it just looks like he's sleeping. Nurse Wendy-weirdo told Mom when she was here earlier that people can still hear you when they are like that. So you can talk to him all you want, okay?"

I have to hand it to Dad for trying to cheer me up by calling out that freakish nurse. He walks over to me and bends down to my level, putting both his hands in mine. "I know this has to be so hard for you. A kid in school goes missing and now this with your grandparents. If you feel like you can't go in and see your grandfather that is perfectly okay. It's whatever you can handle."

Another minute passes, and I tell him that I'm ready. I really want to see Grandpa and say goodbye. I know he'd want to see me, and I feel like I have to do this. I can't not do this, knowing it might be my last opportunity, ever. Before I go in, I ask my father if I can stay overnight in the guest bedroom downstairs. I would just feel better being closer to them.

"Of course, sweetie, of course. Mom will be here, too. We'll call you in to school, and maybe you can ask Autumn or Jeff to collect your homework."

"I'll ask them later." I pause. "And can you tell Mom to bring my phone? Thanks, Dad." I can't believe I even left it at home. I feel so naked without it, like I'm missing an appendage. At that, I approach Grandpa's bedroom door, take a deep breath, and walk inside.

That night as I settle down in the guest bedroom, I don't bother turning on the overhead light, letting the Powerpuff Girls nightlight be the only thing that guides me. My grandparents think that I'm eternally eight years old and made this room just for me when they moved in so I could stay whenever I want. Right now, if I even take one look at these Pepto-pink walls, I will probably vomit. Too much has happened today, and I'm beyond tired.

I replay the strangeness of the day in my head and text Autumn and Jeff about everything—especially the part about the nurse and how it looked like she walked out of the pages of an old encyclopedia from the 1800s, and of course, what I could remember of the old nursery rhyme. I put my phone away and fold my sweater, placing it on the tween-sized white vanity. A paper falls to the floor, and I remember it from earlier today when I crumpled it up to hide it from Miss Carlson in class.

I turn on my phone's flashlight and check out what I've drawn: a crabapple tree from the ugly old orchard in the back of my house. I hate those things..

I remember once when Jeff and Autumn were sleeping over at my house, we sat up for hours trying to name them all. Then we made up stories about how they get up and walk at night and the adventures they got into. Yeah, we didn't sleep at all that night. We almost slept at Jeff's house instead, but it was too late to go sneaking around. My parents never let us play back there; I guess it's not really our property, and they don't want us messing around where we don't belong, which was fine by us. Not to mention, there's a rumor that it's haunted by two little girls with flower dresses and braided hair, who, apparently, like to frolic through the trees. As far as I'm concerned, they can frolic all they want to. I've never had a desire to set a foot in there.

I'm about to crumple it back up and throw it in the trash when I notice something else at the very bottom of the drawing where the roots of the tree pop in and out of the ground. I scratch my head as it looks to be… "A top hat? That's odd."

I throw the paper away, dismissing it, knowing too well that my mind likes to throw me curve balls. As soon as I cover myself with the quilt dotted with strawberries, I begin to sob more than I ever have in my entire life. I think of Grandpa and the rattling sounds his breathing is making, about how there is absolutely nothing I can do to save his life even though at one point, long ago, he had saved mine. I worry about Grandma and how she will be taken care of.

I just want things the way they used to be, but I know they will never ever be the same again. It's a hard thing for me to accept. This is the first time in my life where I realize that I'm not immortal, that I won't live forever, that things can change in an instant. I let my mind reel in circles until it gives up, and I fall into the comforts of sleep, welcoming it like a big dark hug.

What seems like only seconds later, someone shouts my name, and my eyes pop open. I'd recognize that amber voice anywhere. It's Grandpa. I jump out of bed, tripping over the comforter, which is all tangled around my body, and run up the stairs to his room. The next shift's nurse, a male this time, is sitting on the sofa in the dark doing something on his phone, the glow illuminating his blessedly normal face. *At least this one doesn't look like a horror movie character.* I wonder why he isn't heading for Grandpa's bedroom like I am. Had he not heard him? He looks up at me in concern, and I tell him I need to visit my grandfather. He nods empathetically.

I enter the bedroom, clicking the door behind me as quietly as I can muster, excited because I heard him call for me. Maybe by some miracle he has come out of the coma. There is only the soft glow of the television on mute, the changing pictures on the screen making the room grow brighter and darker and brighter again. I can see the reflection in the mirror on the wall behind his bed and look at the words etched lightly onto the glass surface, but even deeper in my heart.

Sometimes the only way to find yourself is to lose everything you love most.

I never did ask him what it meant, but something about it has always resonated with me, like a memory from a lifetime ago tucked away, comforting me like an old friend's photograph.

I slink down on his bed and see that he has not woken up. I had been so deafened by my own excitement that I failed to realize he was still making that horrible noise. That gurgling and bubbling in his chest like a clogged set of sink pipes. I wish so bad at this moment that he would open his eyes so I can see the light in them one more time. The beautiful blue, the happiness, like liquid sky on a summer day. I take his hands in mine and caress them, weathered with age but strong, so strong still. I rub my thumb over the scar that lives on the skin between his thumb and pointer finger and think about the dream I had the other night. About how this hand plunged in to save me from the darkness, how he's always been there to save me, and now I feel lost at the prospect that now it's up to me to save myself.

Mom and I often talk about our sixth sense, that extra sense they never taught us about in school. She said we can use that sense to help us in a lot of ways. Like knowing if someone should be our friend or not. Or to tell if it's going to be a good day or if I should be cautious and tie my shoelaces a little tighter.

Mom also told me that when people die, you can ask for signs that they are still around and usually you will get an answer. Not an answer in the way that I talk to my parents or friends, but something more subtle. It's a fine line though, because I can't read too much into everything looking for a sign. In other words, I can't try too hard. I just have to relax, close my eyes, and breathe for a few minutes.

Apparently, it's supposed to work especially well during those first few moments between awake and asleep. She says that's when the invisible world is the thinnest and that we can learn a lot about ourselves in those seconds by relaxing and "feeling the energy." She told me when the sign happens, I would know without any doubt because my whole body would tingle, the little hairs on my arms would stand up on end, my heart would feel like it's floating in midair, and time would stand still for the briefest of moments as everything feels like it will fall perfectly into place.

I remember thinking of that painting by Salvador Dali that hangs on the wall in my art class when she was talking about this. I imagined using your sixth sense would feel all creepy and dreamy with melting clocks or great ships with butterfly sails.

I've tried it dozens of times but could never quite figure out what she meant by that. She always said to "let go." I didn't know what exactly I was supposed to let go of especially if I'm just lying in bed holding onto absolutely nothing. Needless to say, it was never anything that worked for me.

Now I'm so desperate to find out what Grandpa wants that I'm willing to try anything. I start concentrating on only the two of us in this room. I know that was him calling me even if he can't say it in words. Still holding his hand, I focus on his closed eyes and ask, "What do you want, Grandpa? Why did you call for me?"

I let a few seconds pass, trying to stretch out my ears in whatever way possible, straining as hard as I can to hear something, anything at all.

Nothing. Radio silence. Just the unsettling sound of his... death rattle. I squeeze my eyes so tight that I see tiny pricks of stars on the other side of my lids and feel blood pulsing in my ears. Still nothing but an ache in my jaw from clenching them, vise-like. Frustrated, I open my eyes and ask again, "Grandpa, what? Please tell me, please!" I'm practically begging now, and I don't care who hears me. Mom's words come back to me: *Relax and let go.*

And so I do.

I shut my eyes again, and this time I relax and try not to force things. I breathe deep and sink my bottom onto the edge of the bed. I don't think of anything else except for what I'm doing at this moment, which is concentrating on the space between me and my grandfather, placing my consciousness between the two of us. His energy and mine are the only living things in this room. I direct my attention on my feelings, on how much I love him and how every part of me does not want him to leave. I let our entire relationship play behind my eyelids like a silent movie—the many years of secret birthday candy, the boat trips, and walks in the park. I focus on this as I open myself up to listen.

Then it happens. The wooden clock with the pendulum in the living room stops ticking, the breeze creeping through the open window holds its breath, and the house sparrows on the other side stop their morning song. It's as if a great sweeping breath exhales through the house and shushes everything in its path. I open my eyes and hear the words before he comes back into focus: "Our song."

I don't hear it with my own ears. It's not like he whispered to me again. It's like my heart was talking or more like some sort of receptor from somewhere deep in the middle of my core. I almost laugh at this, remembering how Grandpa was never a big fan of music, saying he has enough clutter in his head and doesn't need to fill it with anyone's depressing stories. But for some reason he latched onto the Beatles. He said they had a song for every one of his moods. One in particular was ours, and he'd sing it to me before bed when I'd stay the night with them.

Frantic now, I run down to the guest room which is a light shade of pale as the sun is just beginning to announce its presence, to find my phone. I press the home button, but it won't turn on. *Damn! Damn! Where's my charger?* I tear through the overnight bag that Mom brought me, but it's not in there. I make my way to Grandpa's office, which has been turned into a makeshift bedroom where Grandma and Mom are sleeping at the moment, and sneak around looking at wall outlets and in Mom's purse, but nothing.

I recall the nurse sitting in the living room earlier messing with his cell phone and go out there to see if he'd let me borrow his charger for a few minutes but am flustered when I can't find him. At this point I'm at a loss and resolve myself to the fact that I'm just going to have to sing to my grandfather, hoping and praying that will suffice. Taped to Grandpa's bedroom door is a note from the nurse telling us what to expect in the next hour before the morning nurse comes in. He wrote that he took Grandpa's vital signs about a half hour ago, which must have been just before I went in to see him. He mentioned that Grandpa's condition is worsening, but we shouldn't be alarmed; this is a natural process. He included his cell phone number in case we had any questions and closed the letter by saying that he didn't want to wake the sleeping family before he left as he felt rest was very important for all right now.

Well that's nice of him. I let a sigh escape my lips. Not because I didn't want to do this but rather, walking back into his room, Grandpa seems so peaceful lying there surrounded by memorabilia of the Buffalo Bills, his favorite football team, as well as countless trinkets and photos from his travels.

I climb in bed next to him and lie down, just like I did when I was a little girl. I wrap his hand over my shoulder and put my head in the crook of his arm. For a few minutes I just lie here, listening to the sounds of his breathing—so shallow now, but he's still here with me. I take comfort in that.

I sing to him in a whisper, loud enough that he can hear me but avoiding any sort of echo. I'm feeling very selfish, not wanting to share this moment with anyone else; just us.

I hold his hand, let my finger trace the line down his thumb to his wrist. I feel his pulse so gentle.

Still here.

I sing another line. I so wish he could hear the instruments in the song as I hear them so vividly in my head.

I listen to his breathing some more.

His pulse starts to lose its rhythm, the spaces between growing longer and then shorter bursts of many beats in a row. It stays like this for a while. I sing another line as my own pulse picks up its tempo. I'm so scared for him and for me. I don't want him to go.

His heartbeat flutters inside his wrist like the wings of a butterfly trying to escape. The last bit of his life is hanging on, but his spirit is trying to break free. "Good night…" I exhale the last bit of song.

Silence. There is no more breath, no movement of his chest. The butterfly has been set free. I try to keep my tears inside, fearing that each one contains a memory that will be lost if I let them go, but I can't help it, there are too many, and I can't stop them from falling over the edge. I cry right from the depths of my stomach where the little girl still lives that needs her best friend more than anything, but she can't have him.

4 CHELSEA

Nine years can be an eternity to some people or the blink of an eye for others. For me it's an event that I've kept in a pocket inside of my heart. Nine years ago, I was only five, and I remember sitting on the cold bench of my grandfather's boat… closing my eyes and tilting my head toward the sun, pretending that I was a mermaid, soaking in the pale heat of a day that promised to be quite warm for November.

I want to stop thinking about it, but I can't help myself— sometimes the memory is so real it's like it just happened. Other times, it plays across my mind like a movie that I saw long ago. It always begins with the shiver. A faint chill runs through my body—the sun hasn't yet burned off the morning dew from the bench that I'm sitting on. A sheet of fog lays itself across the bay, thinning by the minute, it seems. I'm only distracted for a moment as a shadow passes across my face shocking me with a cool breeze. I open my eyes and give a mock scowl to Grandpa. His blue flannel shirt peeks out from a vest full of feathery lures. He reaches down and fastens my life jacket at lightning speed. I remember being astonished that his aging hands could move so fast.

He catches me eyeing him. "Not bad for an old man, eh?" He laughs, and I can only imagine his eyes sparkling as they always did whenever he smiled. At the time, though, I'd been basking so long that everything I saw carried an odd tint of green.

"Ready?" he asks, looking me over to make sure I'm secure. "Let's catch some fish!"

I nod in excitement as I watch him pull the engine cord like he's starting an old lawn mower. He winces and mumbles something about his age. The engine sputters at first, but after a few more deep tugs and deeper winces, it startles awake. I remember thinking it reminded me of Rip Van Winkle, from one of my story books, waking up from his long sleep.

"Yeah, I know, she coughs a few times, but I can always get her purring like a kitten," can't I, Chells?"

I smile and nod, my five-year-old brain not totally understanding the particular connection between that snarling boat engine and my favorite animal but who was I to argue with him? "Ok, Grandpa!"

My heart dances as the boat takes off for the middle of Irondequoit Bay, breaking through the disappointment that we aren't going out on Lake Ontario. Grandpa had told me the water is too rough and unpredictable this time of year. I was still a "tadpole" at the Y, and he said he didn't want to take his chances when my tail was still attached.

The burning smell of gasoline and the mustiness of autumn leaves cements itself to my memory as the breeze whips past my cheeks and tangles my long hair. My body bumps along with the *swoosh-smack* of the boat. I hear something clinking and snatch the tin box sitting next to me before it falls. Its contents are more precious to me than any of my dolls or toys. Special, because contained inside is a secret tradition that not even my parents know about.

Every year, when Grandma Dorothy and Grandpa Jo take their fishing trip to Canada, they always bring me special maple sugar candy for my birthday. The candy is small, about the size of a half dollar, an off shade of beige, and usually shaped like a leaf. The outside might be boring, but inside, the taste is something that Slugworth would pay millions for.

"One for every year you've been alive!" Grandma told me. I once asked Grandma how many *she* eats on her birthday, and she told me that she's old now and will only celebrate with one piece. "Or two," if she was feeling, "especially saucy."

I pop a sugar leaf into my mouth, close my eyes, and savor the warm notes of molasses and maple syrup. Even now, the memory of the flavor's intensity causes the little hollow under my jawline, below my ears to tingle. The clouds in heaven must taste like these maple candies, I thought as I imagined sitting on a cloud devouring handfuls of white puffy maple goodness. On my fifth and final piece, I decide to play a game of seeing how long I can let it dissolve on my tongue without swallowing. Being so focused on my little game I am startled when, seemingly out of nowhere, Grandpa's sharp voice snaps me back into my body, a reverse slingshot with a tight rubber band.

"Hold on baby!" he shouts and tries to reach for me. I'm a little groggy from my daydream, so it doesn't register right away when I see the corner of another boat nail into the side of ours. The fog lifts as I break the frigid glass surface of the lake.

Trapped underwater, suspended between my life jacket and a large piece of driftwood, I don't waste my time trying to break free. I am not panicked and do not have any urge to fight. I'm too small, too fragile, so I let myself go, allowing the gentle movement of the underground current to rock me. I imagine that Vivienne, the Lady of the Lake from the King Arthur stories, is keeping me safe in her arms like a baby.

Beams of sunlight periodically break through the top layer of water like fingers trying to reach for me—God's hands or my guardian angel. I'm warmed by this thought as the light starts to become brighter, the beams melding into each other creating something all encompassing. I remember thinking that maybe Vivienne was coming to take me to her underwater castle in the very bottom of the lake. I wanted to be a princess just like her, and I almost let go completely until an image flashed in my mind. It happened so fast I'm not even sure if it was real, but it shocked me enough to hold me there in that place.

There was a girl in a forest, reaching out to me like she needed my help. She was mouthing words, but I can't hear what she was saying. I don't know who the girl is, but I know that I have to help her somehow. The reality of the situation makes me panic, and I desperately try to rip off my life jacket. My little fingers fumble with the buckles, trying to release the constraints. My lungs scream for air, my chest feels like King Kong's hand is squeezing every drop of life from my body. I try to hang onto the image of the girl as I pull and tug at my jacket, but her likeness is pushed away as my need to breathe outweighs everything else. My body's survival instinct takes over, forcing my mouth open, replenishing my empty lungs with liquid ice.

A harsh light overhead beckons my attention, but my eyelids are lead weights. The image of the girl is still underwater somewhere while I'm becoming conscious to the fact that there is glorious fresh air in my lungs. I take note of the sounds around me. Not the muffled pressure of water in my ears or the beating of my own heart. There is something squeezing my arm at various intervals and beeping from somewhere in the room. My eyes are too heavy to open outright, so I force them into slits and see a rolling table next to me. On top is a dented tin can, overflowing with maple candies.

5 JOSIAH

Josiah awoke in a whirlpool of confusion and a puddle of sweat, plagued by the same nightmare he'd had since always. He was grateful to the rooster, who was still cackling somewhere outside, for pulling him back to his bed. Sometimes he wondered if it was his own fault that the dreams kept coming back. As soon as Papa started getting busy down at the mill processing wheat during the harvest season, they would start back up again and last into early winter.

Rationally, he knew they were just dreams. They had no control over him. They all started the same way. The ground rumbled and the train whizzed by and he ducked before an apple hits him in the face. Then it cuts to the part that truly disturbs him. The girl he couldn't save. She had to be around his age, maybe younger by a year or two. She stood in the middle of a great expanse of old crabapple trees, scared stiff, quite literally—she couldn't move. Her nightclothes were dirty at the bottom, her bare feet crusted with mud. The silhouette of a monster stood before her, holding something in his hands, but it was too dark to see. Josiah could just make out the smile, white teeth reflecting the moonlight, the grin a mile wide, overly proportioned; inhuman.

The horror on her face broke Josiah's heart and made him want to help her, but he couldn't. The more he struggled to get to her, the farther away she became. He'd woken up more times than he could count on both hands and feet, always with that last image of the toothy grin and an incredible sense of unexplainable loss.

"I can't wait for the winter to get here so these dreams can just stop already!" he said to himself as he pulled up suspenders and tucked his white shirt into faded trousers.

Josiah's father had already left for the mill long before dawn. Mama had breakfast waiting, which Josiah shoveled into his mouth before giving her a quick kiss on the cheek and heading out the door with his books in hand, strapped to a belt. A wooden windmill overlooked the far side of the house, its great propellers circling in slow-motion, casting long, swooping shadows from the rising sun. He made a game of jumping through the shadows on the long, flat stones that curved from his front door to the road.

He wiped the dirt from his pants as he walked with a little spring in his step. The path to school was a monotonous hike, but he made the most of it, taking nothing for granted. Endless miles of wheat extended on either side of him like rows of soldiers that bent and swayed in the breeze. About a half an hour in they gave way to an expanse of flat land with a large gap in between neighbors. Once in a while he'd pass empty husks of old barns, abandoned when the fire hit the city.

It had freaked people out, this fire. Probably because no one knew exactly why it happened. Or where it started. It seemed like one day the city was bustling and the next it was up in flames, like God decided right then and there he had enough and the sinners must go. Or Mother Nature just said, "To hell with it, I need to grow more trees, here's a good spot." Then *poof*! She made a clearing. People didn't like to talk about the fire or how odd it was. A lot of people died that day, and many more lost their homes and had to change their lives completely. Josiah had always lived out here in Henrietta and didn't get to the city much at all. He only knew about the fire when his parents told him, and that was just when he started noticing people coming and going at such a dizzying pace.

Josiah hated to admit it, but he was kind of glad it happened. Not because people got hurt, no. He would never wish that on anyone, but because if it hadn't, he never would have met Edgar, his best friend. Edgar Slate had come from the city after the fire with his mom and dad about two years ago. His father went missing not long after they moved in. Edgar seemed to handle it okay, but his mother, well, she barely kept the pieces together. Edgar said he could hear her crying every night.

The road took a winding turn, and as Josiah rounded the corner, the air changed, the smell a strong clue that the Slate family farm was drawing near. Not only did Edgar have to deal with the forced relocation of his family and his missing father, but the children at school constantly picked on him because he couldn't help but to carry the faint smell of the family business with him.

Josiah's papa told him once that a man does what he has to do to survive. And that's how he saw Edgar, wise beyond his years, a little shy, super creative, and a whole lot of fun, but doing what he had to do.

As he approached the Slates' house, he picked up his pace, hoping Edgar hadn't left yet. Sometimes Josiah was late, and Edgar never wanted to be the last one to their classroom lest the air of him walking in followed him to his chair. He much preferred to already be seated before anyone else.

Josiah could see, even from this distance, that the wooden fence needed some repair—the pine that had been twined together had started to topple near the front gate. He reminded himself to ask his dad after school to fix the gate. The Slate house was a one floor home, a perfect fit for their family of five. Beams of wood, piled at the side like tattered gravestones, served a harsh reminder of the extra bedroom for the planned sixth Slate family member that sadly never came to fruition.

He knocked on the front door, and Mrs. Slate called from the kitchen, "He'll be out in a second, Josiah!"

"Ok thanks, Mrs. Slate!" Edgar called back, relieved that Josiah was still in the house. He also knew his politeness made her feel good and taking to heart everything this family had been through, if he made her happy for even just a moment then he was all the better for it.

Josiah paced around their modest front yard until he was bored, then made his way to the side. His eyes skimmed past the horses and barn to the field beyond. Something about that field had always made him feel uneasy; ever since he was a little boy he'd had this habit of turning his head the other way as he passed it when he was walking to school. The grass looked dead no matter what time of year it was, and even when a thick blanket of snow covered the entire area it looked... off. The snow was never fully white, rather it took on an ugly, muddy hue.

There was only one tree way out in the far left corner, and beyond that, the wilderness picked up again with lush pine, maple trees, and vegetation. He'd seen how animals avoided that stretch of land, and he knew even Edgar's horses wouldn't go near it. The birds even seemed to fly around it, and sometimes he could swear that that the clouds parted ways so they didn't have to drift over it.

His stomach turned as he stared at the lone tree off in the distance. From this angle, it looked like a person out there, but Josiah would never consider walking up to it to take a closer look. Edgar's mom wouldn't let them go out there anyway. She said the land was "unholy." *I don't know about that*, Josiah thought, *but it sure makes me feel strange.*

Edgar interrupted Josiah's thoughts as he rushed out the front door with a huge goofy grin on his face, practically running into Josiah.

"Whoa there little doggy," said Josiah laughing. "Why are you so happy this morning?"

"Mama got me new shoes!"

Josiah knew what that meant to Edgar. The poor kid had to wear his work boots to school every day, and no matter how many times he would try to wipe his boots on the ground or scrape them off on trees, the smell just would not come out. He tried trudging through the creek one morning, but the sun was so bright and hot it turned the water to sludge making it that much worse. That was the day the kids started teasing him and coined the nickname "Dung Stew."

The teacher gave the class a lecture hoping it would bring forth some empathy from his peers. It did not—they just shortened his nickname to "Stew" so the teacher wouldn't know. But Edgar did.

"She sold one of her blankets at the market," he beamed as he picked up one foot, turning it from side to side in the air and doing the same with the other.

"That's great!" Josiah said and clasped Edgar's shoulder. Something most of us took for granted made him light up like the North Star. His cheery attitude, always so contagious, made Josiah feel better to just be around him.

"So, you think they will make any difference?" Edgar asked as they walked along the road towards school.

Josiah reached out, plucked a piece of wheat, and caught Edgar wincing as he did so, like it physically hurt him.

He stopped walking and asked Edgar, "Why do you always do that?"

"Do what?"

"You make a face whenever I pull something out of the ground. Like this," Josiah said, holding out the stalk in front of him. "Or the other day, when Ma made me cut down that dead tree in our yard. You went all pale, and I thought you were going to pass right out."

"Itwas'tead."

"What?" Josiah leaned toward him.

"It wasn't dead," he answered, louder than before.

"Well it nearly was... someone had to put that old thing out of its misery. What do you care anyway?"

"I dunno. I don't. I guess." Edgar shrugged and gave Josiah his best vacant look. Josiah exhaled and started walking again with Edgar a short pace behind him, not saying much the rest of the way to school.

Josiah figured Edgar must be still adjusting to his new life and working through all that had happened. He couldn't imagine how he himself would go through what Edgar had: a life of privilege, a happy family, and now no father, a home that was falling apart, and this. He cringed as their school came into view. He wouldn't let the worry get to him, deciding that maybe if he could make his energy feel like armor, perhaps it would rub off on Edgar.

Edgar was a strong person for sure, usually letting the kids' taunts roll off his back, but Josiah knew that somewhere inside, it had to sting. The majority of the jerks at school had had it in for Edgar since his first day. Josiah didn't think it was just the smell that bothered them either. He looked a little different than everyone else, dressing in the same fancy city outfit for his first few weeks because he had nothing else to wear. They thought he was just showing off.

His hair was longer than the other boys, and he wore that ridiculous looking top hat which Josiah finally convinced him to stop wearing to school. Not that not fitting in was so horrible, but he convinced Edgar that the kids' fire needed a little less kindling.

He was also smarter than everyone else; they hadn't even been sure where to place him that first day because he kept answering all the grade level math questions without even thinking about it. In the end they just decided not to teach him math anymore. He wouldn't really need those skills out here in the country anyway.

According to them farming had been handed down through generations straight from the old countries, and if you were born a farmer, you died a farmer. So arithmetic? What's the purpose? You just learned it in the field.

The schoolhouse was forged from cobblestone and it leaned slightly to the west as if it was constantly grasping for the last of the sunlight. Out here in the country, there were dozens of schools like this one, but this happened to be the closest, around five miles from home. Josiah and Edgar paused a few feet before the front door, already late, but Edgar was practically bouncing with joy when, on a typical day, Josiah quite literally had to push him through the door.

Josiah looked down at Edgar's new boots, answering a question he hadn't meant to ignore before. "Yep. I think they'll make all the difference in the world."

This time, Edgar walked in first.

6 CHELSEA

My body feels heavy, like Superman under a blanket of kryptonite. I can hear sounds swirling around my head, coming in waves, rolling in past one ear to the other, but I can't make sense of them. I'm in a void bereft of space or time.

I can't tell if it's day or night. Everything appears dark, but as I strain through the blackness, hints of light show themselves like fireflies that become distorted and eventually disappear altogether. I'm aware but completely detached. The light, I want to reach for it, but I can't move my arms. I feel like I'm five years old again, still trapped underwater, waiting for Vivienne to take me away.

My heart is pounding not only from my effort to get out of this awful place but to try and figure out *who* or *what* I am. I start trying to claw my way out, my limbs moving like Mom's wooden spoon when she used to make play dough on the stove. Slow, impossibly slow, but you have to keep stirring so it doesn't burn. My muscles ache with the effort.

A hand plunges into the darkness and reaches for me, trying to yank me out of this sticky mess. When I see the little scar between the thumb and pointer finger, I know that I'm dreaming. That's Grandpa's hand, the scar accidentally given by a little girl named Maddie that he met on a train a long time ago.

Now, little by little, I can think, can move my fingers and toes. It's like somehow Grandpa Jo is trying to teach me something, but I just can't figure out what it is. I reach for him, but

34

he disappears, and just like that I'm stuck with the difficult task of figuring out how to wake myself up.

I try to pinch myself, but I can't move my fingers at all—they're frozen in odd angles, like claws that developed horribly wrong, or the twisted branches of the crabapple trees in my backyard. I'm running out of time, like all the clocks in the world are spinning backwards.

I need to wake up, to get out of this awful place. Surely there's a hole in my chest where my heart should be, I keep waiting to see it float past. I feel so lost, so out of control. I wrack my brain. *What can I do? What can I do?*

The only thing I can possibly think of is to scream. I open my mouth and prepare to let loose, but only a mouse of a noise escapes, and my voice sputters like the engine on Grandpa's boat. I take in a deep breath and focus on the window which I know is next to my bed. If this is a dream, perhaps I can shatter it.

I try again. I scream and scream, imagining cracks beginning to web their way against the window. I scream for the air I couldn't breathe when I was five. I scream until the noise drowns out the sound of my terrible racing heart. The sound, so distant from myself, awakens something from deep inside, sending a chill that runs from the back of my neck to my toes. Every single hair on my body stands at attention. The sound reverberates in my nightmare of a bubble until I'm transfixed, a human tuning fork in perfect harmony with my own voice.

Light begins to pierce the blackness. My hands are starting to ease out of whatever had been gluing them together. I know soon that I'll be able to bust out of this mold, a baby chick pecking at her egg from the other side. Yet some insane part of me wants to linger, to find out if there's something more to the darkness.

My body springs upright with such force that I nearly fall out of bed. It takes me a full minute to realize that I'm still screaming, except it sounds nothing like it did in my dream. In my dream, it was full-on, blood-curdling, horror movie screams. Right now, I'm unleashing short little bursts of breath and voice that sound like an angry goose. I throw my hands to my mouth to stop the noise and listen for my mother. Mom will want to take me to the dreaded doctor if she thinks that I'm having nightmares again——she's overly paranoid, but I have no doubt that she'll follow through on her promises.

After a minute passes, I decide it's safe to exhale. Relief overwhelms me, and I smooth the wet, matted hair away from my face and reach for my journal where I always record my dreams. It's best to do it when the dream's fresh on my mind.

The cover reminds me of a scene from *A Midsummer Night's Dream*, all dark, mysterious, and ethereal. I trace the fairies and flowers with my fingers, loving the way the indigo cloth feels against my skin. Grandpa Jo bought this notebook for me not long after the accident. I open the cover to read the inscription on the back side, even though I know it by heart. "When you can't get the words to come from your mouth, pen them directly from your soul."

I've been having the same type of dream since then. It changes once in a while, but the gist of it is always there. I'm stuck in the dark, in some mindless oubliette without the use of my limbs, and no matter how hard I try to move them, I just can't. I always wake up before I can get out of that place. I never know when these dreams will pay a visit. I can go a year without having them at all, and then all of a sudden, they'll start coming weekly. That's when Mom gets particularly freaked out. Then another few months with absolutely nothing.

I thumb through my journal searching for the next blank page, and I find it, noting the last entry as November 15th, 2015. Has it really been a year? I pause for a moment, considering this. I start to tap my pen on the blank page as if every tap is shaking a new thought from my mind.

What was different this time? What was different? I look at the last entry for inspiration. "Hmm… the train was new last year?" I recall hearing a train chugging along through the void. Didn't happen this time though, which stumps me a little. "Oh!" An epiphany dances around the four corners of my bedroom. "The scream! Now that was new," I mumble, taking pen to paper. "But how do I draw a scream?"

Grandpa knew I wouldn't be writing in my journal, so he made sure this one had no lines. I have always been an artist, whereas he was always a writer. He used to talk about this one journal he'd lost on a train somewhere, which is exactly when his words would trail off and he'd stop talking.

"Ironic that I drew a train last time... and how the heck did I manage watercolors?" Touching the page makes me think of the smell of leaves and warm breezes.

"Indian summer. I left it on the open windowsill to dry." I look out the window now and feel a frown spreading before I can help myself.

"Definitely not today." A cold white quilt covers everything. I start to doodle as I watch a toddler fall over into a heap of snow the plow left at the end of the driveway. His mother grabs him by the arm in a quick swoop and places him back on his feet.

I often draw with my eyes closed or while thinking of other things. I call it mind scrapping. It's just the way I've always done it, like my hands are automatic or have eyes of their own. I look at my work, and an internal lightbulb starts blinking. As I stare at my rendition of the mask from the movie I watched before going to sleep last night, I wonder if this is why I had the dream. The mask is all black eyes and an open mouth that never shuts, a frozen scream.

"I gotta stop watching TV at night," I say as I put the dream journal away and pick up my doodle one, along with my phone. I carry my doodle journal with me everywhere. It's like my walking diary so I can mind scrap whenever I want.

Two separate texts are waiting for me, and I roll my eyes. I don't know why Autumn and Jeff always insist on sending separate messages when we talk about the same things!

"As soon as I teach them how to text the right way, then we'll be better friends," I mumble to the screen. I write back to each of them, individually, that I will bring breakfast to the bus stop today, as I'd made chocolate chip muffins last night.

A loud click off to the side scares me. The familiar noise usually wakes me up before the music does, and today, apparently, we've all woken up before our alarms. My Little Mermaid clock looks deceptively old-school but has all the bells and whistles I love: a charger, Bluetooth speakers, iTunes, Pandora, Spotify, etc. I used to just use the radio for an alarm, but I kept waking up to annoying commercials for hair regrowth and happy hour parties. I smartened up and made a morning playlist, set on shuffle, so I wake to something that I actually enjoy. Today doesn't disappoint.

When Lorde's voice fills my room, my mind wants to drift elsewhere for a while, somewhere more fun with infinite possibilities. I lay back and listen for a minute. My legs weave themselves into the music, and I'm already halfway across the room singing into my hair brush before I realize what I'm doing.

I articulate carefully one of the lines as a nod to Autumn who made fun of me for thinking Lorde was singing something about vampires.

The song ends, and it takes all of my power not to play another one. I probably could if I didn't set my alarm so late, but I need all the sleep I can get. After a quick change of clothes and smoothing out my hair, I run down to the kitchen to throw the muffins and napkins in a paper bag before heading out the door.

"Hey honey?" A disconnected voice calls after me, with a faint hint of desperation.

I peek my head through the doorway to the dining room where Mom is in total trance mode, gnawing on a pencil.

"What is it, Mom? I'm kind of late, and it's my turn to bring breakfast!"

"What's a seven-letter word for elephant?"

"What? Mom, really?" I roll my eyes, kiss her on the cheek and head for the door.

"No really, Chells!" she calls after me, the panic in her voice reaching maximum capacity. "I've been working on this damn puzzle for like an hour, and I refuse to ask Siri!"

"MAMMOTH!" I yell back to her, then shut the door and head for the bus stop.

***

Ugh, school. The second hand completes yet another orbit, and I want to crawl out of my own skin. I've had a hard time focusing on my classes today, but this one by far has been the worst. Everyone is shifting in their seats and dropping things. I stare ahead at the empty space where Billy McKenzie should be, and a cold shiver runs down my spine. The chatter on the bus this morning was conflicting. No one knows if he ran away or if someone took him from his bedroom.

You always hear reports on the news about missing kids, but for us it feels like a fairy tale or something, not based in reality. Now that it's staring us right in the face, everyone seems clueless how to act. The teachers haven't brought it up in any of my classes today either, which hasn't helped with the tension. The news just sits in the air somewhere above, making everyone jittery and either overly chatty to compensate or unusually quiet.

I want to avoid eye contact with his chair, but that's just impossible. I want so badly to see the number 72 staring back at me, but it doesn't. Billy always wears his football jersey. Like every day for the entire year. He plays defensive tackle for the Pirates, the football team for Penfield Middle School, and every quarterback in the county fears him because he is big, strong, and super good at sacking them to the ground. I was never a huge football fan, but I've started going to home games since he's been on the team. It's like being a part of a reality TV show; he's all everyone talks about the next day. Who needs the news when you've got Billy McKenzie pushing past players like bowling pins! I can't even imagine how a kid that big just suddenly *disappears*.

I keep moving my gaze from the clock to my fingers that I incessantly tap on the desk. That's when I see the note that Autumn left me. I rest my head on my arms to read it as you can only see the whole thing at just the right angle on these black-top desks. Mr. Smoose (or Snooze as we like to call him) was droning on about water pollution as I read her bubbly scrawl:

OMG do not let him come near you today. The coffee breath is unreal!

An audible snort escapes me, and all eyes turn in my direction. My face heats up like a kettle.

"Is something funny, Miss Heiland?"

"Uhh… no sir. I was just…"

"Water pollution is no laughing matter, Miss Heiland."

"Yessir."

He turns his back, and I slump in my chair, relieved that his attention has been diverted. I check the clock again to see we have just two minutes left, so I start to pack my backpack quietly. I get up as fast as possible when the bell rings.

I need to meet Autumn at our shared locker down the hall so I can yell at her for getting me in trouble. As I turn the corner past the droves of kids, I see her long brown hair from behind. I've always admired how thick and pretty it is, reminding me of warm chestnuts; totally the opposite of my plain blonde hair, which thanks to her, is adorned with the perfect streaks of electric blue framing my face.

She was tired of me complaining about it so helped me change it to reflect my favorite place to be, by the water. She's the one out of the three of us that is the most calm and rational, yet so bubbly and almost... hippy-like. Sometimes people think she's a flake because of how happy and carefree she is, but she's one of the smartest people I know.

We had an end of unit math test last week, and while I was studying until 11 p.m. every night, she binge-watched old episodes of *Friends* on Netflix. Binge-watched! When I reprimanded her about it, she flashed her warm smile, saying, "Chelsea, what's the difference? I studied earlier in the day, and if I didn't understand it by then, no amount of stress and worry is going to make me learn any more than I already know." Oh Autumn... if only I could be like you.

"Hey Autumn! Thanks a lot!" I say with as much sarcasm as I can muster.

"What?" She fixes her blue eyes on me. The contrast between her hair and eyes reminds me of a pixie in a fantasy novel.

"The note. About the breath? It made me laugh, and Mr. Snooze yelled at me! Well he accused me of not caring about water pollution."

She giggled an apology.

"Ew, I have Mr. Snooze next. Sucks! Try being in the front row!" says Jeff. His sudden presence doesn't surprise me. His glasses, like his smile, are always a little crooked, but he hides his frames behind shaggy blond hair so you can't see the angle of them until he pushes his hair back.

"He always uses my desk when he has to make a point about something he thinks is *so* interesting. Do you have any idea what it means to be on the receiving end of that man's breath?"

"Enlighten us," says Autumn, amused.

Jeff stretches out his hands as if he's leaning over an invisible desk and starts to speak in a loud whisper, moving his head in a jerky motion as he enunciates each word for effect. "Whispers. Make. His. Breath. Shoot. Over. My. Head. And… Stale coffeee is soooo… grooooosssssssss." He takes his time whispering that last word, making sure to blow air into both of our faces.

"Yeah, well I think you need some strong mints yourself there, Jeffrey," I say as I wave my hand in front of my face.

We all laugh, but it fizzles, the good mood acting like a nail in our tires. I close the locker after grabbing my books and lean my back against it, finally voicing what's been on our minds all day. "What do you guys think happened to Billy?"

Jeff looks deflated and shrugs. "I dunno, Chells."

"I don't know either but it's creepy," says Autumn. "Why would someone take him from his bedroom? *How* could they? He's huge for a fourteen-year-old!"

"That's what I was thinking," I agree.

"Maybe he did run away?" Jeff answers.

"But he didn't take anything with him, they said. There was just an open window." I shudder as I say this. Talking in circles about it doesn't help, just makes it creepier.

The three of us are startled by the bell when it rings. "Ok." I sigh and try and perk myself up with a smile. "One more to go. See you on the bus!" We part ways, but I still have a bad taste in my mouth about Billy. I make my way to class, and it's as if everyone around me is moving in slow motion. I feel like a bottle in the ocean, letting the current of students push me to English class.

I hang my bag on the back of my seat, pull out the book of poetry by Edgar Allan Poe, and slump down in my chair. I flip through the pages until I find "Spirit of the Dead." Miss Carlson starts reading right away, and I miss the first few lines. She's a fun teacher but a big believer in time-management. She never intends to waste it, usually starting as soon as each seat has a butt in it.

I'm happy about this unit on Poe. There's something about the way he writes that is so vivid for me. As soon as I start reading, the words fall away and paintings appear in my head. For the past few weeks, I've upped the ante in my journal doodling, too.

I start copying down the notes that Miss Carlson repeats for us as she stops reading every few lines to explain things or ask questions. Raina Boddington interrupts her with a few questions of her own. This makes me smile because she's always been annoying teachers like this since we were all in kindergarten. She basically has no filter, but no one seems to mind, because she's usually has something very funny to say. But this is exactly how a five-stanza poem can take an hour to read. I've already memorized it but try not to drift too far so I can take notes when I'm supposed to because we have a test on Friday.

"How it hangs upon the trees, a mystery of mysteries!" Miss Carlson lights up at the end and opens up the class for discussion.

Mystery indeed, I think to myself. I start scribbling as I ponder the poem, the mysteries of death, Billy…

I feel a gentle squeeze on my arm, and my body goes rigid, sure that I've just been busted daydreaming. I brace myself for the inevitable lecture from Miss Carlson. I snatch the notepaper before she can see that I've drawn more than I've taken notes. With my eyes on the back of my hands, hoping the evidence is concealed properly, I feel her head next to mine as she leans in to say something.

But instead of her perky high pitch, her voice is low, gravelly, and wrong. I give her the side-eye and can feel my brows furrow involuntarily. I expect to see her light hair out of the corner of my eye, but it's absent. My heart trembles a little as the confusion grows. I realize now that this person is someone else completely, so I face them.

Eyes like great black voids stare back at me, much bigger than any I've ever seen. They're set in a face that quite resembles my grandfather's, but it's as if they took out his eyes and cheeks, carved great gaping holes in his face, and threw some obsidian in their places.

He grips both of my shoulders in each of his hands and leans in so close that I can feel his hot breath against my face, bringing with it the stench of decay, old books, and some sort of ancient mustiness.

"The dark man is coming, Chelsea!" he says in a voice that is as angry and putrid as his breath.

I shake and scream until I feel another set of arms around me. This time the touch is gentler, motherly almost, and I look around the room to find my entire class staring at me. "It's okay Chelsea, it's okay." I hang on to Miss Carlson's voice as I become centered again and familiar with my surroundings.

A phone rings and I jump again, still shaky from whatever just happened to me. Miss Carlson releases me, answers the phone, then makes two more phone calls. The next thing I know, Autumn is at the door with my jacket and schoolwork; she's come to escort me to the office and sit with me until one of my parents takes me home. She isn't saying much, waiting for me to explain myself first, I suspect, but I'm still too shaken up to go into detail just yet.

I feel Autumn trying to tug something out of my hand, and I release my grip, not realizing I was still holding on to the paper. "I didn't know I still had that." A fresh wave of heated panic spreads across my face and down my back. I try to calm myself down and focus on the present in fear of losing my sanity.

"What is it? Notes?"

"Should have been, but I was daydreaming again."

"Ohh…" She uncrumples the paper without asking and stares at it intently.

"What?" I prod, curiosity outweighing the panic.

"I don't know? You tell me?" She holds it up so I can see it, and spots cloud my vision. I try to hang on but the shock is too great. Those black round eyes burn themselves into my vision before my body   hits   the   floor.

7 EDGAR

Edgar couldn't keep his eyes off of his new shoes on the way home from school. They were brown and plain and maybe a little secondhand (even if his mama said they weren't), but that hardly bothered him, they were all his. He watched as the dust swirled over the laces, admiring how it made intricate patterns that changed with every footstep. And to him they were magical; none of the kids picked on him or turned their noses away. He even caught Mary Melinda sneaking a peek at him from his periphery, which made him put his head down, forcing his hair to cover the pale pink that blossomed over his cheeks.

"EDGAR! MOVE!" Josiah's shout pulled Edgar from his daydream at the same moment he was yanked so hard he fell over the side of the road.

"What the?!"

"I've been telling you the buggy's been heading this way for five whole minutes already! What is going on in your head?" Josiah said as he grabbed Edgar's arm to help him up. The smile and the squint in his eye served as an unspoken confirmation that he understood Edgar's unusual personality but liked him anyway.

"Oh sorry. It's just my shoes."

"I know buddy, come on let's keep walking. And pay attention this time! I promised your mama I'd look after you, and I can't very well do that if you're a bloody heap on the side of the road, can I?"

Mama told Edgar almost every morning that Josiah was sent from heaven to watch over him after his Papa left and that he had a better head on his shoulders than Edgar did. Edgar thought he probably should be hurt or jealous by those words but he knew it was true to a sense. Edgar had a nonsensical habit of staring off into space. It's one thing to daydream, but Edgar disappeared more often than he was alert some days.

He often sat alone on the edge of the yard that borders the wheat field, during lunch hour and recess at school. He heard his classmates speculate about his isolation, blaming it on the loss of his father or his predicament of being a manure farmer. If he could just explain things, then maybe they'd leave him alone, or like him better, or even ask questions. But he couldn't explain anything or they'd think he'd gone mental.

The truth was when he watched the wheat dance and sway, he could feel it breathing. Each individual stalk would hum together when they were happy, scream when they were pulled. All plant life did this, as far as Edgar knew. Except fruit. Fruit doesn't usually mind when you pick it because it knows that otherwise it would just rot on the branches or fall down. Fruit's destiny is to be eaten. And best eaten by animals who would spread its seeds.

Seeds are resilient creatures in themselves. A single seed can go through all the harsh acids and whatever else is inside an animal's body and come out intact at the other end. If it's lucky it will bear another fruit. Each piece of fruit knows its own destiny… and they're okay with it. Each tree, he found, was different in its reaction to the fruit leaving. Some trees were more motherly and didn't want their babies to go. Others knew and understood the life cycle, so they gave more freely. And still others, well, those poor things like some people could bear no fruit at all.

The problem was that he couldn't explain it himself, and even if he could, he was pretty sure his mom or the kids at school would kick him over directly to the Rochester State Hospital, and that is somewhere he never wanted to be.

Aside from his own Uncle Benjamin taking his life there, Edgar had heard stories of people who went mad after losing everything in the fire. A tragedy would do that to a person, the way it turns their world into a sinking ship.

Some people drown in a deep depression, some move through the grief and carry on with what they have left. Still others seem to turn into the worst part of themselves. Like Papa's boss, Mr. Amerson. He went nutty and killed his wife and children.

When Edgar tried to rationalize the way he knew what he did, he couldn't decide which was heads or tails. If it was heads, then he had some sort of superhuman power like the strongman at the circus, except all of his strength lay within his ears and eyes and whatever was inside of him. If he did have super strength, he sure couldn't do a thing to prove it.

If it was tails, then it was the earth that had the superpower, and he just happened to be able to hear it because he paid more attention than most, which is the complete opposite of what people said about him. He liked to focus on the minute world around him, the patterns and lines, and subtle ways the little things live their lives. Everyone else paid too much attention to the bigger picture to realize there was a whole other world going on around them. Edgar wished sometimes that people could see how akin to nature we are. But some people are too pig-headed to see anything but themselves, and it made him sad and angry.

He believed that the earth is beautiful and that humanity needs a lot of catching up to see and live within that beauty. While they're busy bickering over the details of the railroad or which side of the land they're allowed to plant corn on, the corn is busy trying to grow, not caring where, as long as it's able to get what it needs to survive.

One time, Edgar watched a farmer dig through a section of his wheat field. There were some old drier pieces that he was trying to get rid of. He was very friendly and asked Edgar if he wanted to give the pulling a try. Edgar shook his head just as you'd expect any little boy to do, except he wasn't shy; he was scared. He was afraid to find out what it felt like to take their life force away from them. The farmer said to him, "Watch this, boy!" then reached for a handful and yanked, his muscles bulging more than Edgar thought they should. *They must be fighting back.*

Edgar got into his zone and focused on the wheat that the farmer was heaving. They started to break free, rumbling out of the dirt like an oil well. The energy around the wheat caused terrible anxiety, as if they were holding their breath and knew what was coming. The earth that harbored them was tense as well. She never gives up her children without a fight. All the things attached to her are her children.

Even people. But she doesn't hold on to them with such a firm grip.

Edgar knew the fight was just about over when a high-pitched scream started welling up from below the soil. It was a horrible noise. Edgar looked from the wheat to the farmer and back, surprised that the farmer couldn't hear it too. Another yank and the sound became so deafening that it made Edgar sick in the pit of his stomach. The roots were now visible as the farmer gave his handful a final tug.

The other stalks around them, all yellow and bright with life and youth, raised up ever so slightly. If they had arms, surely they'd have pulled the others back down. And then the noise stopped. The pain disappeared from Edgar's stomach, and a crow cawed in the distance. There was a shallow hole in the earth where the roots had been, and the remaining wheat had their heads bent low.

The farmer probably thought it was the breeze or didn't care at all, merely standing there, holding his prize in triumph. Edgar knew it wasn't the breeze and he was holding no prize. They were in mourning.

Edgar mumbled his condolences, and the farmer responded saying it was ok thinking he was apologizing for not helping. Edgar didn't mind that the farmer thought he was talking to him. It made him feel more normal.

"So I saw Mary Melinda staring at you at school today." Josiah nudged Edgar with his elbow sending his mind back to the present.

Edgar put his hands in his pockets and scrunched his shoulders up to his ears. "She was probably trying to read something on the wall next to me," he said, hiding his smile behind his hair.

"Yeah right," your face was redder than the teacher's skirt," Josiah poked him again. "What have you got going on this weekend?"

"Umm… let me think." He paused. "I know! I have to shovel shit for five hours. Then take a break and shovel again!

Whooooooo!" Edgar raised both hands in the air and ran ahead as if the finish line was just in sight.

Josiah laughed and jogged to catch up, his solid legs needing extra effort to meet Edgar's long thin ones. "Hey!" he said, a little winded. "Slow down. I have an idea."

Edgar turned around, jogging backwards in place with a big goofy grin, waiting for Josiah.

"Yeah?"

"Yeah, so listen… what if you come over bright and early and help me with my chores and then we go to your place and work on your… shit. Might free up some time that way?"

Edgar tightened his mouth into a thin line, contemplating. He guessed that might make his mother happy. She hated robbing Edgar of a childhood but didn't have much of a choice, and that pained her. "I don't see why Mama would mind that as long as we get it done?"

"All right! I'll wait for you to ask when we get to your place."

The boys continued walking and talking, Josiah handling the weight of the conversation. His Papa had some new project at the mill and needed to travel all the way to New York City to have meetings about it. He went on about what life must be like in such a huge bustling place like New York. Josiah had a knack for being overly detailed and imaginative, a true writer in every sense of the word. Edgar tried to focus on his words but something nagged at him, and he was afraid to mention it to Josiah. He always felt like he was walking a fine line with him anyway, like Josiah was just too good of a person and put up with Edgar's weirdness rather than actually embrace him for who he was. Because of that, he believed this would definitely set him over the edge.

It was this dream Edgar had been having every night since his father left. Lately it had become so intense he didn't want to sleep anymore. The good part of the dream was that he saw his orchard fully realized. It stretched far beyond anything that he ever originally intended, and in the dream he looked after each tree as if they were his pets or children, meticulously pruning and caring for every single one of them.

It made him believe that he really could be a good farmer if it was something that he chose to do instead of being forced into it.

He adored that part of the dream! But his happiness was short lived—there was always some force there that he couldn't handle the weight of. Like something was trying to destroy him and everything that he created. He could never see what this force was, only that it felt like suddenly he was carrying twelve sacks of manure on his back, making his legs want to buckle and leaving him nearly breathless. If he could bear the weight long enough to plant another tree, then he would get a reprieve and a huge sense of relief would wash over him.

And then there was the old man with black eyes. There was something about them that drew him in. If he looked at them directly, they'd pull him into their darkness, and who knows where that is or if he'd ever come back from it.

The man seemed to be connected with the force somehow. When he was around the force would be stronger. He always tried to reach for Edgar but could never catch him. As soon as he appeared and Edgar got a good look at those eyes, he would wake up in a cold sweat.

The only person to whom he'd ever mentioned the dreams was his mother.

Her face would become very stern.

"Witchcraft is for the devil! It's a bunch of old hooey," she lectured him.

"Well then why would you let me go in the field if you don't believe in that stuff? And what about Uncle Benjamin? Apparently, he could commune with nature, but it was a gift from God, according to you, not sorcery!"

Mama squinted him a warning with her eyes, but didn't respond to his remark. She rationalized with him instead. "Maybe these dreams manifest because of your plans for this orchard. And maybe the evil force is telling you that you aren't allowed to go back there."

Edgar smirked, accepting her sarcasm.

"The old man must represent your father somehow and how you are unsettled about him leaving us. Half of you desperately waits for him to come home and the other half knows that he won't. I believe those black eyes stand for the void in your heart because he didn't say goodbye." She put a gentle hand on his cheek.

"Well, Mama, when I feel the force, it seems like it's trying to ruin me and our family."

"It's the struggle between your mind and your heart. Your heart is the force and you are afraid to listen and follow it, because if you do, you believe that something bad would happen, that it would destroy you. So instead, you listen to your head and allow logic and reason to make the decisions."

Edgar knew this to be true and swore his mother should have been a professor or something, so smart that she was. Mama was right about a lot of things. Sometimes, his head reasoning made him do bad things. Like when the kids at school dared him to put a mouse in their teacher's lunch pail. He figured if he did it, then more kids would like him. His heart said not to, but he ignored it. He just wanted everyone to be nice to him for a change. He cried himself to sleep that night. He blamed his heart for everything and decided long ago to keep it under lock and key.

Edgar felt disoriented. He'd been swimming in his own thoughts on their walk so much that he didn't realize they had already reached his home. He was thankful that Josiah was still talking and hadn't noticed that he'd wandered off.

"Well, go in and ask your mama about this weekend, Eddie. I'll wait here." Josiah smirked, as he knew Edgar hated that nickname.

"Be right back, *Jodie!*" Edgar quipped.

Josiah rolled his eyes.

Edgar knew his mother wouldn't have any problem with their plan and was back in a hurry to tell Josiah, who was kicking around dirt in the front yard.

"Fantastic! I'll see you at my place when the… rooster… crows?" He looked around in a slow circle. "I forgot you don't have one."

"Ha! Yeah, my mother hates roosters, says they're too much like men, the chickens do just fine on their own."

Josiah laughed. "So how do you get up in the morning? Farmers can't sleep in!"

Edgar bit his bottom lip, thinking of his dreams but then blurted out, "My sisters! If you had little twin sisters, you'd be awake before the roosters, too!"

Amused, Josiah called out his goodbye and turned to walk the rest of the way home. Edgar watched him go. He was looking forward to the weekend ahead but still contemplative and uneasy. His mother was right about a lot of things. She told him not to blame himself for his dad being gone. But he couldn't help it.

The night his father disappeared; they had gotten into an argument. Edgar had been so upset about losing their house in the city, angry that all of his nice things were gone, fuming that he was left to get picked on out in this middle-of-nowhere school. In the heat of the moment, as he was sitting up in bed, when his parents normally came in to say goodnight, he blamed his father for everything and told him so.

His father already seemed a few inches shorter, shrinking under the weight of what the family had endured. He didn't say anything, but his eyes did all the talking. It pierced Edgar's heart to see that look in his eyes.

After he said those harsh words, Papa looked at him for a long moment and then shut his bedroom door. Not a slam but a very light click that told him he had heard and was processing. Edgar never saw him again. He closed the door on his heart when Papa didn't come home.

He was confused. Papa had always been the cheerful optimist, allowing every little thing to blow right past him as if he carried his own wind and let it out when trouble was around so it never touched him.

His mama was like that too. Edgar guessed that's why he turned out the way he did. You can't have dark without light or up without a down. His parents had too much optimism, so Edgar was there to be the sponge, the void that soaks in the darkness that they seemed to ignore. He kept it close to his heart, a great dark pillow that surrounded it, protecting its feelings from ever breaking free.

8 CHELSEA

It's been one whole month since Grandpa Jo's funeral and a week since that creepy school incident, and I feel like I'll never be happy again. Even though his parents vow they won't ever give up the search, the police have said they soon will call off their own for Billy McKenzie. School life has pretty much returned to normal.

I heard the adults talking at Grandpa's funeral about how kids "bounce back quickly," and it appears they're right. They all seem to be getting on with their day like nothing ever happened. Autumn and Jeff included, even though they are more sensitive when they're with me. To me, however, day blends into night, which blends into long drawn out days. I know I need to snap out of it, but it's just too much. I'm starting to feel like a zombie. I guess it's because I was hit with a triple whammy.

First Billy and then my grandparents. When Grandpa died, Grandma, I hate to say it, went downhill fast. Our parents had no choice but to put her in a home with special care. Grandma goes to that "other place" now more often than she's here with us. I hope she has long talks with Grandpa there. When she does come back, she doesn't seem to recognize anyone; she just stares at the television.

She prefers when the cable isn't working and the screen looks all pixelated. The nice electrical guy figured out how to keep the cord just slightly unplugged so it stays that way all the time. I believe it's more about the noise than anything. She probably likes the TV conversations but can't handle the action that happens on screen. I was going to see her every day after school, but it's getting too difficult for me to watch her waste away like this, so I've limited my time with her to only once a week.

As the moonlight through my window pierces the darkness in my bedroom, I try to let go of all of these things, to steady myself into the here and now. My room has windows on opposite sides. East and west. Right now, the west wins as the moon shines one big eye in the sky, making me wonder where the other eye is—that perhaps the other eye is the sun on the opposite side of the earth and when this universal face winks, it will be daylight again on my side.

Sometimes I will lie on the floor when it does and let the heat of it wash over my face. I imagine I'm on a beach somewhere next to a secluded ocean, just me, the sand, sun, and salt water. You'd think I'd be afraid of the water because of what happened when I was little but I'm not. I still feel a great connection to it in any form, whether fresh or salt.

All of nature has a pulse. Everything is alive, even the non-biological stuff because of atoms, electrons, and the other things they teach us in science class. But the vibe of the ocean is different. It compels me to want to be near it and bask in the energy it carries. It doesn't care what the world is doing. If it wants to knock out a ship, it will. If it chooses to bring another to shore, it will. We think we have the power or the earth has the power, but the ocean is something entirely different. Autumn tells me that my spirit twin is a mermaid, and even though it sounds silly, when I really think about it, she's probably right.

I took a ride up to Maine with Autumn and Jeff a few years back because her Grandparents live there in Rangeley, and she visits for a couple of weeks each summer. It's a seven and a half hour or so drive from our home, and we had so much fun in the car reading books and being silly. But I read this one book that shocked me that it was even in Autumn's collection because she is such a "happy flower."

The book was a little scary, something about a kid seeking revenge on another kid by putting a bubble of air in their veins with a syringe that they stole. That stuck with me, because gross. And now I know just one more nasty thing that can kill a person. I hate death. I'm sure no one likes it, but it scares me to no end. I think of that bubble when they changed Grandma's saline IVs. I couldn't handle watching the solution drip down, imaging what would happen if an air bubble got stuck in there somehow.

When we finally crossed the line into Maine something changed for me. I felt like we didn't just cross into another state, but we were launched into another dimension. The air felt lighter, and the forests that covered either side of the road were buzzing and alive with life as if they were welcoming us into their home.

The smell of cedar and pine drifted into the car windows and made me feel like I was the stuffing in one of those little pillows for your underwear drawer that you can buy at all the country stores. Goodness knows there's nothing more forest goddess than having your bras and panties forged from a great spruce! It was wonderful and exhilarating, one of those many small moments that I'm sure to carry around with me for the rest of my life.

We were forced to stop right smack in front of the "Welcome to Maine" sign. A behemoth of a moose was making a languid journey across the road, which we joked about right away as it seemed like the Universe creating its own live-action advertisement. Then the moose did something we weren't expecting: He stopped in the middle of the road right in front of the car and turned his big body around to face us like he wanted to see if he approved of who was coming into his territory.

He stood there staring at us for a good few minutes as if his eyes were cameras trying to focus, and then something remarkable happened which is still a hot topic of debate between the three of us. He appeared to look us over one by one until he fixated on me, there, in the middle of the back seat. He must have started at me for a solid two minutes until he gave me the smallest of nods. After, he turned around and kept on walking. None of us spoke until we were on our way again, and it was me who broke the ice, hitting Jeff on the shoulder.

"Did you see that? Come on, did you?!"

"See what?"

"The Moose! It... NODDED!" I was transfixed on the road like it was still staring at me.

"Uh, no, you're losing it."

"I am NOT! Come on. Autumn, you saw it didn't you?"

"He just shook his head… they all do that."

"Mr. O'Connor! You're right there in the front seat. Didn't he just nod?"

"If you say so honey." Autumn's dad was distracted with rerouting his GPS directions.

After the BMI, or Bizarre Moose Incident, which I no longer wish to discuss with them, we drove through a path in the woods until a clearing opened us up to the coast which led to the second moment in my life that my breath had been taken away from me. Except this time, I was glad to let it go. I even asked Mr. O'Connor to stop the car because I wanted the moment to last, and it wasn't until we rolled away again that I inhaled. The air I released is probably still suspended in that spot, keeping watch over the beauty of all things.

Right before me was a massive cliff like someone had taken a cleaver fit for a giant and lopped off the edge of a mountain. Far below, waves were crashing into the rocks, filling my ears with a new kind of romance I'd never experienced (not that I've experienced much). On top of the cliff stood a magnificent grey house. It wasn't like one of the newer homes with sculpted angles.

It was more like an old cottage, except larger. Much larger. That house, with its proximity to the ocean—its charming peacefulness… I knew that one day I would have a house just like that one. Maybe even in Maine for all I knew. Maybe it would be that house. I could sit on the edge of that cliff all day, just the ocean and me, basking in her beauty, pretending I was a mermaid. I didn't want to leave, and it still comes up in my paintings quite often. One day…

For now, though, I'm just lying in my bed noticing how the moonlight cuts through the window, when I hear a soft tick. I glance over thinking another depressed bug has just met its demise against the glass when it happens again and one more time after that. Certain there isn't a bug cult drinking spiked juice, I open the window to investigate. Sure enough, it's Autumn and Jeff.

"What are you guys doing here, it's what? Midnight?"

"Come down! We have to show you something." Autumn looks totally excited and freaked out at the same time.

"This better be freakin' important!" I yell-whisper back and then look to my bedroom door to make sure no one is lurking in the hallway as I slip out as quietly as possible. My bedroom window is just over the roof of the porch. After I shut my window, I slither backwards on my belly until my feet hang off, then the rest of my body until it's just my hands on the roof. In the meantime, I feel for the porch railing, which is wide enough to stand on, let go of the roof, and voila! I'm free.

"It's out in the forest," says Jeff, grinning in a way that makes me want to run, not walk, straight back to my bedroom and lock myself under the covers somehow.

I stop before I even start walking. "No way am I going out there. I don't even like it during the day, but at night? Are you crazy?"

The forest is so massive that it forms the backyard for most of the neighborhood and this side of town. It's not a normal forest or even an orchard. I've never been sure how to classify it. It's littered with hundreds of creepy-ass crabapple trees. Like all their growth has been stunted or like, if Tim Burton wanted an orchard, he'd marvel over this one. We're supposed to keep off it because it's considered private property, but honestly, I've never had a desire to "play" back there. Ever.

"So what?" he says smugly.

"So what? Autumn, are you hearing this?"

Autumn nods.

"Oh, let me see, Jeffrey... There's that rumor that a kid's dad died back there and his ghost still walks around at night, particularly during an Indian summer when the fog hangs around. Oh, and the two little girls. How about them? Remember that one time you swore up and down that you saw one?"

Jeff doesn't defend this accusation, he just continues to stare at me with that stupid grin. So I go on, more mad now than anything else. "And it's been common knowledge since we were little that kids go in there and never come back out."

I can tell that I'm going nowhere with this tirade and allow Jeff to become blurry as I focus on the trees in the distance. I feel claustrophobic just looking at them. Without any prompting, my grandmother's nursery rhyme pops into my head, but I can't recall the exact words.

"Damn, what was that rhyme?" I whisper.

Autumn pulls my arm. "No really, Chells, I know how you feel about it. Trust me, we all do. But you have to see this."

"Why couldn't we just do this during the day? Or better yet, why couldn't you tell me about it tomorrow?"

"You know we aren't allowed in the woods. And once he told you, you'd want to go, too!"

I cave, knowing this is true, and start walking toward the back of my house. It takes maybe five minutes to walk to the property line where the forest begins. We've played back here so many times as kids it's instinctive for us to jump over the old, rotted, half-burnt beam of wood peeking out of the ground.

Dad told me this used to be an old farm property and that piece of wood probably belonged to a barn. I used to imagine what life would be like when the farm was around: how many houses were there, what the people were like and so on.

Jeff finally blurts out why he's brought us here: He's been experimenting with the trees.

"You've what?" I say, not sure if I'm more shocked or disgusted. "Why on earth would you even go near those things? They're horrid."

"I know, I know. At first, I was surprised with myself for even considering it. But I was watching this show on bats and really wanted to see one. And since the forest is on your side of the street, I figured I'd take a little stroll and find some.

"At eleven o'clock at night?"

"Sure, why not? I couldn't sleep anyway. And I knew Autumn would be up, so I grabbed her first and debated whether I should show you or not because it's behind your house and I really didn't want to freak you out. Anyway, it's just this one tree here, closest to your property so we don't have to go too far in there or anything." Jeff motions to a blessedly normal looking crabapple tree just a few feet away.

I frown. "Eww though! Why does it have to be my property?"

Jeff turns to me shrugs and says, "I dunno. Cuz it's you, I guess?"

Jeff and I have always had a special bond. No matter how irritated we get with each other, we are still family, and he always protects me, too. He's like the older and younger sibling I never had, all tied into one.

He also seems to look up to me or at least respects my decisions. He usually asks me my opinion when he's battling between two problems and tells me the path I choose for him turned out to be the right one. I consider myself lucky that I have friends like these two. Not many people could have known each other this long and still be so close. Which is why I didn't put up too much of a fight when they said we were going to this godforsaken forest.

Even standing a few feet from my property line freaks me out. I do not like it here. I do not like the energy. It's like as soon as you are standing on the border you enter a vacuum. The sound from the neighborhood is muffled, and your ears hurt like when only one of the car windows is rolled down when you're driving. It's like the trees are so dense even sound has a hard time finding a way in. Whatever it is. I hate it.

"So this… this is the tree, then? The thing that is keeping me of dreaming about Johnny Depp tonight?" I begin to wonder what all the fuss is about.

"Gross! He's so old!" Autumn squinches her nose.

"Welllll…" I elongate this word as I try to think of how to explain it. "My mom has been watching reruns of *21 Jump Street*, and I have to say THAT Johnny is dream worthy."

"*21 Jump Street*, huh? I'll have to check it out!" She snickers.

I can almost hear Jeff's eyes roll as he says "girls" in that tonal mix of disgust and humor.

"Okay, you guys stand here." He's all business now.

"Mlahhhhh." Autumn sticks her tongue out at him. "You're too serious, Jeffrey."

"Psh! If I recall not thirty minutes ago you were shaking in your slippers."

I stifle a laugh. I hadn't noticed Autumn's fuzzy bunny slippers.

She shrugs.

Jeff places us just on the edge of my property line like chess pieces. The moon is completely full and casts a shadow on

Jeff that makes me realize that he must have grown six inches this year. "My god, Jeff, you are so tall and skinny!"

"Right?" says Autumn. "I was just noticing that, too."

"Focus please," he says, agitated. I swear he is going to be a librarian or something. He's goofy enough, but when he flips on the serious switch, he's a totally different person.

"Now look straight ahead at the—"

I see it before Jeff has to explain. "Oh my God! What the heck?" Autumn is looking between me, Jeff, and the tree saying, "What? What?"

After a long moment with my mouth hanging open and Jeff smiling, eyebrows raised in sheer excitement, she sees it too.

"Oh that," she says. "Duh, Autumn. See! Isn't it insane?!"

The moonlight illuminating the trees is casting long shadows. The shadows, which for all intents and purposes should be to the left of the trees, are completely in the opposite direction. I take a step back, flabbergasted.

"But how is that even possible?" Autumn says.

"I have NO idea," he says. "But I have one more thing to show you. And you really aren't going to believe this. Autumn, I didn't show you this before because I wanted you both here for this one. Take a step into the woods and turn around so you're facing the house. And keep an eye on your shadows."

We both look at him like he's nuts, and he reassures us it's only one small step. We do as instructed and see that our shadows are in sync with the ones the trees are casting. I cringe as that weird pressure sensation starts to bother my ears. The look on Autumn's face says she feels it as well.

"Now turn around and slowly walk towards your yard."

Gladly, I think as Autumn and I cross into the familiar territory that is mine, one set of feet adorned with fuzzy bunnies, the other, completely bare. All sounds return to normal the instant we cross into my yard, and as we watch our shadows, we both scream and cover our mouths as if it would erase the sound that just came out of them.

Our shadows have flipped. They've reverted back to the way they were supposed to be. We didn't see it happen, it was just... one second they were on one side, then the next second they were on the other.

Officially freaked out, Autumn and I grab each other's arms. "There has to be an explanation for this," she says.

"Seriously, Autumn, I don't think there *can* be an explanation for *that*!" I point toward the woods with my eyes.

Jeff appears at our side, raising and lowering his eyebrows like Groucho Marx, pretending he's ashing a phantom cigar and says, "I told ya you'd want to see this."

"I've had enough," I say next, waving my arms as if I'm trying to erase the scene behind me. "It's late and I need to process this. Let's talk on the bus tomorrow. Whose turn is it for breakfast?"

"Mine," says Jeff. And I'm making your favorite oatmeal."

"Oh yay!" Autumn chimes in, perky as ever, like nothing completely bizarre just occurred.

"Thanks, Jeff. I'll see you guys tomorrow." We split ways, the two of them crossing our dark street, most of the porch lights having been switched off already which I wonder about in passing as it seems too early but decide I don't really care.

I climb back up to my room opposite the way I came. Before I close my window, I stick my arm out so the moon can cast its shadow on the porch roof, turning my hand this way and that, seeing if it makes any difference with the shadow. I close one eye then the other. Nothing. The shadow is where it should be.

Dragging my tired and dirty feet under the covers, I make a mental note to make sure I shower before my parents have a look at me, and while I'm at it, throw my bed sheets in the laundry, too. The top and bottom of my eyelids are magnets, closing in on each other and I don't feel like fighting the strength of the pull, but I've just remembered I didn't set my alarm earlier. I gather what little ounce of strength is left and manage to grab Ariel and push her tail so the clock illuminates its numbers in neon blue.

I suck in a swift breath and promptly fall out of bed, still holding my alarm clock. It's 6:30 in the morning, and I have to get up for school! I'm just as startled when my phone buzzes with two texts. One from Autumn and one from Jeff, both with the same question.

Were we really outside for six and a half hours?!

9 EDGAR

It was a lazy Saturday afternoon. Edgar had already gone to Josiah's to help him with his chores, and then both of them went to Edgar's to finish his. They had purposefully woken up at sunrise so they could have the day to themselves and do whatever it is that boys do to pass the time. At this moment, they were doing a whole lot of nothing.

They had made a space for themselves in the loft of the barn. The window opened to give them a view of the fields and forest in the backyard. They both let their feet dangle out of the window as they stared at the barren field and the trees beyond it. Edgar was etching something into the wood with the pointy end of a hand cultivator.

"I've been thinking about checking out the field," Edgar said, breaking the silence. Josiah pulled a long thread of wheat out of his mouth and looked at Edgar like he'd lost his mind. He had seen Edgar wince when he plucked the stalk from the ground, but Edgar just said he had some dust in his eye.

"Your mama would skin you and use it to make a pair of new shoes if she knew you were going to do that," he said.

"I know. I just don't see what all the fuss is about. I mean, at least it has something growing on it." He nodded to the crabapple tree perched in solitude to the far right of the field. "I swear I don't remember it being there when we moved in, but that whole time was such a blur for me, I guess I never noticed. I just want to check it out and see if I can figure out why nothing wants to grow. I mean look," he said, pointing toward the field, "there's an amazing looking forest just past all this. Obviously all is good over there. Just why not here?"

"Well…" Josiah paused, launched his wheat stalk over the edge like a dart, then looked out at the field contemplating Edgar's scheme. "I guess I'd say you have a pretty good case to argue about with your mom. Especially if you throw the bit in about your business idea again. It really would be the perfect plot of land to grow your apples or whatever it is you want to do. And if you start now, they should be the right size and bear fruit by the time you're old enough to have a business like that. You would think, anyway. Lord knows we could use more apples around here. I'm sick and tired of tan—tan wheat, tan corn. Dull colors all over this place. There is that orchard down the way that's taking up all the business anyway."

Josiah continued as he mulled over the plan, a spark beginning to alight with excitement for Edgar. "It's not fair that they're cornering the market! You need to give them a run for their money, Edgar. Yeah, that's it. You're good with numbers, right? You should sit down and figure this all out. How much can you really make with a business like that?"

"I've worked it out already." Edgar's pride lifted that someone was finally seeing his vision. "If I play my cards right, Mama won't have to work anymore. Not ever. And the girls can do whatever they want to do. They can help Mama or help me, or whatever. Let them be free… not stuck like I am. I don't want them to grow old before their time…" He trailed off, starting to feel somewhat bitter about his current situation but continued to imagine the possibilities.

"I can see it, you know?" Edgar's heart jumped like a fish in the ocean as his vision took shape, imagining the yellow grass suddenly alive with color and the entire stretch of field littered with rows of trees. Apples, peaches, whatever would grow best here in the Northeast.

"I could have apples here. And peaches over there. Maybe some berry bushes. I could invite people to pick their own, and they'd have to pay me for it. Mama could make pies and fresh jams. That would make her so happy! She never has time or money to do that. Maybe I could go to Buffalo or something and sell bushels to the city vendors there. Wouldn't that be great?"

Josiah's nod was enthusiastic as if he could feel all the excitement that Edgar was laying before him. He looked out over the field for a moment, internalizing the whole of the situation. "You sure do have your work cut out for you. When do you plan on sneaking in the field? Or maybe you should talk to your mother first about it. I think it'd be better to do this the right way. Because you know if you get in trouble, then I get in trouble. And I don't want to get in trouble, especially with Mrs. Slate."

Edgar sighed, reeling the elation back in with an empty hook. "I guess you're right. Maybe I'll bring it up after she puts the twins down tonight."

"Sounds good to me," Josiah said as he squinted at whatever Edgar was carving into the window frame. He smiled as he saw the word "brothers" etched in a choppy scrawl.

***

"I don't know, Edgar, I really don't like it back there! Besides, I always thought you'd be a banker like your Papa. You were always so good with numbers."

Edgar had spent a good portion of an hour pleading his case to his mama about his vision of creating an orchard, and she was remaining as stubborn as ever.

"Yes! And I'll have to use tons of numbers with my trees. I'll have to count seeds, calculate them into rows. Figure out the failure rate of the seedlings, and then when we do get a crop, there's a whole other world of math involved, especially when it comes to money…. And guess what, Mama?"

Edgar, who had been pacing back and forth across the room, approached her and gently put his hands on hers to stop her frantic knitting. She typically hid behind a ball of yarn when presented with something she didn't want to deal with.

She looked at Edgar, her eyes wide and round, matching those of her son except the worry and exhaustion in hers, from being a single mother trying to make the family survive on what little their father left them with.

Knowing he had her attention he said, "Mama… you can bake pies and sell jellies and all the stuff you used to love to do. You can have your own little business with me and maybe the girls could help, too. They'd be older then! Or you know what, Mama?" he said, hoping to deliver the most blazing denouement. "I want to make it so the girls can do whatever they want to do. They don't have to, you know, settle down. If they don't want to. They can travel! And maybe you can go with them this time!"

He hung on to both of his mother's hands and allowed his words to sink in, knowing what it meant that her twin daughters would have the freedom she was never allowed. Edgar knew her life had been laid out for her by her family, who needed assurance, and she was the wax for their seal. His father told him about it once, that she wanted to travel abroad to study literature and poetry. That it was never her plan to marry and he always regretted not being able to take her there himself—even on his lengthy salary they couldn't afford to do all the things that she dreamed.

The faintest of tears became visible rising up from under her bottom lashes, which sent hi stomach fluttering. "We can make a lot of money, Mama! My trees, your goods. The whole town would love us. We'd be a rich family again."

Mom perked up. Edgar knew Mama was a city girl at heart and hated the thought of being stuck here out in the country, though she said she'd gotten used to it and respected its beauty.

Mama freed her hands from Edgar and closed her eyes briefly before beginning. "You know, Edgar, this is really going against my better judgement."

Edgar felt his face light up before he could help himself. He wanted to remain stoic in case his mother changed her mind.

"That field out there, I do feel like something is wrong with it. But I don't believe in supernatural nonsense. Not one bit." She continued to look at him, brows furrowed, eyes brightened by adoration of her only son.

"I guess you can give it a try. But you wear gloves and as soon as you step foot back onto our property, you hose everything off in case there's some kind of illness breeding out there. What bothers me most is you getting hurt. I don't want you to be too disappointed if and when you find out that land is rotten and no good for anything."

"But—"

"Let me finish!" She shook a knitting needle in his direction. "We have had enough heartbreak and sadness to last an entire lifetime. And you better let Josiah help you. I don't want you going out there alone. At least not at first. Promise me, if this doesn't work out, you'll consider doing something more tangible with that gift of yours."

This made Edgar freeze. He tried to balance a voice that had the potential to come out shaky. "Uh… what gift?" He was terrified that she might know about his… oddity.

She put down her needles and stood up to give him a big hug. "Honestly, Edgar, sometimes you scare me. Your math skills, silly. You have an amazing gift for numbers."

Edgar, visibly relieved, sunk into his mother's hug. He thought she was the best mom ever, and he told her that.

Edgar couldn't sleep that night. He tossed and turned and eventually went out back to the barn, stopping to say hello to each of the horses and give them apples that he snuck from the kitchen. Mama would most definitely notice, but he was too excited to care. The horses deserved a treat once in a while, and he figured he could pay his mother back with thousands of apples in a few short years.

He made his way up the tall ladder and opened the window so he could take in the whole of his new project. He knew he should try to sleep, but he was too excited to go inside. He made himself a bed in the hay, something he and Josiah did quite often for sleepovers. He made himself comfortable and warm and lay down with the window still open so he could stare out into the moonlit field. The field was amassed in shadow, and the forest behind was backlit by the glow of the moon. The contrast between that area and the forest behind it didn't faze him one bit.

For hours he lay there, plotting and planning. He imagined what each tree would look like. He saw his twin sisters as girls his age running throughout the trees with matching sundresses and pigtails in their red hair. He imagined the apple blossoms smelling so sweet and beautiful that it would overpower the old funk that lingered here. He cherished the thought that his orchard would make it so that he would never have to shovel crap again. Better still, he'd open all the windows of the house so that the blossoms would fill every space, pushing out the old smell and replacing it with glorious new life. The blossoms would come through the back and mingle with Mama's cooking. People would walk past and smell everything they'd created. It would be inviting and alive and wonderful!

Edgar thought for a moment that he really wanted to experience everything, not just from his imagination, but from a very deep and personal level, and was about to take his guard down to allow his gift, the one his mother didn't know about, the one that she shared with his Uncle Benjamin to take over. But he didn't—and wasn't totally sure why. Maybe part of him didn't need to know all the secrets. He wanted to uncover things himself, the real normal way, like his Papa would have done. So he continued to imagine his plans coming to fruition until his mind became tired and the blanket of sleep covered him tight.

10 CHELSEA

I watch the neighborhood houses as they disappear behind our bus. One by one they pass, until we pick up speed and they start to blend into each other turning into a blurry string of color disappearing to some unknown place beyond my periphery. It's like our bus is some magical spaceship leaving a black hole in its wake. Until last night, *or was it early this morning?* I never thought much of space, the stars, or what lies beyond, much preferring to keep my proverbial fins in the water.

I'm the kind of person that takes everything at face value, was never one for the supernatural. I mean ghost stories are fun and all, but I never believed that any of those things could be real. But now I'm not so sure.

I look down at my full cup of oatmeal, and my stomach turns, still uneasy from the events of last night and the fact that I'm completely exhausted. I twist it around in my hands and see a smudge forming on my fingers; I'd been doodling on the cup and didn't even realize. I hate when I do that. I try to inspect my work a little closer, but it's hard to make anything out anything besides blobs of blue ink that I can't rub off with the edge of my sweater sleeve.

I snap out of my daze and look to Autumn sitting next to me. She's picking at her oatmeal as if inspecting it for bugs. Jeff, on the opposite seat from us, looks so chipper it's frustrating. He catches me staring at him, and he stares right back, saying nothing,

67

just making his eyes wider and wider, obviously trying to make me smile. Really, it just makes me want to punch him.

"Ugh, Chelsea, are you in one of your moods, again?" he says. "Snap out of it, girl, it's a beautiful day! The birds are singing, the sun is shining, and we haven't slept in twenty-four hours! Ahhh, glorious!"

"Seriously, Jeffrey?" Autumn pipes in. "Doesn't it bother you in the slightest that whatever we saw last night makes it seem like the laws of physics are just little bendy straws?"

I'm taken aback by Autumn's remark, not realizing it had affected her so deeply. "I can't believe this is creeping you out this much, too!"

"Well yeah. I mean come on, that was craziness! And besides, it's worse for you because you have to live with that behind your house... sorry." She's apologizing because she knows I have a tendency to overthink things, but it's too late now.

"Yeah," is all I can say, and I go back to twirling my coffee cup, making new pictures out of the smudges. I do this for a while, trying to think of nothing at all and give my poor brain a break, when a particularly interesting smudge stands out and gives me an idea.

"Autumn!" I shout out, and she is so startled she dumps her oatmeal on the floor.

"Hey, I worked hard on that." Jeff looks at the cup with dejection.

"Aw, shoot, I'm sorry," I say laughing, not able to help myself. "I just had an idea. Check out my cup."

Autumn takes the cup, turning it around and around, examining it like an ancient artifact. "Looks like a little pen bomb went off."

"I concur, doctor," says Jeff, pulling down his glasses to get a closer look.

I take the cup and point to a rectangle shape. "Right here. It looks like a piece of paper! Or a file folder, or a... trip to your dad's office to research that property!" I shoot a sly grin over to Autumn who seems to be on board with my thoughts as she immediately takes out her phone to text her dad.

Jeff looks confused for a moment but catches on quick and nods with enthusiasm about the budding plan. Autumn's dad works for the city and has lots of access to things that are tough for people to get into. We can only do so much research on the internet or at the library. What we may be able to gain from his computers goes beyond anything we can get from our own resources.

Three-thirty can't come fast enough. When the bell rings, I almost forget to grab my homework from my locker. Jeff sees me whizzing by and with one long arm snatches my coat to pull me back like a human yo-yo.

"Hey there, lady! Where ya off to? The homework police will fine you big time if you forget your bio study sheets."

"You know, sometimes it's a curse to have us in the same grade." I sound annoyed but have a smile on my face. I can never be mad at him. "Seriously though, thanks. I hate missing homework. I guess I'm just excited to do some research!"

"So it's game on, then?"

"Oh, I thought you knew. Autumn's dad is totally into it. He thinks we are doing research for a local history project. So you better think of a place you want to research like, now.

"I love me some last-minute decisions!"

I walk with Jeff out to the parking lot and see Autumn already waiting in the car with her father.

"Come on in guys! How was school?" Mr. O'Connor calls from the window.

"Hi, Mr. O.! Thanks for letting us shack up in your office," Jeff says as we squeeze into the back seat of his Mini Cooper.

"Of course. I love having you guys for a visit. You learn so much more by getting out into the world, rather than sitting in school and reading books all day. That's why I drag Miss Autumn here with me to work whenever I can," he says, beaming at his daughter in the front seat. "Now explain to me more about your project."

I tell him, "Our history teacher wants us to research local historical sites. We all had to choose a place around town and find out more of its history and see if we can uncover any stories from its past. She says that sometimes uncovering the past in something can revive life in something else. She's weird like that, you know? Always talking about ghosts and mysteries."

"Yeah, Dad, I think she's a ghost hunter or something when she isn't teaching," Autumn says.

"Ghosts, huh?" says Mr. O. "I don't know about ghosts, *but* I do know the three of you will get an A on your projects. So which location did you decide on?"

I tell him that I'm picking my own yard, that I want to find out about the barn and what happened there. I want to see if I can dig up any ghosts from the past. I'm trying to be funny and ironic, but it's lost on him. He grows quiet for a moment, mumbling something about letting sleeping dogs lie and then diverts his question over to Autumn and Jeff.

They both blurt out, "Mt. Hope Cemetery!" and I see his eyebrows scrunch in a puzzled sort of way in the rearview mirror as we had mentioned that two people couldn't have the same subject.

Jeff quickly perks up and says in a disgruntled voice that he thought maybe if he said it first this time he'd be able to get the project.

"Ha! That only works in class!" says Autumn, while Jeff makes a big show of slumping low into his seat.

We arrive at City Hall without any more project talk, and Mr. O'Connor leads the way into the records room.

"All right then," he says. I still have lots of work to do, so I'll leave you guys here. Just stay out of this section here." He points to a glass door on the far side of the wall protecting what looks to be mountains of file cabinets. "It's restricted. Anything else is fair and at your service," he says, bowing low at the waist while making a sweeping gesture like he's taking off an imaginary hat.

He pauses in mid-bow, then stands up straight like someone just goosed him, but the look on his face shows sheer confusion. "I can't believe I just did that... Wow. Well okay, you have two hours. Let me know if you need anything. I'll be just down at the end of the hall."

And with that, he vanishes into the field of fluorescent lights. We all look at each other our eyes saying the same thing. *That was weird.*

Autumn and Jeff make sure to spend at least half an hour researching their own projects so as not to raise any suspicion. Jeff chose the subway. We live in a smaller city, and at one point there used to be a small subway system. Now it's home to graffiti, the homeless, and probably Pokemon Go hotspots, but we've never tried it.

Autumn really hit the jackpot with Mt. Hope. It's a beautiful old Victorian cemetery with famous residents—women's rights activists, abolitionists, and the like. Come to think of it, I wouldn't mind researching it myself sometime.

"So this is really interesting," says Autumn as she taps away on a computer keyboard. "But I was thinking, why didn't we just tell my dad the truth?"

"Which part, that my backyard is a black hole that moves time and changes the direction of light?"

"Point taken," she says as she pushes off the desk with her feet, the wheels letting out a rebellious squeak, and starts spinning in her chair. Jeff joins in the fun, and I watch them for a few minutes until they decide to start racing around the room in their swivel chairs.

"Come on guys. This is serious!" I yell at them but change my tune. "I mean... it is. Isn't it? Don't you want to know more about the orchard?"

"Honey," says Jeff in his best faux girlfriend voice. "It's more than just your yard! It's that whole lotta land with those scary-ass trees and probably the forest behind it, too."

"Ugh, don't remind me."

"Don't worry, Chells. We'll get to the bottom of this," Autumn tells me as she puts a reassuring hand on my arm.

"Really? How can you be so whatever about this? Didn't that flip you out as much as it did me?"

"Yeah I guess, but it's been there for how long and we never knew about it? So it'll probably be there for another who knows how long. We have time."

"Easy for you to say. You don't have to live with it," I tell her. "And damn you Jeff and your crazy expeditions!" Still spinning in circles, his moppish hair follows behind his head like a cat chasing its tail. He stops when I address him and holds on to a desk for support.

"Whoa, spins," he says catching his breath. "Oh come on don't damn me! Consider this an adventure. If it weren't for me, we'd never have any fun. Amiright?" He's managed to wheel himself over to me and jabs my ribs lightly with his elbow.

Autumn chimes in. "Heck yeah! Remember that time when you wanted to prove that the power of running would keep you from ever being cold? So we bet you five bucks to run around in the snow with only your undies on?"

"Yeah!" I add. "But you didn't want our money because you knew you were right. So what happened? Huh?"

"So we spent a few hours in the ER while they got the blood pumping back into my fingers and toes. Big deal. And hey. They froze their applesauce so it was all slushy. Tell me that wasn't an awesome hospital perk."

A smile breaks free even though I try to fight it.

"Yeah," says Autumn. "And they felt bad for keeping us so long and gave us vouchers for free breakfast in the cafeteria. And we'll never know what sort of meat was really in those sausages. Hey, Jeff, maybe your next experiment would be to see if worms or bugs tastes the same as pork."

"Ew, Autumn, you're a vegetarian."

"So?"

"So what made you go all vegetarian anyway there, Auto?" It's Jeff's nickname for Autumn. The funniest part is how much she hates it.

"Your cooking," she says, sticking her tongue out at him to which he responds by throwing a wad of paper at her.

"Okay, seriously, where should we look first?" Autumn says.

"But the restricted section of course!" At this Jeff pulls a key card from his pocket. Autumn does something next that I've never seen her do for as long as I've known her, and that's a very long time. She yells at him. Like truly wholeheartedly yells at him. And that isn't all she does.

"Jeffrey August Mendon! You STOLE from my father? How could you?!"

With that she starts to beat him with everything she can find within reach while simultaneously mumbling under her breath, "Grounded. For two weeks. Stack of papers. Lost. My. Homework. Empty water bottle. Ate my last Ring Pop when we were six…"

When I see her reach for the stapler, I know I have to work fast to get it out of her hands. I don't think she is paying attention to anything she is grabbing.

"Enough you two!" I say and manage to grab the stapler before we end up back in the hospital for stitches.

Autumn glares at Jeff breathing heavily... Jeff is covering his head with long arms yelling, "I give, I give! Dang, Autumn, I didn't know you had such angst against me. You are normal after all!"

Autumn continues to give him the evil eye, saying nothing, so I take it upon myself to break the ice. "Okay, how on earth did you get this card?" I snatch it out of his hands, turning it over to check out the picture on it, which brings me a small amount of relief. "This isn't your father's card, Autumn."

"What? Let me see," she says and takes the card for inspection. "Huh, one of these desks must be his. Who knew?"

She sheepishly apologizes to Jeff, telling him to forget about the Ring Pop thing citing that she stole his last Jolly Rancher that same day.

"Truce?"

"Of course!" he says then grabs her head, nuggie style, rubbing her scalp with his knuckles like she's his annoying little sister.

"Okay well now that we have this…" I shake the card in my hand and bite my lip.

"I'm surprised at you, Miss Practical," says Autumn.

"Right?" agrees Jeff.

"I know… but maybe just a peek wouldn't hurt. Jeff, you guard the door. Autumn, come with me?"

"Why me?"

"You've been in this room more than we have."

"Yeah, but I wouldn't know…"

I shoot her a look that makes her stop talking, and now it's her time to bite her lip.

"Okay what's this all about, hmmm?" Jeff says wiggling his eyebrows like a detective trying to coax information.

"One time I sorta snuck in there when I was little. My dad caught me and gave me a warning. I'm sure he would have yelled at me, but I didn't really know I wasn't allowed to go in there. And he probably figured I wouldn't understand anything I read in there anyway. Which was mostly true. But I found something interesting. I'll see if I can find it."

"Well alrighty then. Now this should be fun," he says, rubbing his hands together. "I'll watch the door." He sneaks dramatically over to the office door, stretching out his legs one by one as far as they will go. Then he drops to the floor and rolls between two desks, crawling the rest of the way on his stomach.

"Here it is. Check this out!" As I was watching him impersonate Ace Ventura, Autumn had already made it to the restricted room and pulled out a file. "Yes this is it! It's like our own X-Files right here in Rochester. It talks about the big fire."

"What fire?" I'm puzzled.

"The one that burned down Old Rochester."

"Oh yeah! Didn't they say they didn't know what caused it? That it just seemed like everything was fine and then the next minute everything was up in flames?"

"Yes! Well it says here there was a lot of investigation after the fire, and it uncovered tons of seeds under the ashes."

"Seeds? That's random. What kind of seeds?"

"Not sure, but they couldn't do much with them; the technology wasn't around back then, of course. They thought maybe the town was built on an old farm or something. They kept a few here, see?" She produces what looks similar to apple seeds, except smaller and black, reflecting the overhead fluorescent lights. "I guess the evidence was inconclusive."

"Wow. That's crazy! I have never seen anything like those. I wish we could steal some and take them to school... but I guess that would be bad."

"Chelsea Joyce Heiland. I am surprised with you. It's one thing agreeing to the restricted section, but stealing?"

I sigh a long, drawn-out breath. "I know. I blame Jeff. He's turned me into a monster." I look over, but he's not paying attention at all, just staring down the hallway. We both laugh.

"So they never did find out what happened?"

"I guess not," Autumn says. "I heard my dad talking to my mom about it once a few years ago. They thought about opening the case up again but figured that it was so long ago there wasn't really any point, aside from curiosity. Besides, they'd have to dig up half of the city, which doesn't seem like something that could easily happen, you know?"

"He's coming!" Jeff alerts us.

Autumn jumps and almost drops the key. I grab it and race out of the restricted room before I have time to think. She closes the door behind her, and I place myself in front of a desk pretending that I'm writing down the details of important research. Jeff sits at a computer desk and punches up Google, because it's all he can think of doing. Autumn trips over the stapler that almost left its mark on the side of Jeff's head. Her dad walks in with three cans of soda and a brown paper bag.

"Hey guys, I brought you some sandwiches." He puts them down on a nearby desk and says, "Where's Autumn?" Just then an arm pops up from behind a desk brandishing a shiny silver stapler.

"I've got it!" she says, and her head appears over the desk as well, red-faced and hair disheveled. "Oh, hi Dad!" She starts to staple every piece of paper in front of her. For the third time today, her dad gives us a weird look.

"Um, okay. Well, you guys have about another hour here. Try to make sure you get what you need," he tells us before walking back out.

Autumn is staring at the collection of stapled papers thoughtfully. "It's modern art," she says to me, and I just laugh, hoping it wasn't anything important.

I turn my resolve back to the matters at hand. "One hour. Let's see what we can find." I jump on the computer and start looking up my address. Autumn heads for a file cabinet labeled "deeds," and Jeff sits to eat his sandwich, telling us he can't work on an empty stomach. I mumble that his stomach is always empty and keep digging through the search results.

"Awesome, I found it! 77 Mohawk Drive. Used to be Wheat Grove Ave. Here's Dad's name. And before him… P. Tucker… He must be the guy that built the house we live in now. How cool! Okay before him… looks like the land sat empty for a massive number of years… and then the Slate family. Hey, isn't that the name of the employee on the key card?" I check it again, and sure enough it's the same. I click a link that reads <u>Mysterious Disappearance of the Slate Family</u>, and it brings me to this article:

More Devastation and Heartache in Henrietta

Michael Edgar Slate. Missing November 15,1893.
After the devastating fire of the city of Rochester, the Slate
family relocated to 17 Wheat Grove Ave. Mr. Slate,
esteemed banker in Rochester then operating in agriculture.
Son Edgar Slate, 15, Mary Elizabeth Slate, 35 and her twin
daughters, Melinda and Maureen, 7, assumed perished in
the house fire Saturday, November 1, 1895. Bodies not
recovered. Fire determined from natural causes due to high
storm activity.

"Oh my god!" Jeff and I say at the same time. I look at Jeff,
who's holding a paper in his hands. "You first!" he says, heading
over to me with Autumn following behind him.

I show them the article. "Wow! That's *your* property,
Chelsea? Do your parents know about this?" Autumn says.

"I have no idea," I say. "But that would explain the piece of
burned wood sticking out of the ground in my backyard." I shudder
at the thought. "I just wonder why, after all this time, no one dug it
up?"

"I wonder if they knew each other," Jeff says, handing me
the paper he has just printed.

Another Missing Person in Henrietta

Josiah Heiland, 15. Missing, November 1, 1895. May
have perished assisting the Slate family. Body not
recovered.

"You have the same last name, Chells!" Autumn shouts.

My head is spinning—one part full of excitement, the other
part a true skeptic.

"You know, maybe the storm the article referenced had
something to do with the shadows back there? Like… making
everything all electrical or something," Jeff says. "That might
explain that weird ear feeling we get if we stand in there."

"I was kind of thinking that, myself. Maybe? But how? And besides this was all on my property. Not back there in the forest." I hit print on my own article then close the computer.

"Good point," Jeff says.

"I found the deeds to some of the houses in the neighborhood," says Autumn, smiling. She produces the list. "I already made a copy."

"What is this? Oh my God, you found my Grandpa Jo's old house! I knew he lived in the neighborhood a long time ago, but I guess they tore down his house and put in a 7-11, so I never got to see it. How cool!" I'm over the moon seeing something that somewhat belonged to my grandfather. It's like a little gift from beyond.

"Look, here it talks about Great Grandma Georgina and property lines. Looks like he had quite a yard. I wish I could tell Grandpa about this!" My face falls for a minute, remembering his laugh and all the stories he would tell about his mom. "I remember he told me about how she would let him and his best friend—oh what's his name? I forget. Anyway…Oh… nevermind. This deed makes me so happy. It brought me closer to him again, for a few minutes, anyway.

"Oh thank you, Autumn," I say, hugging her tight.

"You're welcome. Even though it's not really about your property, I knew you would appreciate it. I know how much you miss him."

I don't want them to see my eyes are welling up, so I quickly unhitch my arms from Autumn and pick up a paper clip I find on the floor, wiping my eyes nonchalantly on the way back up. Jeff, however, has a big tear rolling down his cheek. He quickly blames his dry contacts.

11 JOSIAH

The field was no longer empty and rotting, but was full of trees, trees that resembled that one in the way back, all mismatched and thrown about, twisting and turning like a maze that had no definite beginning or end. There were a few clearings here and there, which seemed to be the way through the maze. In the dream, Josiah seemed to know precisely where the clearings were, and that was how he figured his way around. He made it a point to keep his eyes on the ground, away from the gaze of the trees—he couldn't shake the terrible feeling that they were staring at him.

What light there was diffused through the shadows of the arm-like branches. There was no moon, sun, stars, clouds, or sound. Except for the footsteps. The footsteps he heard crunching in the distance were not his own, of that he was certain, because in his dream he wasn't a real person. At least he didn't think he was. He felt more like a ghost or someone stuck between worlds.

No, the footsteps belonged to the man with the dark hair, here too somewhere, probably trying to find the little girl. Josiah knew this because he had practice rationalizing his dreams: The dark-haired man was an extension of himself. And the little girl. She was always just within reach, but he could never quite grasp her. She represented some vulnerable part of himself that came out when his "dark side" manifested. Maybe that's why he couldn't save her? He thought about this for a bit with his eyes still closed, allowing the sounds from the outside to bring him back to his bedroom.

Josiah got out of bed and poured some water into his hands from the porcelain pitcher his grandmother had given him. He splashed his face, allowing the water to drip into the basin and mingle with the remnants of his dream, both splattered to the sides and disappeared. He needed a clear head to focus on Edgar today and what was to become of his field.

Josiah had to hand it to Edgar. He was creative and ambitious, quite the opposite from most boys their age. Out here, when the kids are old enough, they go off to help their fathers. The boys, anyway. The girls would stay home to be with their mothers and learn house things like cooking and sewing. And having babies, he assumed. He honestly didn't know what girls did.

But Edgar was always going on about the city and all the people and fancy places to eat, their clothes, and the people with different colors. Josiah thought it sounded exciting, and maybe one day he'd venture out there, but he much preferred the simplicity of the country, which suited his uncomplicated personality.

Josiah helped his mom with breakfast, sampling it while they cooked. He loved the smell of the sausages frying on the pan. His mama stirred the eggs, scrambling them in a way that only she knew how. His papa would joke that her eggs were so good it must require a form of sorcery to cook them.

"I was thinking about your friend Edgar and his family," she said as she stirred. "Their land bothers me something awful."

He moved the pan from the heat source with a towel, careful not to burn himself. "It does me, too, Mama. But I feel like we might be able to do some good with it somehow. I…" He transferred the sausages to a plate and continued thoughtfully. "You know, Mama, I can't decide who's more blessed. Edgar for finding us or us for finding him. It's like as soon as I met him, I've wanted to help him, but sometimes I feel like he helps me more than he realizes."

"The Lord works in his own way," she answered. "Go and work with the Lord; see if you can help breathe life back into that field."

He liked the idea of "working with the Lord." It made him imagine God as a farmer or a working man like most of the other men around here. He pictured God as a muscular and proud man with black hair and bright eyes picking up hay with a pitchfork in a field with all the other farmers.

Josiah's family was religious, never missing a Sunday at church. Josiah, however, was unsure about everything they said. He agreed with the pragmatism of honesty, loving everyone, and treating people how you want to be treated. It was the scary side, the things about the devil and evil which made him uneasy. The idea that one wrong move would send him somewhere to burn forever and ever made him shiver.

Josiah definitely believed in angels and was certain that his mother was one. He knew beings like her walk among us and are just meant to take care of people. Before setting off to Edgar's, his mom packed a basket of freshly baked cookies for him to take over, saying something about staying in Mrs. Slate's good graces.

"Wait," she said, "I got some dates from the market to add to that basket. I bet it's been a long time since Mrs. Slate has had a good date!" She flashed her beautiful smile, then made a thin line of her lips when she realized what she had just said. "Oh my goodness, I'm sorry." She crossed herself.

"Oh Mom… it was an accident. Honestly!" Josiah winked because his mother had drilled the word "honestly" into him for so long he was surprised it wasn't his middle name.

"Okay go on then, come back before supper."

"All right Mom! Love you!"

The early morning sun was growing ever higher, predicting a warm fall day. Josiah loved days like this, especially so late in the season, and he found himself practically skipping down the road, basket in hand. All the leaves were already brilliant shades of red, orange, and yellow, as if nature had grown tired of the greens of summer and decided to add some color, taking her magic paintbrush and doing a meticulous job on the leaves. Then she drew a deep breath and let the color spray on the ground.

He liked living where the seasons change and found it hard to imagine the parts of the country that never got cold. He liked the cycle of the seasons, the whole idea of birth and rebirth, life and death. How the fall leaves give way to the frozen winter, succumbing to new life in spring.

He planned his life around the seasons. He had to. How would his family get through winter without the food they stored in the fall? Days like today made him wonder if there were some sort of invisible internal struggle with Mother Nature and Mother Earth. Maybe one was actually the daughter and one was the mother and they butted heads. Or maybe they were old friends vying for position of being called "mother." He imagined the seasons themselves as their own entities, battling over wills, hanging on to dear life as the next one takes over.

Today it seemed that way. By all means he should be wearing a jacket. But Josiah was wearing only a shirt, work trousers, and boots. Summer had won the battle today, but the signs of fall were scattered everywhere: farmers working hard to harvest what they could, kids jumping in leaf piles higher than they were tall. If he were asleep all spring and summer and had just woken up and looked outside, he'd know it was fall despite the weather. The sky had the iciness of impending winter, and the clouds, puffy and white, were somehow reminiscent of the proverbial calm before the storm. It was early afternoon, and where just a few months ago the sun should be right overhead, now it was off to the side casting long shadows on the road already, like it was just too tired to fully make it out of bed.

I hope this weather lasts, Josiah thought as he inhaled the warm air, which smelled of straw, wood, and burning leaves. If tan had a flavor, it would taste just like this. Decay but not rotten. A hint of dried corn came in from the distance, and something sweet drifted past which made him think of fresh pies being left on windowsills to cool. Pumpkins adorned the few doorsteps he passed, and were splayed out by the hundreds in the fields.

Josiah stopped at Mr. Stoken's farm where Martha Stoken and her great grandkids sat out front selling some of their harvest. Josiah traded some cookies for a cup of cider. They had so many apple trees on their land, and from them they made gallons of cider, pies, applesauce, and baked goods and sold them at the market. On the off days, they had this little stand to tend to.

Josiah drank the cider down in one gulp, not realizing how thirsty he was. He put the cup down on the stand and stepped back to study the fantastic orchard full of fresh apples adorning the trees and piled high on the ground below them.

"You know, Mrs. Stoken, my friend Edgar Slate dreams of having an orchard like this one. Except he wants other fruits too. He has the perfect property right down the road a few miles. But his stretch of land… nothing seems to grow on it at all. I'm actually on my way to help him figure out if something can be done about it. Tell me, are there any tips you can give to budding farmers like us who are trying to turn over the land?"

Mrs. Stoken crinkled her eyebrows a bit. "Oh, that poor dear, he's the one whose father went missing and now his poor mama is all alone raising three kids, right?"

"Yes Ma'am."

"Tut, tut, such a shame, that family. It's the land you know. Ain't right by any stretch of the imagination. I been by that farm but try to stay away from it because the smell isn't good for my lungs, you see. But I see that patch o' land back there. And not a thing be growin' on it. Not a thing. Even the birds steer clear. And you'd think that'd be good worm pickin'. Just that one lone tree back in the corner. Crabapple. I can tell by its branches. Devil's fruit you know. Devil's fruit."

Josiah vaguely remembered a rhyme he learned when he was little with those words. Her mentioning the devil's fruit had sparked the memory of him at a family gathering, probably for someone's birthday. The kids were all sitting in a circle singing and passing an apple to each other. After the last line whoever had the apple was out.

The dark man under the soil in spring
Mother Nature's spoils she brings

Full of fruits through Autumn's first frost
till summer's end and harvest lots

Gourds and apples we do share
Bright and round then well we'll faire
till winter ushers in the frosty air.

A vibrant year from seed to harvest

cold to warm to hot to cold darkness stands at its furthest.

Yet when warm winds overtake the air
tis the season to beware
Indian Summer then gives rise
to the dark man in his guise.

He hadn't realized he was staring off into space until her voice drifted back into his ears.

"You know what I mean?"

"Uhh...yeah. Sure." He shook the fog out of his head.

"I mean it, boy, tell him to come talk to me if he wants an orchard. I got some land he can practice on; he can work for me, and I'll give him some profits. Tell him his land ain't good for nobody, you hear?"

"Thanks, Ma'am. Fff—er the cider."

Josiah started back on his way toward Edgar's house in a daze. He could feel Mrs. Stoken's eyes on his back, and he couldn't wait to turn the next bend. He was half trying to remember the rest of the poem and half thinking about the stories he'd heard of the old woman. How she went mad a few years ago when half of her grandchildren had gone missing and were never found. They had been playing in the orchards and did not come back. That's all anyone knew.

There were rumors that Mr. Stoken might have done it. Nobody ever saw him. All the kids joke that he wasn't a real person and Mrs. Stoken made up a pretend husband Whatever the case, it was nice of Mrs. Stoken to care enough to have Edgar come work for her and see if it's something he'd really want to do. But Josiah knew Edgar well enough. He wanted to do everything himself.

As he continued to walk, he kept getting stuck on her words about the devil's fruit and tried to remember the last half of the rhyme.

"Devil's fruit. Devil's fruit," he repeated to himself as he walked, now past the bend and away from the penetrating gaze of Mrs. Stoken. "Devil's fruit." He kicked stones and let his mind focus on the words instead of his surroundings. Truth be told, he could walk this stretch of land with his eyes closed. "Devil's...

83

OH!" He stopped as Edgar's house came into view seeing the crabapple tree in the distant back corner before the house came into view.

> *The land shifts back, the moon is slight.*
> *The devil's fruit appears overnight.*
> *Lock your horses, tuck your children tight.*
> *The dark man will come to you at night.*

"Huh," he said. Where he should be relieved that he'd finally remembered the end of the rhyme, he felt chilled instead. That last bit about the dark man used to scare him to no end. It still did, now that he thought about it.

A long time ago a bunch of children had disappeared, and some people said they swore the night before they had heard soft music, like accordions playing a slow lament, and children laughing, the cheer barely a whisper in the early morning breeze. Parents thinking their kids were being naughty by sleeping in late went in their rooms for a lashing but found they had completely vanished.

Come to think of it, Josiah wondered, maybe Mrs. Stoken's grandkids were part of that rumor. He wouldn't dare ask her about it though. Mostly it was hearsay anyway. None of the grownups would admit one way or another what happened or what they remember.

Josiah didn't care if was real or not. The story used to give him all sorts of nightmares. He shuddered thinking about the different scenarios that used to play in his head about the dark man. Then he started to wonder if maybe this rhyme had something to do with his dreams.

He had somewhat of a eureka moment as he considered this. "I can't believe I'm such a ninny. How could I have never realized that before? The dark man. The stupid nursery rhyme! That's why I have been having these dreams my whole life!" A huge wave of relief swept out of his body with his breath. "I bet I'll never have that dream again! Now that I know the truth that it's all a bunch of made up stuff to scare little kids!"

12 CHELSEA

I've circled this beam of wood I don't know how many times. If I keep going I'm sure I'll bore a hole to China! I reach down to touch it, feeling how the char has worn smooth over time, hoping maybe this will reveal its secrets. Staring at it doesn't seem to do much for me.

What happened to the people who lived here? Why did that Josiah person have my last name? Is he related to Grandpa Jo? He'd probably be old enough to be his father, given the dates in the article. Most of all, why, if this place has such a horrible history, would my parents choose to live here? Maybe they don't know about it... but was it really that long ago?

There are so many questions in my head I can't think straight. The one that stands out most right now though is what in the ever-loving heck is wrong with that orchard? I glance behind me and try not to look up the trees. They all seemed to have faces etched into them, horribly moody faces that hate the dark as much as I do right now. It's like the man in the moon—once you see the face, you can never unsee it.

I sit down next to the beam of wood and place my hands on it, thinking of the intuition stuff I talked to my mom about and what happened when Grandpa died. How he spoke to me without words. I look around to make sure my family isn't watching me and decide to shift so my back is facing the house just in case. I'm sure they'd be ready to have me committed or something if they saw me having a conversation with an inanimate object.

I put my legs over the beam so it's easy to place my hands on it, while making it seem that I'm just sitting here, thinking. I caress the old fibers with my fingers wondering if maybe this process only works with living things. But I've heard that wood is alive, or at least it used to be. That it holds memories or retains information. I don't know whether that's true or not or if it would even bother talking to me. Then I debate my own thought. I'm a likable person, why wouldn't it talk to me? "As a matter of fact I would be offended if you ignored me!" My face flushes as I look around, then laugh at myself for being so crazy.

Deep breath and relax, I tell myself. I close my eyes and focus on my breathing, trying to quiet my mind of any thoughts other than the sensation of wood under my fingers. I laugh when an image comes to mind of Jeff running into the door at school then shake it out like trying to erase an Etch A Sketch. *Okay, serious this time.* I allow myself to breathe normally and then take in a deep breath, holding it for a couple of seconds before slowly letting it out. As I do this, I pose a silent question to whoever can hear me right now: *Can you tell me your secrets?*

I repeat this mantra over and over. Fast at first, then pausing a few seconds between each repetition, waiting for some sort of answer. I do this for a while until I become drowsy. I start to think this is pointless, but I'm pretty comfortable here, so I stop asking and just hold this space, the blank canvas between sleep and wakefulness.

And then a flash of something crosses behind my eyes like a memory that isn't mine or at least one that I can't remember. Blue eyes sparkling in the sunrise, carrying a feeling of hope so strong it fills my own body. A teenage boy standing on the edge of a barren field. A wave of sheer joy passes from him to me as he runs into the field, alone. Darkness. Another boy comes out of the field, looking confused, disheveled. Limping. The smell of smoke is saturating, suffocating, I can hear the faint echo of horror-stricken screams, like stars that burned out a long time ago but you can still see their light.

I jump to my feet, shaking myself out of the images. I'm out of breath like I've just run a marathon. It's dark now, and my mother is calling me for dinner. But I can't move, I grasp the tops of my thighs for support as I try to replay everything that I have just seen, not wanting to forget a thing. I collect my composure, run into the house and past my parents, and yell an apology that I'd be down in a second. Slamming my bedroom door, I pull out my journal and draw frantically, my hand snarling with painful cramps as it's trying to keep up with my mind.

I can still smell the smoke and hear the scream so vividly that it makes me want to take a shower with music on loud enough to drown it out. But I don't. I just sit here for another minute and try to rationalize it. Then it dawns me that I'm a complete idiot. *Oh really, Chelsea! Be serious. You just read about the fire in the article and the names of the people who died or whatever! The wood didn't give up its secrets, your crazy brain is on overdrive.*

Ever since I was enrolled in art classes, I feel like it woke up some weird part of my imagination that is hard to turn off once it starts. When I begin to draw or use my imagination, the colors and pictures I see are so lucid, it reminds me of a Dr. Seuss book where everything is dreamy and eccentric. Still shaking from the experience, I tell myself I'm not going to embarrass myself again with this intuition crap.

At least I tried, I think as I head for the dining room and see my parents sitting there with empty plates and impatient faces. The TV is on in the other room so they can hear the news. "Whatever were you doing out there?" Mom says as she passes me the sweet potatoes.

"Oh… just making an etching of that barn wood."

"Well, you were out there for a long time. I was getting worried! Don't ignore me like that, Chelsea!"

"I'm sorry, Mom, I guess I was in the zone." I'm thankful she doesn't press the issue as I have no proof.

"It's ok, pumpkin," she says and turns her attention over to Dad, telling him about some DIY house fixer-upper ideas she saw on Pinterest.

I eat a small bit of chicken then immediately go to work on my sweet potatoes, turning them into a volcano. It reminds me of some movie I saw where a guy was doing the same thing and then his son was abducted by aliens. *I feel like an alien in my house,* I think as I make buttery lava swirls with the tongs of my fork.

Everything that I've always believed and felt was true has abandoned me. I'm not even sure what kind of world I live in anymore. I can explain away my visions by the old barnwood, but I cannot rationalize what I saw with Jeff and Autumn about the shadows or how even going into that area makes me want to rip my own head off.

I could tell my parents about it. I mean, really, I probably should, but I'm afraid if I even mention something like this, they'll send me straight to a psychiatrist. They love that I've channeled my fears from the boat accident and depression about my grandfather into my art, but I know they worry that I'll go overboard at some point. Like one day I'll just snap and run naked through the streets playing bongos or something. This thought makes me laugh out loud.

Both my parents look at me smiling, and I realize they must have said something funny and thought I was listening. *Great timing!* I take a bite of my volcano, and they go back to talking. Personally, I think kids have a better grip on life than our parents do. Parents always seem too stressed out and worried. When something happens to us kids, it's a big deal in the moment and then we just let it go. We don't let the weight of it hold us down.

Not parents; they suck in their worry until it has no place to go so it sprouts grey on the top of their heads. My father is growing his very own worry farm up there as they speak!

"Chelsea! Earth to Chelsea! Ground control to Major Chelsea! Are you in there?" Dad has been throwing pieces of napkins at me. I immediately turn red when I realize I'd been daydreaming. Definitely not what I need them to see right now.

"Ha, sorry Dad. I think I'm just tired. Maybe I'll just go to bed early tonight," I say as I get up to put my plate away. I give them each a kiss on the cheek before I turn in. Mom gives me a quizzical look, but I rub the lower half of my stomach away from Dad's eyes and she nods, winks, and tells me to grab a Hershey's Kiss and the heating pad on the way up to bed.

***

The radio is on in the kitchen like it is every morning, playing some show on NPR. Mom and Dad are in the dining room. He's shuffling through emails, and Mom is reading one of her crazy romance novels. I picked one up once and tried to read a few lines to see what the fuss was about. Mom must have thousands of these books lying around. The part I read said something about the guy's long, luxurious hair, bulging muscles, and passionately kissing his mistress while his princess was tending to her embroidery. I couldn't stand it.

"God awful...bleh, Mom!" I say as I plop down at the table with a piece of toast. "How can you read that stuff? Especially here. Where we eat! And with the radio on! I mean, look at this cover." I start to laugh as I pull it from her hands. The cover is a poor depiction of a Scottish guy with wavy brown hair and muscles bigger than the Incredible Hulk. "It's like Braveheart gone horribly wrong."

Mom laughs back. "Gimme that!" She looks at the cover, "You know? I never really pay attention to the pictures, it's the fantastic storylines," she says rather loudly while staring at Dad, who's still typing away at his computer. She was obviously expecting a reaction but doesn't get one from him. My parents are weird.

A screeching noise fills the room and continues, irritating like nails on a chalkboard which even makes Dad look up from the computer, and for a moment none of us can figure out where it's coming from.

"What is this?" Mom questions as she picks up her cell phone. "Oh! huh... Amber alert." "Is that what yours says too, Don? Don? Donovan!"

"Huh? Oh I don't know let me see," he says. He picks up his phone. "Yep, amber alert." Then he goes back to his computer.

"Mine says the same thing." I'm frantically trying to click the link they provided for more information, but my technology is being all glitchy again.

Mom clicks the link then and her face goes blank.

"What, Mom? What is it?"

"Hmmmm," she says as if picking the exact words she wants to use from an invisible list up on the ceiling. "Honey, do you know a Raina Boddington?"

"Yeah, she's in my English class. Wait, why? Is she missing? What?!" I try the link one more time, but it freezes as texts pop up from Autumn and Jeff.

Did you hear about Raina?

Confused for a second whether to respond to them or click the link, I send out a fresh garble of words, courtesy of autocorrect:

`Cat out of the tree.`

The link finally works.

Raina Boddington, 14, of 12 Clearview Drive missing. Last seen 9pm in her home. Please call this number or text AMBER INFORM with any information. Twitter: #amberinform

"My god, Mom, that's so scary! What could have happened?" I was trying to think of what I knew about Raina. Her family life, did she have anything weird going on, could someone have taken her? She doesn't live with both of her parents. Maybe one of the parents lured her away? She's such a sweet girl, small frame, mousy brown hair. I don't know her very well, but we do talk in class once in a while. She has the cutest smile and multi-colored braces with awkward facial features that confirm she still has some growing to do. My guess is that she will grow up to be a model, albeit a short one. She even has one of those little moles on her cheek like Cindy Crawford or Marilyn Monroe.

"Not sure baby, but it does worry me. I know you don't pay attention to the news but there have been a lot of missing kids lately from other towns not too far from here."

"Where?" My heart goes from a slow jog to a sprint.

"Like Canandaigua, Naples… the Finger Lakes area. I'm surprised you haven't heard about it in school?" She squishes her mouth to the side like she's chewing on a tough piece of meat. "I think we parents have been trying to shield you guys from it. You guys are too young to worry about this kind of thing. I'm hoping it's just one of those things, and the kids will all come back once they realized the prank has gone on long enough. Like those darn clowns that were everywhere. I'm so glad that's over!" She laughs in a dismissive kind of way to soften the seriousness, but it doesn't work.

"Why didn't you tell me?!" I turn to my father before she can answer. He has long been listening to our conversation, and I didn't even realize he had put away his computer.

"Dad?"

"Honey… I'm in agreement with your mother. We didn't want to say anything and bring up needless worry for you."

"Jeeze! You know? I'm so tired of this!" I'm bubbling over with anger and not even sure why or where it came from. "Yes, yes, I had a boat accident when I was five years old! Yes, I almost died! But I'm alive! And to be honest, I barely remember it anyway. Yes, Grandpa died and yes, I'm working through it! But you guys don't need to treat me like I'm this little fragile creature that needs to live in a box segregated from the outside world!"

I'm flustered and breathing heavily, partially wanting to stick to my guns while also wanting to collapse into my father's arms and have him comfort me while I cry like I'm two years old again.

"Are you sure you don't want me to homeschool?"

"MOM!" I scream at her, taken aback by the fact that she seems to have heard nothing of what I just said.

She puts her hands on mine, and in her calm mom way apologizes, telling me that it's not me she's worried about; it's her. That I'm her baby girl and she couldn't forgive herself if anything ever happened to me.

"Homeschool, though?" I say to her as I let the air out of my anger balloon. "You're going to think I'm crazy for even admitting this, but after Billy went missing, the thought actually did cross my mind. But I like going to school. I'm kind of a social butterfly, you know?"

"Yes, I guess you are. Just… please don't forget to bring your phone wherever you go. You can text or call whenever you want. And there is an emergency app I want you to get that I just read about. You don't need to press the button or anything, just say the code word you set for it, and it will dial either the police or whatever emergency contact you program in there. It sounds pretty neat, actually. Well worth the fifty bucks to buy it don't you think, Donovan?" Dad nods.

"And what if I say the code word by accident?"

"Well, make sure it's something you wouldn't normally say. She pauses. "Like… Fabio has great hair!" She doesn't even crack a smile when she says this.

"Oh my god, Mom!" I start laughing. She is such a goof.

We sit in contemplative silence, Dad back on his computer, Mom with her book, and me texting Autumn and Jeff.

91

"So hey," I say, talking to my parents but still looking down at my phone. Do you mind if we take our bikes up to Sherman? Have big plans today." I don't have to tell them who "we" is. "We" has meant the three of us since before we started our elementary days at Sherman School.

Mom seems flustered about my question, no doubt because of the amber alert, and looks at my dad who just shrugs.

"Not until you download that app," she says.

"Ugh. All right." Anything to appease the repetitive beast that is my mother.

I head out to the garage and grab my bike, a rusty and faded old ten speed. I half expect to see Autumn and Jeff on the street or at least coming out of their houses, but there's no sign of them. Either they made it before me or haven't made it out yet, which is fine, I could use some time to cruise alone. I love riding my bike, feeling the wind in my hair.

Driving around to the back of the school, I drop my bike next to the swings. I sit on one and let my feet dangle, touching the ground with my toes, not really swinging, just sort of rocking myself back and forth, losing myself in thought. I'm trying not to make a big deal of Raina missing, but couple her disappearance with what Mom said about the kids from other towns, and I can't help but to wonder what could be going on, if there's some sort of connection.

"Boo!" someone yells in my ear, and I'm so startled I fall flat onto my face.

"Damn you, Jeff!" I'm more embarrassed than anything, but know I shouldn't be because I'd probably have done the same thing to him.

"Sorry," he says then offers a hand to help me up. Autumn is just parking her bike with a sour expression planted on her pink face.

"What's wrong?" I ask her.

"I dunno, really? I just feel… off. And this whole thing is scary!"

"Did you hear about the kids from the other towns, too?"

"Yes!" they both answer. Autumn continues. "Well, my dad mentioned it, and I told him," she nodded in Jeff's direction.

"It's kind of freaky," Jeff says as he looks around. "Maybe we shouldn't even be here?"

We are the only people here at the playground, which pretty much sits in a wide-open expanse of land.

"Meh," I answer. "I think we're pretty safe here. We'd have time to get out if anyone strange comes to visit. Plus, there's safety in numbers, right? Besides, you're so tall, from far away you kind of look like an adult."

"I guess?" he says, soaking in my observation of him.

Autumn looks to us, her eyebrows furrowed in desperation. "Okay guys, I have to be honest here. I have NOT been able to get much sleep lately. I know, I know," she says holding up her palms towards Jeff and me as if to block the looks we are giving her because we all know that Autumn could sleep for an entire week if she was allowed.

"The problem isn't so much that I'm scared. Well, okay that's a lie. I kind of am now with the recent news about the other kids. What's really got me all bunched up is the shadow thing and those seeds I showed you at my dad's work. I've been overthinking everything, trying to come up with some sort of an explanation. I mean, what do crabapple seeds look like? Maybe that old orchard has something to do with the city? Maybe the entire town was one giant orchard and they built the city on top of it and the trees got really, really angry and somehow made the city catch on fire? Or maybe…"

"Autumn, Autumn, Autumn," Jeff says as he puts a gangly arm around her. "Turn off the brain! We'll get to the bottom of the shadow thing. Maybe it was the street light and the angle where we were standing. We didn't spend enough time on it, right?"

"I don't think so," I say. "It's not like we were spinning in circles or anything. We walked forward and backwards in a straight line. Not to mention we lost an entire six and a half hours somehow." My own wheels start turning as fast as hers.

"Always so logical," Autumn says, and I know she was ready to cling on to any explanation that she could. "I kinda wish we could see it all again and really do some detective work this time you know? Then if there's still no explanation… well, I don't know what. Maybe we should consider talking to our parents?"

"I was thinking about that last night," I confessed. "I just… well here's the thing. Does it really matter? No, no hear me out," I say to Jeff as he steps forward and opens his mouth to talk. "We've lived here our entire lives and have never noticed the trick with the shadows. We have never been able to tell how strange it feels when you walk inside there, right? Now that we know, has anything changed?" Autumn and Jeff say nothing, so I continue.

"No. The only difference is that we know about it now. It doesn't seem to be hurting anyone so we shouldn't worry about it. Right, Autumn?" She nods.

"It is what it is." I go on. "That being said, I still want to know more. Does that land hold any other mysteries that we haven't uncovered? Or, as you said, Autumn, maybe if we go back there again just maybe we'll see what's really going on, and it could be more simple than we think." I pause again, allowing this new information to soak in for them. "What do you guys say then? Sleepover tonight? Wanna try it again?"

"Yes, absolutely!" says Jeff. "I've been thinking about it lately myself. I have an arsenal of things I want to bring and experiment with. Flashlight, mirrors, shadow puppets."

"What," Autumn says, laughing, "will a shadow puppet do to help us?"

"I don't know," he says. "But they're fun!"

"You are SO weird, Jeffrey!"

"I aim to please." He smiles.

"Ok, I'm in," she says.

Out of the corner of my eye, I see someone walking out of the school. It's Miss Parker, our English teacher. Without even thinking I yell, "Hey Miss Parker!" then run out to greet her. Autumn and Jeff look at each other like *what is she doing?* then run after me, well versed in my spontaneity.

"Hi guys!" Miss Parker says. "Beautiful day for a bike ride, eh?" She unchains her own bike and notes ours by the playground with a nod.

"Sure is," I say, a bit out of breath. "I didn't know you worked on Saturdays?"

She smiles saying that a teacher's work is never done. "I have papers to grade, syllabuses to write, groupwork to sort out…"

She stops herself because she could tell she was losing me. "Sorry, what's up? Just saying hi?"

"Actually… I was wondering if you heard about Raina?"

"Yes, I have! I've contacted both her parents to see if there's anything I could do."

"You did?" My eyes light up, hoping she can tell us some good news.

Seeing my anticipation, she gently tells me that they aren't sure what happened to her and are obviously very scared and devastated.

My heart sinks. Between Raina and Billy, I'm starting to think that maybe someone kidnapped them. Miss Parker reaches out and pats my arms.

"Listen guys, I've sure you've heard the other reports by now from the news or your own families, but I'm willing to bet this is an isolated incident. The best thing you can do right now is send good thoughts and intentions to Raina for a safe return. Maybe you can write a note to her parents saying you're thinking of them. But please stay positive and keep your chins up. In the meantime, be alert and safe. Stay together, don't go out alone. Not to worry you, but it's a good practice to have."

"Yeah my mom just made me get this emergency app thingy."

"Good! I've read about that. That's a great start. Listen, try not to worry, and I'll see you guys in class next week, ok?"

"Okay, Miss Parker, have a good weekend!"

"Bye," said Jeff, his voice weak. Autumn just stares after Miss Parker, not saying a thing.

***

The doorbell rings, and my mother runs to get it like a giddy teenager. "Hi guys!" She's practically dancing. "I'm SOOOOO glad you are staying the night! I threw in a pizza for you already, and have the TV all dialed up."

"Aw thanks, Mrs. Heiland, you're the best!" says Autumn.

"Thank you!" says Jeff. "Here… my mom sends you her support." He produces a bottle of wine from his backpack.

"Ha! We moms have to stick together, don't we? Thank her for me, will ya?"

"I will," he says.

Not ready for movies just yet, the three of us sprawl out on my bedroom floor. Jeff is leafing through a romance novel he must have swiped from the bookshelf at the bottom of the stairs.

Autumn gives him a distasteful look. "Glad you are doing your... uh... research?"

"Well actually, Miss Autumn, this is a piece of historical fiction! I'm learning about the commander of the Civil War and how he has a very large..."

"Give me that!" she says. Indeed, right there on the cover is a man with bulging biceps and exposed chest, wearing a Civil War–inspired hat and blue trousers. He's riding on top of a behemoth of a horse with his beautiful maiden reaching for him as he strides off to war.

"Oh lord! Honestly, Chelsea, why does your mom read this stuff?"

"I ask her that all the time! I have no idea."

Jeff takes it back. "Because it's hysterical!" He leafs through it again for another minute before throwing it on the floor. "So," he says, "you want to see what I brought?"

"Sure," I say and slide over next to Autumn while he produces a toolbox.

One by one he pulls his arsenal of detective gear out for display. "Mirror, flashlight, thermometer, infrared spy binoculars, candy bar, paper, granola bar, pencils, string cheese, and stencils."

"Hungry much?" Autumn asks.

"I get most of this stuff," I tell him. "But stencils?

"For shadow puppets, silly!"

Autumn giggles and then grabs the spy glasses. "Do you really think these will work? They look like a toy you get at a fast food restaurant when you're like... six years old," she says while peering through the red lenses, the glasses far too small for her face.

"Okay, okay." Jeff takes them back from Autumn. "I actually downloaded a night vision app. These are just for effect," he says and throws them back in the box.

***

In the middle of the Harry Potter movie, Mom announces that she's going to bed and tells us to be good. Dad's overnight at a conference so it's just us tonight.

"Don't stay up too late, and please don't go sneaking around outside!" she warns before heading to her room.

I feel a pang of guilt as that's exactly what we plan to do as soon as she's sleeping. *At least we are just going in the backyard*, I reason with myself. *It's not like we're running off to some party.* I leave a note saying that we are just looking for something in the back so she doesn't freak out if she wakes up and sees that we aren't there.

Jeff suggests that we try a different spot than last time. I'm a tiny bit nervous but more confident that we probably blew things way out of proportion last time. Jeff's looking at Autumn and me, hammering his toes on the ground. Just as before, we lock arms and stride in together.

I'm hit with an intense pressure as soon as my feet touch the ground, like I'm sucked into a bubble. This time it's followed by ringing so forceful that I feel like the pendulum inside the world's largest church bell. I immediately put both hands on my ears to stop it as if it was coming from the outside, but I know that it isn't. I would have heard something a moment ago when I was standing in my backyard.

I try to uncover my ears, but I can't. I double over, squatting on the ground, and look to my friends who seem to be just fine and are not even paying attention to me. They're talking so fast to one another, but I can't hear what they're saying, as if their words are being swept up in some invisible breeze.

I'm in a daze and want to get out of here. I can't figure out why Autumn and Jeff don't seem to feel this way. I try to force myself to stand up straight, and as I do I see someone in the woods—looking directly at me. Her long hair and short stature is so familiar…It's the tell-tale beauty mark on her face that is the giveaway. *Raina.*

My joy is short-lived as I notice her eyes. Big hollowed eyes like two black holes in space that aren't letting any light escape. In one swift motion she snaps her arms up and out, bending one up at the elbow so her fingers point to the treetops and the other low, fingers toward the ground.

She jerks her head to the side, opens her mouth, and something streams out of it. *Glitter? Pebbles?* I squint to see better as I'm too frightened to react any other way. Seeds? Black seeds? *Like the ones we found in the files at Autumns dad's office?*

I try to focus on the ground where these things are falling, but I can't. The curious side of me wants to run up to her and shake her as if that would knock the freak show out. But everything is happening too fast, and I'm rigid with trepidation. I start seeing spots in front of my eyes as I try to reach for Raina thinking maybe I can just take her with me, that bringing her out of this place will make her normal again.

Before I take a step, I'm knocked onto my back, all of the pressure whooshing out of my ears along with the air in my lungs. And then Jeff and Autumn are standing over me asking if I'm okay. I wait a minute for my breath to come back, recovering from the shock of what just happened.

"I... I don't know." I hold up a finger gesturing the number one as I try to catch my breath. Taking my time rising to a sitting position, I wipe my sweaty forehead with the back of my arm and tuck my hair behind my ears. I do a quick body scan with my hands to make sure I'm no worse for the wear. And then I yell. "WHAT IN THE EVER-LOVING HELL JUST HAPPENED?"

"First, tell us what happened to you!" says Autumn, her eyes wide. "We were calling you and... you were just staring off into space with your hands over your ears. Then you reached out and started screaming, and well, that brings us to now, pretty much. If Jeff hadn't yanked you out of there..."

"Yeah, uh, sorry about that," Jeff says, scratching his head. "Are you ok?"

I nod, then fill them in on what I saw. They, too, noticed the exaggerated silence and a small amount of pressure, but nothing as intense as what I described. When I ask what their conversation was all about, they don't seem to know what I'm talking about. They had both been pacing back and forth between the trees with a flashlight because the moon wouldn't stay out of the clouds long enough, but both the flashlight battery and Jeff's iPhone went dead.

The clincher is when I tell them about Raina. They did not see her. AT ALL. And that freaks me out. I'm starting to think that maybe I really am crazy. Mom always wanted me to see a shrink, but I sincerely believe that even a shrink would send me away if I told them about this.

"How long were we in there?" I asked, getting up, feeling lightheaded.

"I don't know for sure because my batteries bit it, but I would guess, oh, I don't know… ten minutes? Maybe fifteen? Does that sound about right, Auto?"

"Yeah I think so? Probably. Are you sure you're okay, Chelsea?"

"I guess so."

"We have a lot to talk about," Jeff says.

"Yeah," Autumn says. "Besides that, it's freaking cloudy tonight. We can't play with the beams if there's nothing to chase."

"I've got something to chase," I mumble.

Autumn and Jeff pass out as soon as they crawl into their sleeping bags on the living room floor, but I can't stop thinking about what I saw. I start to shake all over when a flash of recognition jars my memory so hard I have to grasp the edge of my couch to keep myself steady.

Raina. I had seen her like this before. It was her calling to me when I was five, underwater. *That was the same image that made me not want to drift away and become a mermaid with Vivienne.* She kept me here, I have to help her somehow. But how? Was it really Raina in there? I don't think I'll ever sleep again.

Ever. I decide to go upstairs and draw it all out in my journal. I don't really want to remember this night, but part of me doesn't want to forget, either. I feel like I need to be alone. Something else happened in there that I don't want to mention to Autumn and Jeff. I'm starting to worry that my friends will think I'm cracking.

I'm caught up in the notion about how yes, I was frightened, but I was also taken over by this immense curiosity. I almost felt… safe. It sounds like lunacy, but I wanted to go in deeper and explore. It was more than a curiosity too. It was an urge, like a moth to a flame. I think that frightens me more than the hallucination of her does.

I'm also thankful that I unplugged the cable box in the living room before anyone noticed and that Autumn and Jeff just crawled into their sleeping bags and drifted off like nothing ever happened... like they didn't even care what happened to me. That's why I didn't want them to know that the digital clock I hid from everyone read 5:00 a.m. We weren't outside for fifteen minutes or even an hour. We were outside for six hours. Again.

I'm starting to not care what they say. To them it's no big deal, a mild curiosity. But I know there is something horribly wrong, and if I'm to make peace with living in front of it, I need to do something about it. I'm just not sure what yet.

There are so many pieces to put together. The boy with my last name in the article. The burned up old piece of barnwood lodged into the ground in my backyard and the random visions that come with it. Hearing Grandpa's voice asking me to sing his song when he was clearly on his way out of this earth. Grandma and her nursery rhymes. My parents... completely oblivious to everything. How is it that this property sat here burned and empty for so long and then suddenly there was a house on it. Why was there no property deed? Why didn't I even consider this as we were going through the files at Autumn's dad's place. Who the hell built this house?

I squeeze my eyes so tight, hoping it will erase my roving brain. I'm starting to become bitter towards everyone and everything in my life. I just want to be a normal kid. Why can't I be normal like everyone else?

Through the bitterness I feel the adrenaline still racing from this evening's events, I never expect sleep to come again, but it does. I feel myself drift away just as the birds are waking up. And I dream. I dream of falling through endless swirling black holes that sling me off into space, further away from my ultimate destination, the warm comfortable light of the sun. I dream of upside-down trees and Jeff and Autumn dancing in slow motion, of my mother falling off a cliff and of me trying to stop her but failing, of Dad opening and closing the door over and over and over until it scares me. And finally of Grandpa, of his arms around me as we sing about saying goodnight. And then my fits relax, and before me is a few hours of blissful nothing.

13 JOSIAH

Josiah wiped his feet and tiptoed inside, saying "Hello?" while looking around the room. He didn't want to be too loud in case the twins were napping. When no one answered, he closed the door behind him and walked into the living room. He was taken aback by the sight of Mrs. Slate sitting on the sofa, staring off into space and holding a raggedy top hat, her face pale as moonlight.

Josiah ran over to her and bent down to her level, knees on the floor.

In a loud whisper he said, "Mrs. Slate, it's me. Josiah." He put his hand on her shoulder. "Are you okay?"

She didn't answer.

This situation did not seem right at all. Not one little bit. "Mrs. Slate, what's going on? Why do you have Edgar's hat?" He tried to take it from her, but she clutched it to her chest quickly like it was her baby and Josiah was a stranger trying to steal it. She looked at Josiah, wide-eyed and said, "It's all that's left. He's gone and this is all I have left!"

Josiah rolled off of his knees as his heart started hammering.

"Gone? What do you mean? Where is he? Where's Edgar?"

She didn't respond. But Mellie, one of the twins, appeared from around the corner, her long red hair in strings past her elbows. "He didn't come in for breakfast. Mama went to the field to find him. She said there's two trees out there. Two trees. And a top hat. That's all Mama said. Jo-Jo, I'm scared!"

"No, no shhh… it's okay. Everything will be okay." He hugged her to try and calm her even though he was feeling shaky himself. "Where's your sister?"

"She's in the other room playing."

"Okay, go and get your things. I'm going to take you to my house. You can stay with us until we figure this out. Pack stuff up for your Mama, too. I'm going into the field."

"Can we come?"

"NO!" His yell came out stronger than he anticipated. "Sorry," he said with less intensity. "You need to pack, okay? I'll be right back."

Josiah stopped at the barn where he had a hunch that Edgar probably slept last night. Sure enough, when he climbed up, the window was wide open and the straw was fashioned into a bed. He wondered when Edgar made the decision to go out there and then yelled into the air, cursing him for not waiting.

He made his way out of the barn and then stood for a moment on the threshold to the field. He knew he had to go in, most specifically to that tree (or two trees according to Mellie). He was sure Edgar must have gone and done the same. Probably to inspect the fruit, if there was any. It was hard to tell from so far away.

As he toed one foot over the line, he felt his world shift in a way that he didn't totally understand. Something about the air here was strange. His ears felt like they did in the summer when he would try to swim to the very bottom of the pond, knowing full well they'll never find the bottom before needing to come up for air. The pressure from swimming that deep made his ears feel like they were going to explode right inside of his head.

There was also a slight ringing sensation, and he took note that there wasn't much sound apart from what he heard inside of his own head. It made him dizzy. His pounding heart made the spins worse. He wondered if he should go back but knew he couldn't.

He turned back to the house to see Mellie and Maureen looking at him from the back window. Each with opposite arms pressed against the glass like mirrors side by side. He smiled and waved so they knew that everything was okay, then turned to make his way out to the tree. The dirt against his feet didn't feel like normal ground. It was more like he would imagine a cloud to feel, if he were to walk on one. It sucked his feet in with every step. He stopped to touch the ground and the soil felt just like it was supposed to: gritty, stony, and dusty. *Odd.*

As he approached the tree, he looked back and wondered if the girls were still watching or could even see him. The house looked so small from this distance, a floater in his vision. The tree looked like no other tree he had ever seen before. Crabapple or otherwise, it was hellish. There were two, just like Edgar's mom had reported. One must have been easily six feet tall. The branches twisted in sharp angles. The smaller one maybe a third of that in height, housed the same type of branches.

The longer he stared at them, the more fearful he became, as he focused his gaze mostly in the center where the bark was mangled in wrinkled patterns giving the appearance of a face petrified in mid scream as though it literally froze while being absolutely terrified. Josiah took a step back, rubbed his eyes and ears, and told himself that he was crazy. That these things were some hideous abomination, Mother Nature's scrapyard for when she had a bad day.

He started looking around for any sign of Edgar as a light fog began rolling around the barren field. Around the trees he circled. Back and forth he spanned the area within a ten-minute radius, looking for any sign of his friend. He walked to the end of the field and over the line of the forest beyond, opposite to the comforts of Edgar's home. As soon as he stepped into the forest, he felt instant relief like he has just been shot out of a cannon and landed safely on the ground.

He called out Edgar's name, which ruffled some of the birds from deep inside the wall of pine that stood before him. Save for that and the snapping of brush against his heavy boots, there was no sound. He caught sight of a clearing in the distance and headed in that direction with a new burst of optimism hoping maybe Edgar decided to go exploring there, too.

As he approached the clearing, he made a sudden stop and switched his gears to pedal backwards as fast as he possibly could. Josiah tripped over himself, scraping his hands in the brush, but he didn't notice the cuts or blood pooling and spilling down the palms of his hands, wrists, and forearms. His body screamed with the urgency to get out of there. He dashed back towards the field from where he came and felt the eyes of hundreds of squatty crabapple trees staring back at him, their mouths twisted in chilling horror.

He crossed the threshold into the field in a panic, confused by what he saw and how he felt now, back under the weight of this awful field. The fog had grown so thick that he worried he wouldn't be able to find his way back to the house.

He managed to find the two trees and let out a low sigh as he knew from here he'd be able to find his way back. Even though his head reeled with questions, he decided to take one last look at the trees before turning back towards the Slate's house.

Catching his breath, he ran his fingers along the rough bark, and an unexpected sensation graced them. He anticipated the bark to be rough and to crumble under his touch, but it didn't. It was smooth, like a baby's skin—he jerked his hand away. He touched it again, and the same thing happened. He couldn't wrap his mind around it. *Why does it feel like this? What on earth is this?* He didn't think he could handle any more surprises today, so he started to back away.

As he did, he felt something latch onto his right foot and pull, knocking him to the ground. He looked to his feet to see that a human hand had broken through the soil and was pulling at him, trying to bring him under.

Terror choked his senses, and he froze between decisions he didn't know how to make. He tried paddling backwards with his hands to get away, clutching fistfuls of soil, but there was nothing to grab on to. The hand was on his knee, he felt his foot sinking into the earth, being squeezed, a vise grip robbing it of life.

He kicked with his other foot, trying to release his body and heard an awful snap like he stepped on a twig. Only this was no twig—he had broken one of the fingers, causing it to release its grip on him. Josiah screamed, heaved his foot out of the earth, and ran as fast as he could. The fog was heavy like a white shroud, and he couldn't tell which direction he was going, but he kept running, his right leg in agony. He had no time to look and see what damage was done. His only instinct was survival; he had to get back to Edgar's house, to his sisters and mother. Josiah kept pushing forward with them in the center of his vision.

14 EDGAR-PREVIOUSLY

Edgar wasn't asleep more than an hour before the horses below started whining for their breakfast, and he didn't care. He could barely contain his excitement for his first day of exploration. He stretched his long legs and bore witness to the infant streams of sunlight just birthed from the sky, sitting low through the tops of the trees way beyond the barren field. The clouds gave an ominous feel to the morning, but Edgar could tell the sun would be high this afternoon, burning off any trace of darkness. Even if it didn't, nothing could dampen his mood.

He whistled as he fed the horses and sang while he did the shoveling. *Mama sure will be surprised when my chores are done before even she and the twins wake up,* he thought as he worked. After the shovels were put away, he paced awhile, waiting for Josiah, who should be here at any moment.

"Hmm…" He looked to the house, then back out to the field, then to the house again. He walked to the edge of the field and spotted the crooked tree in the distance. Surely it wouldn't be such a big deal to go and inspect the tree, then come right back? No harm done?

He laced up his boot, the right one that was always untying itself. Twine really, too stiff to hold a proper knot, so he decided to just tuck the lace inside of his boot.

"Oh! I can't leave without my lucky hat!" Edgar made a beeline back toward the barn, skipping every other rung on the ladder. He uncovered his top hat, scattering hay in every direction, and placed it on his head with one hand as he slid down the ladder. He snatched the old suit coat off the rusty hook he keeps for colder days, and found his way to the edge of his property and field. Slightly out of breath, he took a peek behind him to see if Josiah or his mama was around. A crow sat on the fence adjacent to the barn, but he wasn't looking at Edgar, almost like a silent protest against Edgar breaking his promises to stay put.

Edgar couldn't take it anymore and poised to jump right over into the field with both feet, thinking that the whole business of the barren field being "unholy" or "creepy" or whatever was nonsense. Why did he really need Josiah to escort him in here anyway? Granted, he did think that sharing the adventure would be fun, but Josiah would catch up with him soon anyway so why not get a head start?

He pushed his hat down a little further so it wouldn't fall off, then counted to himself. "One. Two..." He looked back at the house and the road one last time and turned his body so he would go in backwards. "Three!" Edgar bent at the knees and leapt over into the field.

The dirt swirled around his feet like the dry sands of the Sahara. Something happened to his view of the house when he crossed over, like heat waves in the distance on a hot summer day.

His senses, flooded by the energy that surrounded him, permeated every cell in his body making him feel like he had drank a cup of euphoria and was simultaneously bathing in it. His body tingled, and his eyes widened with wonder and amusement like a child tasting cotton candy for the very first time. He couldn't believe he had waited this long to come here. It felt as if, for the first time ever, he belonged somewhere. He turned his back on the house, not caring anymore if anyone saw him.

This place isn't dead. It's not evil. It's...

Edgar was overcome with a sense of welcome as if his favorite person in the world had just given him a hug after a lifetime apart—that they'd always been here waiting for him and he'd been waiting for them, even though he didn't realize it until now.

He swooped down and picked up a handful of soil, grinding it between his fingers, then allowed it to slowly drop back down. He repeated the process again and again, and as he did he could feel the fertility that was contained with each and every particle knowing without a doubt that he could cultivate any crop he dreamed of.

Shoot, I could have an orange field in this place if I really wanted, he thought, amused, though he couldn't attract that much attention because who ever heard of an orange grove flourishing in New York State. No, this was different. He felt like this place was an extension of himself, an extra limb, or the very depths of his soul realized and expanded beyond imagination.

Edgar set his sights on the crabapple tree in the far corner but took his time getting there relishing in the joy he was feeling. His feet savored every connection they made with the earth, each step rich and purposeful like a morsel of expensive chocolate.

He wished he could stay here forever, but at the same time he didn't want to keep his discovery a secret, he wanted to share this land with the world! But, he thought, best to start things small. Maybe just with his town to begin with. *The kids at school! They would absolutely love this place! I can't wait for Josiah to see!*

Edgar was hit with a revelation so hard that he almost lost his footing, which actually wouldn't be so bad he thought as he paused to pick up each foot and put it back down. Like a scientist looking at a slide, he watched as one foot sank into the earth then the other. He speculated what it would be like to lie down, to let his whole body feel the earth: His body would probably melt into it, or it would melt into him. What an odd realization.

He looked around, picturing the land chock-full of apple trees. They would surround the perimeter so thick that the inside wouldn't be visible from any direction. And in the very center, a carnival!

Edgar remembered his father taking him to the State Fair a few years ago on the other side of town. Now he closed his eyes and listened to the memory of children laughing and carrying on. He caught the scent of roasted peanuts and sausages cooking somewhere in the distance.

Yes, a fair! A carnival! His mind was alive with excitement as he chatted to himself. "You'd have to get through the maze of trees to get there. I can set up a clearing over here." He ran towards a point in the field and carved out a large open area with his feet. "And it would only be open in the fall. Because that's when apples are at their peak. I could have Josiah help me with the details. More people will surely come to my orchard if there's a carnival there. I would have a million friends. And the town would be proud to have us here! And Mama could spend all of her time doing the stuff she loves. We could tear down our house and build another one, a bigger one. And hire someone to take care of it so Mama doesn't have to anymore. And the girls can ride the horses just like the princesses they always wanted to be. I will have the best farming field this side of the state! Maybe in the entire Northeast!"

Edgar's mind was reeling with possibilities, and he was not quite sure how a fall carnival and an orchard would actually produce that much money, but he remembered his father telling him that once you are brave enough to open one door, others would open after. He was sure this would be the start to something wonderful and meaningful and he would never again have to worry about being disliked or smelling rotten. Visions of carousels, candy, and happiness danced feverishly until his foot caught an unruly root that sent him head over heels.

"Oh, this is heaven!" Instead of getting up, he lay there on the ground, legs and arms far apart like he was getting ready to make a snow angel. He laughed at his predicament and figured why not? Staring up at the sky, he allowed his legs and arms to brush the ground in unison. The sky above was now as blue as he predicted it would be, crisp in the fall air. He stopped his angel motion to have a moment with just the earth and sky which eventually disappeared, replaced with thoughts of a rich and happy life with his family: Mama baking and quilting, the girls with their long red hair flowing behind them as they ride their horses through the orchard. And Edgar, the shining star of the fall carnival, the ring leader of the circus, the industrious farmer with the most famous orchard in the country!

The only thing missing from his vision was his father. His father would be so proud of him. Wouldn't he? He tried really hard to remember him, but his likeness was fuzzy at best. He could see his eyes though, because they shared the same color. He covered them with small round glasses and said he didn't mind trading his banking things for a rake and shovel. "Because a man does what he has to do for his family. Never forget that, Edgar. Never."

Edgar promised he wouldn't and meant it. He knew that his papa would have been in charge of all of his bookkeeping here, teaching him the tricks of the trade. Papa lived for numbers and was only truly happy when he got to work with them, or help people work with them. "Numbers save lives," he would say.

All this thinking about Papa was starting to bring Edgar down fast from the high he had been on since the conversation last night with his mama. He closed his eyes and allowed his father's image to dissolve in his head. He then took a deep breath and exhaled the memory away. When he opened his eyes again, his heart leapt straight out of his chest, as there, next to his head, was a shiny pair of black ankle lace-up shoes.

He rolled over as fast as he could and shielded himself instinctively, not bothering to look and see who was attached to the shoes. He allowed a silent moment to pass before he dared a glance—the shoes had disappeared. There was no one in sight except for himself and the tree. He released a shaky breath, trying to make his heart beat at a normal pace, somewhat relieved figuring he must have been still lost in his daydream.

Edgar shook the experience off like a layer of dust, literally sweeping it all off with his hands, and rose to inspect the tree in front of him. He stared at it for a long time, using all of his senses, even that odd gift he'd been keeping a secret. He had no problem turning it on and off, but here, he couldn't turn it off. From the moment he stepped onto this land, it had been on full blast, a faucet with a broken tap.

This field was alive, rippling with energy and activity, and subsequently, so was he. He focused on the fine lines of the bark, on the waves of current running all through it. Hues of blue, red, and brown streaked through the trunk to the ends of the branches like a microscopic raceway full of miniature horses. He followed one band of energy down to the ground. The ground made a subtle movement at the base of the trunk, like it was drinking whatever the tree was giving it.

He found it interesting that the ground seemed to be taking more than it was giving back. As a matter of fact, at this angle it didn't look like it was giving back anything at all. Usually when he let himself go and focused on a blade of grass or a corn stalk there was a pretty obvious exchange of energy. The earth energy had a muddled appearance like fog, except lighter... more like steam on a kitchen window. And usually the plant did seem to take away a bit more energy because it needed the extra nutrients from the soil. It depletes the soil, but it doesn't mean to. It's just the way they work together, and the earth understands this and does her best to replenish herself.

You can always tell a proper farmer that took his time caring for his crop rather than one who tried to produce as much crop as possible in the least amount of time. The proper farmer uses fertilizers and special foods, and the ground eats it up like a holiday meal after a long fast. And the crop responds heartily, while the other farmer's crops rebel, looking depleted and decrepit. Bearing no fruit at all.

The earth cares for her plants like a child and is never too keen on letting go of her children. Even the weeds mean something for her, though Edgar couldn't quite figure out why she would hang on to those ugly things. But as he looked to the crabapple tree, which to him, seemed itself like a giant weed, he could see how all of nature, even the weeds, were beautiful in their own way. Kind of like people.

Edgar took a crabapple that fell to the ground and rubbed it against his black suit coat. Normally he wouldn't touch the bitter fruit, but something told him to take a bite and he did. His senses became so overwhelmed that his knees felt weak. It was like all the good and wonderful things in life filling his body, digesting, being released into and nourishing his cells. He devoured it, but before he took another apple from the ground, he inspected the core resting between his thumb and forefinger and plucked out one of the seeds.

They were smaller than what he expected and seemed to radiate a sheen from within themselves. He pinched and rolled it between his fingers. It felt more like a mineral with a grey hue, like hematite. Fascinated, he plucked them all out, putting them in his pocket before he got to work on the rest of the fallen apples not knowing or caring how they all had gotten there in the first place.

He reached out to touch the rough bark of the tree and traced a line of energy all the way from earth to branch and back again, not surprised that it didn't feel a tree should. Instead of bark, its texture was the soft flesh of a person or an animal. His finger sank slightly, and he found himself to be as gentle as possible. Not wanting to scratch it with a fingernail, he acted more like he was tickling this tree.

Overcome with emotion, he reached wide with both arms, giving the tree a hug before quickly releasing and stepping back, looking around embarrassed as if someone would see him and call him more names. But he couldn't be weird here, not in this place. This place was magic, a dream realized. It was… home.

He closed his eyes again and listened close, hearing two distant heartbeats, one much fainter than the other. He assumed again that this must be the life force of the tree and the earth working together, dance partners perfectly in sync. He opened his eyes, blinking in rapid succession trying to erase what he was had just come into view but it didn't work. It was real.

Eyes, like the meadows near his home, staring down at him. They were not attached to a person, but they belonged to this tree. Edgar gasped. His adrenaline pushed his other senses away and he was left to stare into those eyes. So familiar, so…

"Dad?!" Edgar said as shock washed over his body.

Something grabbed hold of his feet, yanking him from his trance. Roots grabbed at his ankles, trying to pull him into the soil. Both feet sunk below the earth followed by his ankles, knees, and thighs. Edgar looked down in horror, unable to make sense of what was happening to him.

He tried to push the roots down and away from him, but they were too strong. He felt like his body was being squeezed through a tiny hole. As his chest went under, his vision blurred, and he found it harder to breathe. His hands had already been pinned to his sides by the rope-like roots. And as his head started to go under, he took one pleading glance up at the tree—at those eyes—and caught a tear escaping from one of them, sliding between the folds of the bark as he slipped away into the darkness.

15 CHELSEA

The clock reads 11:45 a.m., and I almost have a heart attack that I'm late for school, but then I realize it's Sunday and sink back down into my covers like a bear willing away the spring. I can hear the TV blaring downstairs, so I know Autumn and Jeff are awake.

"Damn you, Jeff, and your experiments!" I yell to my slippers as I ease my way into them. If he hadn't gone wandering around pretending he was the science guy, then none of this would ever have happened and I'd just be Chelsea... grieving over my grandparents and scared about the missing kids. I put on a sweater, noting how sore my arms are. Being scared shitless must really take a toll on the body. I also resign myself to the fact that what Jeff actually did for me was a service. If I wasn't so focused on the twilight zone in my backyard, I'd probably be having full-on panic attacks right about now.

I breathe in a few times to stop my mind from wandering, then make my way to my friends with a plan percolating from out of nowhere.

"Hey guys!" I call out, startling Autumn and Jeff. "Sorry. Listen, let's go over what we have so far. Raina is in that forest somewhere. Or at least I think she is. I saw her, and can't explain that one away. Not entirely, anyway. And those seeds, they were everywhere! And everything was moving in slow motion and..." I let my words trail off because they are looking at me like I just sprouted another head.

"Well hello, sunshine," says Jeff with the slightest touch of sarcasm. "And did we replace the milk with coffee in our Coco Puffs this morning?" Autumn just sits there, brows furrowed in silent agreement with Jeff.

"I'm sorry... I guess I'm just anxious to talk about what happened last night. It feels like a very weird and surreal dream."

"Or nightmare," Autumn interjects. "I don't know what you saw or what we didn't or what happened to you, but it's freaky as heck. And apparently exhausting too because we slept until eleven o'clock!"

I look away from her because I don't want to tell her what I did with the clock. Just then my heart skips, and I check the cable box. *Still unplugged.* I walk over there and plug it back in, mumbling about loose cords, thankful that they'd been watching a movie on my PlayStation.

"How exactly freaky is heck?" Jeff says now, lightening the mood. "And most importantly what is heck?" He pulls out his phone, taps away with two thumbs then says, "Ah here! The internet says it's an intensifier. Oh, Autumn, would you like some heck in your tea? Nope. Don't think so. Doesn't sound freaky to me!"

"Sometimes it's hard to say anything at all around you, Jeff," Autumn says and throws a pillow at him. He crinkles his nose and tips his head back in a little show of smuggery.

"Heck or no heck, there is something absolutely not right. We have already established that. And it makes me wonder if all of our parents know about it," she says.

"Well it is private property," I remind Autumn. And they're grownups. I'm sure they obey signs and stuff."

"Yeah I know, but all of our parents have been so adamant that we don't go in there. I think we've figured out why. But do they really know or are they just that crazy about following rules? I can tell you my parents aren't so into rules, having had me before they got married and whatnot."

"Remember, Jeff?" she goes on. "When you tried to get your dad to build us a treehouse back there?

He snickers. "Well I didn't really want a treehouse, I just wanted to push my dad's buttons because building stuff isn't his thing. He probably knew that. We are always picking on each other."

"Or," she says, "he knew something else."

"Like that land is from Neptune or something?" I say.

"Yes! I think we should just ask them…what do you think?"

"That's what I was trying to tell you guys until Jeff started talking about coffee in my cereal. I just am not totally sure if it's worth it, entirely."

"Well personally, I doubt my parents will know anything at all, since they were born and raised in Buffalo."

"Oh, right," I say, my face falling. "I forgot about that part."

"You never know though. Maybe they heard something from somewhere."

I smile at him. "Ok then, it's a deal, tonight we'll talk to our parents. Let's just agree to *not* say anything about what has been happening with us. My parents will totally kill me if they knew we were going back there."

"Ditto" says Autumn. Jeff gives the thumbs up.

***

After I stow away the last plate from dinner, I figure now is as good a time as any to approach my parents who have just started to shuffle a deck of cards for their nightly game of Pinochle. They tried to teach me how to play once, but I could never figure it out, even when they wrote out the instructions. They are always more open and relaxed when they play, so I often take the opportunity to tell them my stories about school or whatever else. I sit down next to them for a little bit, watching them, trying to formulate my words.

Dad doesn't look up from his cards, but he can tell I'm agitated because I'm fidgeting in my chair, crossing and uncrossing my legs as I watch them.

"Is there something you need to talk about, Chelsea?"

"Not really, Dad, why?"

"Well because you have this look on your face that makes it seem that you want to say something."

"How can you even tell?" I say, bewildered. "You haven't even looked at me since you sat down."

"Parents know these things, Chells." He lays a few cards down on the table.

"Damn." Mom's flustered already by her first loss.

I stand up and walk to the window overlooking the backyard, the trees just visible by the streetlight in the front yard. It's too far away to tell which direction the shadows are pointing. *Huh, I guess this is probably why we never noticed before.* I remember staring out of this same window when I was little, the dim light cast over the trees making them look like real people forever frozen.

I squint, wanting to see the outline of them, the twisting branches, the bark opening in the middle just so, like an open mouth. I suck in a quick breath as I think I see something between the trees, a small patch of white just visible from the reflection of the streetlight. I put my forehead on the glass, hoping that extra inch would help me see better, blinking a few times to try to bring it into focus, but it's gone after the third blink. I'm seeing things.

I think of Raina, of how she looked when I "saw" her in there, and chills run through my body. She didn't say anything, didn't call my name. She just reached out to me, but what could I have done? Was she even real? Why did I have that same vision when I was underwater? And if it's not disembodied people it's disembodied voices.

I'll never forget the first time I heard a voice. I was in the fourth grade, walking home from school. I just made it to the little path that led to my street with the chain-link fence on either side. Someone called my name so loud that I stopped and turned around to look behind me. That's when I realized the voice hadn't come from behind. It was "in" my ear or inside my head somehow.

I still can't explain it, but it's happened many times since then. That time, though, as I rounded a corner, there was a hearse in Mr. Violet's yard. I remember wondering if it was Mr. Violet that called me to say goodbye. He was such a great neighbor.

I ignore the voices now. I just don't see how that stuff could fit into my world and don't really want any part of it.

Especially now, with Grandpa gone. We used to read each other's minds in strange little ways, as crazy as it sounds. He would be thinking of something, and then I would say it out loud.

Like when I was little, this one time he was babysitting me, and I swear I heard him talking to himself about going to the playground that I loved. So I stood up and yelled, "Grandpa! Bring my shovel!" The look on his face was the same my father gave when I drew all over myself with green marker; one part shocked, another amused, with a splash of confusion. He then told me that he was just thinking about taking me to my favorite park, the one with the sandbox, but he knew that he hadn't said it out loud.

It happened at least once a week with him and me. Mom said it was my gift and Grandpa probably had it too. But I just figured it was a coincidence because we're family and I see him a lot.

After everything I've been witnessing lately it's pretty much taking all that I have to not get down on my knees and beg my parents to move away! I tap on the glass lightly with my pointer finger and ask my dad why anyone isn't allowed to go back there. I don't see the look that I know he and my mother give each other, but I hear them put their cards down, and he says, "Because it's private property. And technically you'd be trespassing if you did."

"Well, why did we move here if we can't go past our yard?"

"Because the house was the perfect size for us and we have a big enough backyard that you can play in. There were all the new families here too, and besides aren't you glad? You have your two best friends on the street who you've known since you were all babies!"

"Well yeah, of course. It's just… I dunno. The trees. They scare me, Dad!" I turn around to face them and see their cards on the table, still in perfect fan shapes. My parents are looking at each other in a strange way that's making me uneasy.

"What?" I ask but I'm not totally sure I want them to answer. I just stand there gawking at them, the endless silence making them seem more distant than the couple of feet they are away from me.

"Well... Donovan?" Mom sounds resolved. "I think she's old enough."

Dad sighs and tells me to sit down. I do, and I don't even feel the chair underneath me because I'm hanging onto the electricity that is sparking in the room. I have no idea what he's going to say next, and I tell myself not to speculate.

"Do you remember that nursery rhyme your grandmother told you a few months ago when you visited Grandpa when he was sick?"

"Oh no, jeez, Mom told her that?" my mother says, mortified.

"Well yeah, that's a whole other story I forgot to tell you about, Steph."

"Kind of?" I say. Truthfully I only remember something about a dark man and some fruit but I didn't want Dad to know that, and I'm not even sure why.

He clears his throat. "The dark man under the soil in spring. Mother Nature's spoils she brings. Full of fruits through autumn's first frost. Till summer's end and harvest lots. Gourds and apples we do share. Bright and round then well we'll faire. Till winter ushers in the frosty air. A vibrant year from seed to harvest. Cold to warm to hot to cold, darkness stands at a furthest. Yet when warm winds overtake the chill air, tis the season to beware. Indian Summer then gives rise to the dark man in his guise. The land shifts back the moon is slight, the devil's fruit appears overnight. Lock your horses, tuck your children tight, the dark man will come to you at night."

I finish the last sentence along with him, remembering that last line because it makes me think of Billy McKenzie... the little girl in me thought that maybe the dark man got him. I roll my eyes at myself.

"And?" I say as an awkward silence passes between the three of us.

Mom's been quiet through this whole thing, but she watches Dad thoughtfully. She always looks at him like she is a schoolgirl with a crush. Sometimes I think it's gross, but today I think it's kind of cute until wonder if she imagines Dad in those books she reads. I don't have a poker face, and I realize that I'm looking at him with a very sour expression.

"Right. Well… first of all don't worry. I didn't mean to make a big deal of this because it's really not. It's actually kind of silly… But there's a legend about that orchard. Supposedly it was owned by a very bad man who had a house around here somewhere."

Mom nudges him with her elbow. He glances at her out of the corner of his eye and continues. "Ok, it was this property." His words mumble into each other like he didn't want me to hear what he just said. But I did. And with everything going on, it didn't scare me.

"Apparently he lost his father during the big fire of Old Rochester which made his mother insane with depression. So much so that she killed her two daughters, set the house and everything else on fire, then killed herself."

"My God!" I say, just realizing my mouth has been hanging open.

"Right?" Mom says.

"When the young man found out what his mother had done, he lost it, just went completely nuts!" Dad throws his arms up in the air and swipes Moms cheek, sending her chin-length blonde hair into her eyes.

"Hey!" Mom says, annoyed. She wipes the hair from her face, and little strands stay stuck on her cheek like fine spider webs.

"Oh, sorry honey!" Dad covers his mouth with one hand and chuckles.

I smile too before I can help myself.

"So anyway," he continues with a soft touch, rubbing Mom's arms, "he was so upset about losing his sisters that he didn't want any kids to live if his family couldn't. So he used to lure kids from their beds and take them out in the orchard… and"——his chest stops moving, and I imagine he's the big bad wolf sucking in a puff of air ready to blow my mental house down. He lets it all out with a great release—"kill them." The winds of his breath and the words pass right through me in a fury, but alas, this house is made of brick. I stand up straighter, proud of myself that my willpower holds. Like I'm finally learning to compartmentalize my emotions.

"Now this was a very long, long time ago. I think maybe around when your grandfather's father was a boy—could have been anyway, and it might have even been a rumor then, too. All hearsay… I reaaaaally don't want it to scare you because like I said it was so long ago. And besides, here's the kicker that pretty much proves it's fake Apparently, the story goes that he only lured the kids away during an Indian summer." He does air quotes with his hands.

"So, really?" Dad puts the wooden spoon on my emotional boiling pot. "Why would this man only hurt people then. At that time? It's not real, babe. Just a boogie man made up to scare the kids or give ol' Stephen King an idea for his next monster." He laughs. Dad loves Stephen King books.

A thought bubbles to the surface, and my parents are being so open that I let it escape without thinking.

"You know, actually, I read that they died because a lightning storm caught their house on fire!" I immediately feel like Hagrid telling Harry, Hermione, and Ron about Fluffy the three-headed dog. *Shouldn't've said that!* They didn't know I was researching our property's history.

"How did you know that?" Mom asks, raising a stern eyebrow.

I continue to look down at my fingers, noting that I should have put another coat of polish on them. I can see straight through to my nail beds. I rub my fingers. I can't get myself out of this, but maybe I don't have to tell them the whole truth. I certainly can't lie. I'm the worst liar ever.

"Well…" I say. "We went to Autumn's dad's work the other day, and I tried looking up the history of our property?" It comes out as a question… mostly because I'm testing the waters on how far I can go with them. I figure short and sweet sentences are the best way to go. And, according to my English teacher, when someone answers with a question mark, it can often be understood by the other person as a sign of immaturity. I guess school is good for something…

"Why on earth would you do that?" Mom sounds more intrigued than angry.

"I dunno? Because I was curious I guess?" *There I go with the questions again. I have to stop that.* "Seemed like a fun thing to do." My voice has grown so small I'm surprised my parents hear me at all. I keep waiting for them to start yelling or giving me a lecture or something.

But then something unexpected happens. Both my parents' eyes light up like they just got new batteries. Dad speaks first. "Oh really? Did you find anything out?"

"Not really. Oh! And this!" I run upstairs to grab the papers I brought home the other day.

"Here's the article, Dad." He takes it and nods, sets it down on the table, and starts reading it over. "And Mom, I totally forgot, Autumn found this."

"Oh my goodness!" Moms voice croaks. "Donovan, will you look at this! It's my dad's property deed!"

"No kidding!"

"I knew he grew up around here somewhere but he never liked to talk about his childhood much. Where is this, Don, do you know?"

"It looks like the 7-11 down the street on Bailey," I tell her.

"Yeah, honey, that's exactly right. Boy you sure did your research, didn't you?" Dad beams at me. "Any plans to work with the FBI when you grow up?"

"Ha ha, Dad. I don't know. It's just interesting to me is all. We learned all about history in school like the Erie Canal and Susan B. Anthony and stuff. I just thought it would be cool to see more about where we live." I'm surprised all of this babble is falling out of my mouth like a ribbon of story unspooling.

"Hey Steph!" Dad says looking to Mom. "Look at this article. It talks about a Josiah Heiland. Funny, that's your dad's name."

"Let me see that!" She takes the article and reads it over herself, thoughtfully. "Well I think there were a lot of German settlers around here back in those days. I'm sure there must have been more than one Josiah Heiland. Besides that, this was a bit before Dad's time. I mean, if he had been a teenager here then he'd have been what... 121 years old when he died? Maybe it was relative or something though? How cool."

Dad smiles in agreement then turns to me. "Hey," he says, "Did the story about the man scare you at all? Can you see how a hundred and some odd years can misconstrue real information and turn into silly stories kids tell to scare each other?"

"Nah," I say, waving my hand to dismiss him. "He's dead. It says so in the other article. At least I'm assuming that's him if it matches what you told me."

"Right, true. But it probably is just a fable. People make up all sorts of things when they can't explain what's really going on. It makes them feel better, more able to cope with their lives."

"I guess so..."

"Look if this makes you think of your friends from school, the ones who are missing, don't you worry about it. I'm sure there has to be a really good explanation." He locks his eyes with mine, unblinking, so I know he means every word that he's saying.

"Yeah, I know, Dad. I'm sure there is." I want him to feel that I believe him. I really think he needs me to. I'm his daughter, and he's always protected me from the boogeyman. In my heart I know my closet monster or rabid dust bunnies under the bed weren't real. But this... this nursery rhyme, the kids missing, the dreams or hallucinations or whatever they are, there's an answer, and it doesn't lie in shutting this out and ignoring it. It's out there somewhere where the shadows turn in on themselves and the air pressure makes your ears want to bleed. It's hiding in those trees, and I'm going to find it. I don't know why, but I just feel like I have to.

"Well thanks, guys. I have school in the morning so I'm going to bed," I say as I stand up and kiss them both. Mom, on the cheek, and Dad, on the forehead.

As I slip into bed, I grab my phone to text Autumn and Jeff to see how their conversations went.

Jeff: Nada.
Autumn: Neat stuff, talk tmrw!

"Okay," I whisper as I set my alarm and put the phone on my nightstand. Tomorrow is a new day.

***

Lunch is always the best time to have a longish conversation. I tell Autumn and Jeff the whole story, including the part where I informed my parents what we've been up to with our research and how relieved I was that they weren't mad!

121

Autumn then tells us that she didn't have to tell her parents a thing, that her dad was more than happy to share everything that he knew. And he knew a lot, considering where he worked and everything.

"Well crap, some detectives we are," says Jeff. "When in doubt just ask Autumn's dad!"

Autumn and I laugh.

"Truth," she says.

"So what did he say?" I ask.

"Well," she begins, the fluorescent light making her hair shine like smoldering embers, "Dad said the fire in Old Rochester drove everyone out to live in the country which is now the suburbs. So this whole area was full of city people who had to start over. Some of them moved to other cities, but a lot of people lost everything, so they found themselves trying to make the best use of what they had.

"That's why there are still so many crafts and independent store owners around even today. People taught their kids, who taught their kids, and so on. And they never lost their trades... Anyway, back in that time period there was another tragedy." She looks at me and continues, her eyes squinting as though she knows I won't like what's coming next.

"My dad said there was a maniac that used to lure kids out of their houses and kill them in the orchard. Investigators back then didn't have all the stuff they have today for solving cases, so they never found out who was doing it. And it stopped just as mysteriously as it started. No one ever found the bodies of these kids."

"Yeah.. Dad kind of mentioned it to me..."

"Oh ok, phew then.. so they tried to search that orchard, but the root system of those trees was so intense that no matter where they looked it seemed impossible that any one person could actually dig a hole deep enough to put anyone in there. AND, get this!" Her instant volume makes Jeff jump and knock over his chocolate milk. It was empty, save for a few drops that met the floor as the carton bounced. She watches Jeff pick it up while continuing, her eyes wide as she funnels her story like a tornado.

"The soil is so crazy tough that one of the investigator's shovels broke completely in half!"

Jeff looks between us like he's gauging our reactions. "I don't believe a word of it!" he says.

Autumn is clearly annoyed. "Why not?"

"I just don't. I mean if that many kids were gone, they'd surely have popped up somewhere. And there can't be *that* many roots. And what about the soil? What's it made of? Concrete? Did they even have concrete back then? How about the article that said that kid went missing along with his mother and sisters. He couldn't have killed everyone if he's dead. It just seems like too many holes."

"Well maybe it was someone else, not that kid in the article?" Autumn retorts defensively.

"No, I'm starting to think it was him," I say. "I mean if the rumor my dad told me has any merit, the story said he went crazy after his family died. But in the article, if it's the same family, which I really think it is, then he died, too. And the rest is just a messed up… mystery." Trying to put all the pieces together in my own head is making me anxious.

"Well he does have real evidence sort of. In old newspapers and stuff," she says.

"And I'm sure these, like the one Chelsea's dad was talking about, grew legs and walked so far no one really remembers what happened," Jeff responds.

"Maybe," Autumn says. "But still… it does make sense. Especially with that rhyme Chelsea's grandmother was talking about."

"I suppose," he says. "It just seems odd. And that rhyme. It's just creepy. But I guess not any more so than 'London Bridge is Falling Down' or 'Ring Around the Rosy.'"

I shudder as I remember reading about the possible origins behind those nursery rhymes: the plague, child sacrifice, bans on dancing, Viking attacks. I thank my lucky stars we were born in the twenty-first century.

She sighs. "You know? We can talk circles around this thing. I wish we could just let it go."

"Well, we can always do the smart thing?" says Jeff.

"And that is?"

"We can pretend none of this ever happened, never go into that orchard again, and get on with our young adult lives."

"True..." says Autumn, but she doesn't sound too convinced. "It's just not an easy thing to let go of, but I also think we are starting to get in a little over our heads here. And frankly Chelsea," she looks at me with stern eyes, "I don't think this is healthy for you at all. You scared the crap out of us the other day."

"I know...you guys are right," I say, always the one to speak before thinking. I didn't mean what I just said. I feel like I owe it to someone to figure this mess out. I'm not even sure why. Because of the promise I made to Raina when I was five?

"So what then?" I ask. "Should we just drop it? Pretend it never happened?" I'm more annoyed than I thought, probably revealing to them the emotion I was trying to hide: the fact that I'm not ready to give up.

"I'm kinda over it, Chells, really... I'm sorry that I started us on this mess. I just don't think we should get ourselves any more involved. I really don't." The sincerity in Jeff's face is so earnest that I almost get sucked back into the giving-up void.

"Well," Autumn says, "I do not like to give up on things, personally, but after all we've uncovered, I don't think it's a good idea to keep going either. Ever since this started, I can't sleep and am worrying about everything. I know what you're thinking, big deal, right? Everyone worries, right?"

Jeff and I just look at each other, shrug our shoulders, and raise our eyebrows. "Well I know it's cool to dye your hair grey these days, but I don't want to start turning grey for real, you know?"

When the bell rings signaling the end of lunch, I've hardly touched a bite of anything. I thought for sure that they'd caught on to my reluctance to let go, but at this point it doesn't seem to be the case. From now on, I decide, I need to go at this alone. A sharp ache of guilt or sadness streaks across my chest. I'm not sure which. Maybe both.

"Okay," I tell them with a manufactured smile. "I'm ready to call it quits." Autumn looks visibly relieved, and Jeff nods. I gather my things and head out to class, not happy with the person I'm starting to become. I can't believe that for in the first time in the history of our friendship, I told them a lie.

16 JOSIAH

Josiah ran blind and furious until his feet were on fire and his calves on the brink of explosion. His lungs felt like dragons that at any moment would exhale a blazing inferno. In front of him as he saw a break in the fog, with green grass in the distance. Home. Edgar's home. *Please God, let this be it.* He let out a yell as if that would propel him over the threshold even faster.

At last he broke free of the fog, crossing over the property and falling onto the grass. He watched, incredulous, as the fog, so heavy he could barely break away from it, shrunk back into the middle of the field then disappeared as if it had given up the chase or was going back into hibernation, ready to attack should someone else come and disturb it.

He stared at it without a single thought in his mind. Whatever had just happened was too much for him to process. He stood up and dusted himself off. Pain in his heart about Edgar, pain in his body from running, confusion everywhere else. He set his mind on the twins: He needed to go and comfort them and Edgar's mom, to pack them up and bring them to his house or at least the girls if Edgar's mom had things to tend to. Josiah knew all the Slates had was each other, and he was willing to help out in whatever way that he could. He was as close to extended family as they could get, and his mom always said to "love they neighbor."

He turned his back on the field, new mission at hand, but it was short-lived. The entire farm, the house, the horses, the… *smell*… was gone. It was replaced by a new smell of stale wood and char, old char that had been covered by sun and rain and snow many times over. Remnants of something that used to be… but through this mess if he hadn't known this property like the back of his hand, he would have no idea what used to be here. *Where are the girls? Where's Mrs. Slate? Where the hell are the horses?*

Josiah was overwhelmed with dizziness and such nausea that he could throw up, but he couldn't remember the last time he'd eaten—maybe the cider from this morning? He started to believe that the old lady poisoned him. *She is a little backwards, what if she finally cracked? Maybe I'm dying!*

He doubled over and tried to catch his breath in sharp inhales and sputtering exhales. Hot tingles caressed his spine like a battalion of fire ants on their way to wage war. *No, no, no*, he reasoned with himself. *She had a market stand for anyone to just walk on up and buy something. There's no way she would poison the entire town.* Or would she? Josiah didn't know what to do with himself. Sometimes when there's too much to handle your body goes numb to protect itself from over-stressing to keep the heart from seizing, and Josiah succumbed to this, his body too confounded to filter anything anymore.

So he walked. With vacant eyes and his body on autopilot, he leapt past burnt beams of wood protruding out of the ground. The only thing that was left of his and Edgar's fort, where Edgar's vision had been born thriving, now lay in a long, out-smoldered heap, a mast fighting to regain composure as the rest of the ship is pulled to the bottom of the ocean. He walked over whatever remained of the house, a splintered graveyard of hopes and dreams that would never manifest.

The day was bright and warm, in sharp contrast to the carnage he was walking past. Numb. Blind. He kept going, his feet doing the work by themselves—his brain had shut off. He didn't notice the wheat fields had gone sprouting massive corn stalks in their stead. He didn't blink as he passed the For Sale sign in front of the old lady's house.

The only thing on his mind was home. He just wanted to be home with his family. He didn't know what he would do when he got there. He didn't care how he would explain what he had just been through or if he even should. What he thought about was being in the comfort of family. Of his mama's cooking, because his stomach felt like a dry well. THAT he could feel. But it belonged to someone else. It was just a feeling in his body that he was vaguely aware of. A noise or an annoying cry from somewhere deep inside.

He didn't hear the car behind him, its loud motor sputtering dark fumes, the family of four visible on the top, facing both front and back, the mom holding onto her hat as they whizzed past, city folk spending an afternoon in the country. He was oblivious to the breeze that lifted his hair and covered his eyes as it whipped past. He just kept going.

Before long he saw it as he rounded the bend. Home. The little house with its perfect manicured lawn and its wooden swing held strong by the arms of the old willow off to the side. The windmill with its constant turning, circling even on breezeless days. Home. This vision alone lifted him from the numbing spell cast from the fog of the Slate's barren field.

Josiah remembered his daydream of God working alongside him, and he wished right now that he would carry him the rest of the way, depositing him into his bed. His stomach twisted in empty knots, his heart and body ached. He let the curious music coming from the open windows draw him closer to his front door, its uplifting strings and chipper male voice something that he never heard before. *"There's a time in each year that we always hold dear, Good old summer time; With the birds in the trees-es and sweet-scented breezes, Good old summer time..."*

He listened vaguely at first, then intently, amazed at how the music brought him back to life, allowing the flood of emotions and pain to slither through his body. Soon, he was overcome with the most unbelievable fatigue. He dragged his feet the last remaining yards to his door, wishing he could crawl but fearing he'd fall asleep right there on the road.

He made his way up the porch steps, his feet feeling like bricks encased in quicksand. "In the good old summer time..." he heard the radio announcer pipe in about the Haydn Quartet, an unfamiliar group, and then another upbeat song filtered through the door he had managed to crack open. Just the comfort of knowing his parents were there was all he needed.

There they were, sitting in the living room, Mom rocking on her chair with needlework, Dad's eyes closed as if he too had been lost in the music coming from the radio. Josiah didn't recognize the radio either, but that was the least of his concerns. He walked past them and made his way up, the stairs protesting their age under his weight.

He closed the door to his bedroom and fell onto his bed, insanely grateful that it was still there and as real as could be. It made him want to believe that everything he had just witnessed was just a dream, sure that he'd wake up just like he had that morning, with Mom making cookies to take to Edgar's, looking forward to seeing Edgar with his proverbial tail wagging with excitement for the adventure ahead.

Josiah wasted no time drifting off, knowing all would be right again soon. Drunk on the promise of home, he didn't notice the silence that had filled the house when his footsteps echoed in the living room. He didn't hear the sound of his mother hitting the floor when she fainted at the shock of seeing their son, who has been missing for so long, come back just like he never left. He didn't see them now standing over him not knowing if they should touch him, not sure if he was alive or dead, the rise and fall of his chest being the only indication that he was very much alive.

He didn't hear his mom crying for hours not wanting to wake him in case he disappeared again, his sleeping form being the only reality she could cling to. She believed that she too, must be dreaming. That maybe it's a lost stranger with her son's matured face and hints of stubble, his sleeping shoulders broader than when he left.

"They took my son, and gave me this young man," his mother whispered. "But why did they give him back? Thank God they gave him back." She crossed herself and then looked up at the ceiling, past the watermarks and traces of mold on the wooden beams. "Why didn't you give the others back?"

***

"Josiah, as God is my witness, I will not let you go, do you hear me? I won't!" Josiah's mom was beside herself as he shared the news that he needed to leave and find answers. She had one knee on the floor, the other bent and upright. She held onto the arm of her rocking chair for support. Her heart had grown weak after the first time he went missing. And now, she found it difficult to catch her breath.

His father stood beside her with his pitchfork-sized hands on her shoulder. He was a giant of a man but quiet and gentle as the breeze that graces the wheat fields on a warm day.

Josiah instinctively reached out to his mother but retracted his hand like a scared tortoise, rethinking this moment of weakness. He stood slightly taller than average, a stocky, muscular young man with dark blond hair pushed back behind his ears. His stance was solid on the floor under the heavy boots, an old pair he had to borrow from his father. Nothing fit him anymore.

He didn't want to look at his father, knowing this conversation would be too painful; he had only been home nearly a week. He feared hurting his mother again, but he'd been through this for days in his mind, intuiting from deep down in his heart that this was something he had to do. He needed answers.

Everyone else had moved on from the tragedy and seemed to accept the explanation of the twister that ripped through town picking out homes to destroy, ruining great expanses of fields, and apparently setting things on fire. He knew that last explanation was total shit. No one else saw what he saw. This only happened to him a week ago. Others had had time to mourn. He did not.

"Seven years, Jo. Seven. Do you know what that was like for us? For your mother to have buried some of your things in our plot in honor of the body we could not find, and now here you are standing in our own parlor like you never left?" He was pointing to the little cemetery bordered with a white fence in the back of their land.

Grandpa Charlie had been the first to take residence there, choosing that exact spot because he found a stone in the shape of a crucifix. He saw it as a sign of protection, as some sort of entrance to heaven. He had fashioned the old fence himself and built the house after. They were even more religious than Josiah's mom back in those days.

This was the first time Josiah had heard exactly how long he had been gone, and he was dumbfounded. The surprise registered in a slight furrow of his eyebrows, even though his heart was unravelling inside of his chest.

"Dad. Why are you working at the mill? I know the crops changed from wheat to corn. But why did you stay? Why didn't you go back to wheat? Find another mill to work at?"

"You know I can't just uproot our family, Josiah. I did it because I had to. For all of us."

Josiah took a step closer and peered into his father's eyes. He placed both hands on his father's shoulders firmly, as if he were trying to place his resolve into his father. "Dad, so do I."

Josiah bent down to help his mother back into her rocking chair. She pulled something from her pocket and put it into his hands. It was a rock shaped like a crucifix. "Take this, baby. Take this and be safe. Grandpa Charlie and the gates of heaven will protect you. They won't let you leave me again."

"God, I love you, Mama." The gravel in his voice surprised even him. He hugged her close, feeling her shoulders tense up for a minute before she melted into his arms, becoming the child.

Josiah left home before the first hint of sunlight crept its way across the countryside. It had only just begun to stretch its arms as he was nearing the halfway mark to the train yard. He walked with more vigor today but was still shell-shocked. His first plan was to get as far away from here as possible. He felt like he was beginning to go mad and he didn't want to take his family down with him. He didn't want to wake them to say goodbye, but they said their farewells in their own way last night. As he was leaving, he tucked a note into his mom's apron, but to his surprise she had tucked one in the same pocket just for him. It made his heart ache how well she knew him.

Her note to him was folded neatly and contained a small sum of money to get him through. The only words that were written to him:

> I love you and trust you are doing the
> right thing. Come home, Josiah, as
> soon as you find what you are
> searching for.

Always God be at your side,

Mama

He tucked the letter and the money into a brown leather
satchel before hoisting it over his shoulders. Part of him wanted to
leave her the money… he didn't feel like he deserved it, but he
knew it would tear her apart knowing he had nothing with him. He
wished he had a better explanation to where he was going, but if he
wanted to be true to himself, he had to admit that he really had no
idea.

Josiah figured that the railroad was his only means of
escape, that maybe the memory of what he'd just gone through
would stay here as if the winds rustled up by the speed of the train
would erase all that had passed—that he could leave it all behind.
He paused as he walked, picturing the red rocks of Arizona, of
their majesty and spirituality, but also of the landscape: dry, crisp,
a spattering of grass here and there. No, no that would remind him
too much of Edgar's house, the family lost somewhere in the
rubble, the sinister field that sweeps your soul right out from under
you.

He shuddered then stopped near a small pond and studied
his reflection, squinting his eyes which formed wrinkles that made
him appear much older. He took note of his wide shoulders and
shoulder-length hair. He smirked at the irony in that—he used to
make fun of Edgar's long hair. Now look at him. He broke through
his reflection and scooped up a handful of cool water. He
continued to walk, his back longer, shoulders higher, setting out to
find himself, the man that he'd become.

His heart ached for his mother, for leaving her and his
family again. But to him it felts like he'd hardly been gone, and he
had his sights set on finding some sort of answer to questions that
he just couldn't form. Whether they lay within the railroad ties he
had no idea, but he needed to try.

He had been following the tracks by keeping them in his
periphery. There was a winding path, a shortcut that led away from
the track and met back in the train yard. He used to play on them
when he was little and had discovered this path quite by accident

when he was pretending to go on his own foraging expeditions like Lewis and Clark.

Arriving at the yard, there were only a few trains to choose from, and Josiah settled on one whose underbelly was coated with a thick layer of mud, a sure sign that it traveled often. Trains could sit in a yard for weeks at a time, but he was hoping this one was active.

He opened a car that felt right to him, did a quick check to make sure it wasn't already occupied, and settled in, placing his bag close by but far enough from the sliding door that it wouldn't fall out. He left the door open awhile, allowing the sun to soak into his face and hoping it would sooth his restless spirit and burn off the dirt inside of his soul.

He blamed himself for Edgar, thinking that he should have just stayed overnight with him and had the conversation with his mother together. Edgar probably would have convinced them to go into the field that very night. There was no stopping him when he put his mind to something. Even if Josiah agreed, at least they'd have been together, and maybe that would have stopped everything from happening somehow.

The train started to rumble like it was yawning from a long sleep, and he was grateful for his impeccable timing. The dust in the train yard unfurled from the ground like an old blanket, and then Josiah realized he had been hoping this was just a respite. That perhaps he had parked himself in an immobile train, realized he needed to be home, then gone there. *I must be what,* he thought. *Twenty-something? I should be in the mill with my father and have my own family by now, probably.* He cursed at the ground for erasing so many years. *I could still jump...* He held on to the door, scooting closer to the edge, allowing his feet to dangle. His pulse started to quicken, fed by adrenaline.

But he had picked the right train, one that seemed solid, with a destination known only to whoever was driving it. Perhaps it was fate or destiny. God must have wanted him to go. Josiah's mom would love this for him. She would have told him it was a sign that he was on the right path. She always told him he was destined to travel and see faraway places.

For the first time in a long time, a smile crept across his face and he settled back in, comfortable with his choice and unknown destination. He felt stinging tears begin to form, and it surprised him. He took his small notebook from his back pocket and the pencil that was attached by a string and started to write.

> November 24, ~~1895~~ 1902
> Sometimes the only way to find
> yourself is to lose everything you
> love most.

He tapped the pencil on the paper, hating what he wrote because it was the truth and it hurt. The train started chugging faster along the track past houses, some familiar, some new. Past the orchard of the Stoken family now in shambles with a For Sale sign dangling by a corner. He wondered how long it had been on the market. Wasn't it just the other day that he was drinking cider over there and offering Edgar a job or apprenticeship? It was hard to work through this time change—everything still felt the same but stood so remarkably different.

An uneasiness began to build as the train approached the Slate property coming just around the bend. Instinct wanted him to turn away from it. He didn't think he could handle seeing it again, but at the same time, in his own way, he wanted to say goodbye, even if from a distance. He wished this was another crazy dream and that maybe he'd see Edgar out there inspecting the field with a smile on his face. Even though he couldn't see it from this far away, he just knew Edgar would be smiling.

As the property came into view, grief rolled through him again. He didn't realize that he could psych himself up in only a few minutes, but when it happened the weight of it nearly stole his breath. Everything was gone, a shell of what it used to be. He could barely make out a single beam from the house frame, a slab of wood from the barn. And that field with its two rotten crabapple trees…

"What the hell?!"

Josiah could not believe his eyes. He jumped up as if that would help him get a closer look, holding onto the side of the door handle for balance lest he was thrown from the train. As it zipped past Edgar's property, he could see clearly that there was not just one single tree. There were more. Dozens. Hundreds? But how?

He thought back to the memory he'd been trying with vigor to suppress. The pressure and the fog, inspecting the trees, something attacking him. There were two trees. Only two. Except for the mess of them inside the forest itself beyond the field. But that was in the forest. In the actual field, it was just the two. He ran both his hands through his thick, dirty-blond hair. "What is happening to me?!" He screamed so loud he thought the conductor would stop the train.

A tap on his shoulder startled him so immensely that he turned around and threw a punch that connected like a hammer with someone's face. His shock changed to horror as he saw that it was just a young girl.

"Oh my god. Oh my god!" He crawled over to her to make sure she was okay.

"Jeeze, mister, I just wanted to find out what yer cryin' about."

He wiped his face, just now noticing that he had tears streaming down both sides, and looked at her, exasperated. "Did I hurt you, honey?" he asked as he took her face in his hands turning her head slowly to the left and the right. "I swear if I had known, I never would have—"

"Nah! I'm fine," she interrupted, removing his hands from her. Her scraggly dark locks hung down over her cheeks as if they were protecting her. "Had a bunch of brothers and a father. Ain't got a mama. So here I am. 'Cuz I ain't lettin' no one beat me up ever again, you hear?" She held a fist in the air.

Josiah put his hand up palms out saying, "Whoa I give, I give. But I think I deserve a punch in return."

"Nah," she says. "You're too pretty. And besides you didn't mean to hit me, right? RIGHT?" She bent down and put her face within an inch of his.

"Of course not!"

"Well all right then. I'm Maddie. And you are?" She stretched out her hand to him.

"Josiah," he mumbled, and a pang of guilt lingered in his chest that made him thankful that he felt anything at all.

She squinted at him.

"Josiah," he said again snapping out of his trance, then took her hand.

"Let me help you up," she said and made to stand but fell over as the train shifted. He caught her before she hurt herself, and they both laughed.

"Maybe I'll sit instead." She squatted down and crossed her legs. He reached for his bag and pulled out an apple. "Want one?"

"Uhh no," she said. "I can't stand those things. Devil's fruit, you know? At least that's what my papa told me."

He looked at it, smirking. "You're right, nasty little buggers, aren't they?" He sent two apples out the door which were sucked up and sent out by the wind.

Maddie stood again and made her way to the other side of their train car. She heaved two burlap sacks out of her way to uncover two oversized wooden crates hidden beneath a tattered quilt. From another sack, she reached in nearly to her shoulder and pulled out an iron rod which she used to try and pop open one of the crates.

Josiah moved closer to offer a hand if she needed but she didn't. There was a loud clank as the cover hit the floor, revealing an arsenal of food, enough to sustain a few people on their own for quite some time.

Josiah looked from her to the crate of food and back again, incredulous. "How long have you been here?!"

Maddie threw him a long strip of jerky and a tattered jug filled with water that he caught on instinct.

"These crates been here since I moved in. Every time we stop, I find my way to bring more back and save it here. Mostly food I know won't go bad."

"Smart," Josiah said in awe, trying to figure Maddie out, partially entertained, partially astonished, one hundred percent certain he'd like to stay by her side. He cringed, knowing it was his nature to automatically want to protect people and make them see the better part of themselves. That's what he had tried to do for Edgar. But he failed. He certainly wasn't going to fail this time. He made a pact to himself that he would help this girl. No one should be forced to hack through life all alone, especially a girl who couldn't be more than eighteen years old.

"Okay, Maddie, what's our plan then?"

"*Our* plan?" she responded with raised eyebrows. "I been hacking it out here just fine on my own, thank you very much. I don't need no man to help me. Especially a pretty one like you."

Josiah stood expressionless for a moment, his body visibly shifting back and forth with the train. He approached her, bent down to her level and whispered. "I'm sorry little ma'am. But maybe you're not the one that needs help, here."

Maddie held on to her squint and refused to blink as she stared at him. "A'right then. You can stay. But you try and call any shots, and I'll push you off of this train before you can say Amen!"

Josiah gave a small smirk in response and turned his back to look at the world passing by. "Amen," he whispered.

17 MRS. SLATE

Mrs. Slate watched Josiah disappear, a tiny speck in the expanse of field behind her home. She wiped tears from her eyes and bit down on her bottom lip, hoping the pain would stop her racing heart. As she placed her hand on the window, feeling the contrast between the cool glass on her side and the warm sun on the other, her knees shook and she knew that she had to get a grip on herself if she was going to take care of her family.

"Girls!" she called out to Mellie and Maureen. "Go to your rooms and change into your church clothes, please."

"Why, Mama? It's Saturday!" they chimed.

"I want you to look nice for Mr. and Mrs. Heiland. You are going to stay at Josiah's for a little while."

"But Mama!" said Mellie. "I don't want to go, I want to stay with you!" She hugged her mom tight around the waist. Maureen stood in the doorway in front of the hallway that led to their bedroom. Mrs. Slate gently pried Mellie's little fingers from her waist and bent down on her knees to see her daughter eye to eye.

"Listen, Mel. Mama has to find your brother. He could be playing a trick on us, for all I know, albeit a cruel one. I just need to be alone for a little while and to make sure you two are well taken care of. And we can trust Josiah's family, right?"

Mellie nodded trying to blink back tears.

"Listen. When you get back, which will only be in a short while, I'll teach you how to sew that teddy bear quilt you've been asking about." She wiped Mellie's cheeks with her thumbs, and Mellie allowed the corners of her mouth to turn up.

"Really?" A little spark made her bright eyes absolutely glow.

"Yes, really." Mrs. Slate gave her a hug and a little pat to scoot her off to their bedroom.

"And you too, Reenie!" She turned to face her other daughter. Maureen gave her mom a look of distrust and said, "Come on, Mel, let's get dressed," then turned her back on her mother while grabbing her sister's hand.

Maureen

Maureen was uneasy. All that she knew was that her mother was totally fine this morning, humming to herself while folding the dough for biscuits, ignoring Maureen whenever she asked where Edgar was. Biscuits were his absolute favorite, and it was rare that he joined them for breakfast, so she was hoping to see him. But he never showed up, which wasn't unusual because he was always so busy working or being at school. The girls weren't allowed to go to school yet as Mrs. Slate wanted to keep them at home for another year "to adjust" she had said.

When Mellie announced that she saw Josiah coming toward their house, Mrs. Slate turned strange. She ran into her bedroom digging through her husband's wardrobe until she found an old hat that looked just like the one he had given to Edgar. Then she lit one of the lamps on the kitchen table, walked to the living room, and sat there on the sofa silently staring at nothing. Her actions frightened Mellie who hunkered herself down in a corner to cry. Maureen, the stronger of the two, reacted by separating herself from the situation. She walked past Mellie into the family room to play with her dolls.

Maureen took Mellie to their bedroom to find their best dresses like Mama had asked. Hers was white with blue flowers. Mellie's—white with pink. She heard her mom clunking around in the kitchen and was comforted by the sound, bringing with it a sense of normalcy amidst the chaos.

Mellie finished dressing first and braided her long red hair into two neat ropes that hung past each shoulder, then ran out to the kitchen to show her mother how pretty she looked.

Maureen called after her, trying to summon her back because one of the pink ribbons she used to tie her hair had fallen out. She shook her head as she picked up the ribbon, citing Mellie's uncanny ability to be just a little bit disheveled at all times. Mellie didn't respond, but she wasn't surprised: She also had a habit of paying no attention to Maureen. Maureen tied the ribbon around her wrist so she could put it in her sister's hair later and took time deciding if she should braid her own hair or not. She twirled in front of the mirror, watching the skirt of her dress fan out all around her, making her feel like a butterfly sitting on a flower in the wind. Finally, she twisted her hair into braids just like her sister's as she knew it would make Mellie happy. Mellie loved to dress up the same as Maureen, so even their Mama couldn't tell them apart. It was a fun game.

Growing tired of twirling, Maureen began to wonder why Mellie hadn't come back in the room. She called out again, waited, and heard nothing, so she poked her head out of the doorway and called out again. Maureen stepped lightly with stocking feet down the hall to the kitchen, careful not to make a sound. She had a good idea that Mellie was going to jump out at any moment to scare her, so she mentally started to prepare herself thinking maybe she could scare her sister first.

She heard a creak in the floor in the direction of the kitchen, so she slowed her pace and put her hand to her mouth to stifle a giggle. The noise came from the right side, so her plan was to jump out in that direction and yell "Boo!" At the end of the hallway she paused and counted to herself. "1. 2. 3!"

Maureen jumped out of her hiding place, swinging herself in Mellie's direction, but her yell stopped abruptly as something caught her eye on the floor. She tried to run backwards, to step away from the sight, but her stockings had no traction. Maureen couldn't move. The sound that rushed from her body was high pitched and automatic, and it pierced through the house. She couldn't look away from the blood that pooled around her sister's head, pouring out slowly, covering the floor like it was eating everything in its path.

She continued to stare and unleash emotional anguish into the air of the tired old house as something connected with her own head. A brief moment of unbelievable pain, a flash of light, and her world grew dark. The echo of the scream had been silenced but was still palpable.

Mrs. Slate

"Oh my beautiful girls," said Mrs. Slate, dropping the cast iron pot as she sunk down on the floor, turning Mellie around and placing both of their heads in her lap.

"I'm so sorry, babies, I had to do it. I had a dream about your brother... but it wasn't a dream. It was real, I swear on all that is holy, by God!" She fished the crucifix dangling between her aging breasts and kissed it as tears poured down her cheeks. She unwrapped the pink ribbon from Maureen's arm and undid Mellie's braid which was caked and sticky with blood, retied it with sure fingers and secured it with the ribbon.

"He told me this was the only way we could all be together again. If he did it the other way, had us become a part of his orchard, it wouldn't work the same way. Edgar made a promise to me, and I have never had a reason not to trust him." She looked to Maureen's hair and smiled because as always, her hair was immaculate.

"You'll understand soon. You will, I promise." She kissed both of them and then dragged them by their arms through the kitchen, down the wooden stairs and out to the backyard. Leaving them by the barn, she went back into the house and came back toting a canister of lamp oil. With it, she began to saturate the entire barn with most of the contents, saving the rest for the house. She tipped the lamp over that was burning in the kitchen and watched for a moment as the whole house started to burn. Using the flames to light another lamp, she followed suit with the barn. She'd been waiting for the day a good storm was brewing, and by the looks of it today wouldn't disappoint, noting how the golden sun was starting become smothered by a pillow of grey clouds.

We don't get many twisters this part of the country, but they do happen. And this weather looks ripe for twisters, she thought. She just hoped the rain would hold off long enough for the house to burn to the ground.

She stood by the girls and watched the flames devour her whole life, the tongues of the devil licking away all the joy and all the sin that was carried out in their home. She knew the rain would hold off, sin would do its work first. It always did.

She took up the girls' hands and dragged them past the blazing barn and into the field, their little feet bumping along on the rocks, their hair making trails in the dirt. The moment their blood touched the soil, the ground responded, the fog rising as if it had just woken up from a nap. Mrs. Slate paid no attention, placing her daughters in front of the two crabapple trees like sleeping babies. One girl in front of each tree. "I'll see you soon, my little sweeties," she said as she looked down at their bodies cradled by the soil, sprouts already forming at their feet.

Mrs. Slate removed the sewing shears concealed in the pocket between the folds of her house apron. She opened them and wasted no time ripping a gash in her own neck, sending red prayers that it really was her son that had come to her in the dream and told her to do this unforgivable thing to her family. Her blood soaked the earth and her body dropped.

As her life soaked away, one word slipped past her lips. "Edgar."

18 BENJAMIN SLATE

Green eyes burned in his mind as his face sunk under the soil. *They can't be my father's, can they?! How is that possible? How can a tree have eyes?!* As the roots held tight to his body, he closed his mouth, squeezed his eyes, and hoped for a quick ending to his life. He just wanted it to happen. *Please don't let me suffer.* And for the first time in his life, Edgar prayed. *Dear God, please get me out of this mess. Take me fast, don't let it hurt. Take care of my mother and the girls. Watch over Josiah and the farm. Let me live or let me die swift.*

As his body continued to be pulled deeper inside of the earth, his lungs began to burn. He tried to wriggle his fingers, and toes, to twist his ankles in circles, but he was wound too tight, like a mummy becoming sealed in his tomb. Down, down he went into eternity. Edgar's body became warmer the deeper he was carried. He had no idea roots stretched this far into the earth, and he couldn't help but to think of why they hadn't just squeezed him to death already? Was he going to be pulled all the way to the other side and fall right out of the earth? He wanted to panic but figured there was no point. He was powerless, and there was absolutely nothing he could do but to keep feeling himself being lowered. To what? He couldn't even fathom.

Sweat pooled inside of his clothes, turned the soil to mud that caked his body. The pain in his chest was unbearable, and every cell screamed for air as his body filled with toxins that he was unable to breathe out. What choice did he have? As he continued to sink down into the earth, he tried his best to calm down. The last thing he needed was the shock of miles of soil entering his lungs.

He opened his mouth just enough to chance an exhale and was surprised by the fact that he could at least do that. A tiny exhale. A small release of poison. The unusual moment of hope made him lose control, he let go of all of his breath, and his survival instinct took over. Edgar inhaled, and his body prickled with the pain of fear as the soil found its way into his mouth and he waited for the inevitable.

It didn't happen. The dirt that coated his mouth and found its way into his throat and lungs wasn't gritty and suffocating. It wasn't even "earthy." Edgar couldn't wrap his mind around the texture. *It's like... fog.* He remembered the expression "Fog so thick you could cut it with a knife." His father would say that when twilight graced the water of the Genesee River in the summer, and it would come in swift sheets that mingled with the shoreline of Lake Ontario. He'd imagine it was the souls of the boatmen lost on the water during the War of 1812 coming back to find their families.

Yes, that was it. Fog. In his mouth, in his lungs, and it felt... good! He no longer had any control and began to take in huge gulps of this soil as if grasping for both food and oxygen, simultaneously. The more he brought in, the stronger his body felt as if the soil was reacting with every single cell inside of him. Warm tingles spread through to his core, reminding him of the time he and Josiah made a campfire and slept next to it. The smoldering embers made him feel safe. This is how he felt now. Oddly comfortable, bizarrely safe. Lower he went and lower still. Breathing in, gulping the earth.

Edgar's descent began to slow, and the pressure increased as though he'd been put inside of a machine that separates seeds from their hulls. Crackling sounds which were distant a few moments before had grown more robust akin to hundreds of trees all cracking and falling at the same time.

He squeezed his eyes tighter, bracing himself against the noise and the jarring pressure as his body was forced through some sort of barrier. His pulse quickened again as he braced himself mentally, the only way he could, and he exploded through a barrier deep inside of the earth.

Edgar waited for the inevitable pain that was bound to happen when he landed, and kept expecting that he would transition to death right away or burn alive like in those old Bible stories. But no, his ending could only be described as "satisfying," and the deafening silence that followed was welcome.

His allowed his eyelids to part into a subtle squint, and found that he hadn't landed anywhere because he was suspended in midair. He was free of the crushing earth, farther down than any mortal could ever be, and encased within a layer of something else. He tried to guess what it was that surrounded his body, thinking perhaps it was the fog keeping him in some strange purgatory. He chanced a look around his cocoon, to the roots that were still holding onto him but had loosened their grip.

They appeared old and tattered but sturdy. He imagined that a shipwrecked sailor could use them to fashion a solid raft and find his way home. His eyes followed them up through the translucent layers that were his walls and took note of how they burst through the earthy ceiling of what he realized was some sort of chamber. A fiery glow pulsed in waves around him, and he panicked, looking for lava or some other heat source but gratefully found none. He prodded the encasement with a cautious finger, curious that it had a slight give. He expected it to pop like a soap bubble, but instead it felt more like a balloon.

The little hairs on his arms stood at attention, an alert from his survival instinct that he was not alone. He looked around desperately trying to see who was with him. He started to kick the walls of his bubble, to stretch the sides with his arms, but he just couldn't do it. He gave up, his body too exhausted from his descent into this place. He could feel the presence of many closing in on him as though trying to get a closer look. Even though he was certain they were there, he wasn't able to see them. Instinct told him to use his gift, and he listened as he closed his eyes and let go of himself. A voice flitted through his ears as if it were a feather sweeping through a gentle breeze.

"Welcome home," it said.

Edgar smiled, closed his eyes, and succumbed to his situation. Consciously, he knew the voice was correct. Indeed, he was home. He'd always belonged here. He had never been able to make sense of his life above ground, never feeling comfortable in his own skin, but here he already felt loved and accepted. By whom, he wasn't entirely sure, but at the same time he was. It was as if he'd known since the beginning of time and he'd just forgotten until now. In his cocoon of fog, suspended in a fiery chamber glowing with the energy of all the souls collected from above ground, he slept.

***

Edgar didn't know how long he'd been wandering in this field alone. His eyes strained past the impenetrable fog. He didn't remember coming here, or much of anything at all. He could have been born here for all he knew. He kept stopping to pick up the soil and drop it back down. He picked it up, tasted it to see how fertile it was, spit it out and began to pace again. What was it he was supposed to do?

He only knew it had something to do with the soil because why else would he keep repeating his actions? He grew more restless like he'd been waiting for something or someone but couldn't recall what he'd been waiting for. He strained deep inside of his own aching head as he tried to recall something, anything of himself. There, he caught glimpses of a man whom he believed to be his father because when the images popped in, his heart warmed like a kettle.

He held on to this image of his father, who, in his mind's eye started telling him about how to care for the land saying that it was plenty fertile, that it just needed the right person who knew how to take care of it. "It needs different nutrients," he said as he beamed at Edgar, proud that he wanted to create an orchard.

"Yes! An orchard!" The image hit him like a speedball. "With a fall carnival. And candy. And kids, lots of kids!" He beamed as he picked up the dusty top hat that had materialized by his feet and placed it on his head.

"Sounds like you want to help them, Edgar?"

Seeing his father now in the flesh standing next to him didn't shock him at all. It was as if he'd always been there, just waiting for the right moment to say something. "I do. I want them to like me, Papa. I want them to be my friend. It's been so hard here on the farm with just me, Mom, and the girls."

Oh! I have a mother! A family! The realization kick-started a new emotion that was short-lived when he questioned their whereabouts. *Why is it just me and Papa here?*

"Listen to me closely, son." He placed his hands on Edgar's shoulders and looked directly into his eyes. "You are a part of this land, and you have to be real careful who you share it with." His voice was stern, lacking the enthusiasm that Edgar had admired his entire life. This made him feel empty and confused. This man looked just like his father and talked like his father, but the light wasn't there. It was like someone else was wearing his father's skin.

"What do you mean I'm a part of it? It's not my mother or my father. It's just… dirt." Edgar kicked the soil, and a burst of dusty earth rose in protest. At the same moment, a thousand screams rung in his ears, and a deep pain sliced through the very pit of his stomach which made him double over and fall with his face in the dirt.

"It's been waiting for you, Edgar. You're special. You are as much a part of it as it is of you. Why do you think we moved here to the country?"

"Because of the fire in the city," Edgar said through clenched teeth.

"And what caused the fire?"

"I don't know."

"It did." Edgar's father raised his hand and gestured to the open field. "Can't you feel it? The energy here?"

"Well yes, Papa, I do. But… doesn't everyone?"

"Not in the way you do. It needs you to survive, Edgar. To work it like you've always wanted to. It chose *you*. You are its protector and provider. But it needs special care, son, special care."

"Like?" Edgar wasn't sure he really wanted to know the answer, but he figured his father was going to tell him anyway.

"Souls, buddy. Like the ones that inhabit those greedy kids that you want to befriend so badly."

"Souls? What do you mean, souls? And how are they greedy?!"

Edgar could see his father's face turn red as he chewed on his next words before he spoke them. "Don't they make you do things, Eddie? Terrible things? Because they know you want them to like you SO BADLY?" Edgar thought about it and couldn't help but admit that he was right. He continued to stare at his father, hanging on every word.

"They used you Edgar! Can't you see that? They don't really want to be your friend. They feed on your energy, they're leeches! They think it's funny that they can make you do things for them. They laugh at your expense. You aren't really their friend. You know that don't you? They talk about you behind your back. Shoveling shit, smelling like shit. They think you're a joke. Has one of them ever had you as a guest in their home? Do they ever sit with you at lunch hour?"

Edgar was going to protest that he liked to be alone at that time, but he felt a fire in his heart, making his ears burn. His mind was alighted, and he knew how to prove his father wrong.

"Oh yeah? What about Josiah? He's my best friend!"

"Ohhhh Josiah," his father said in slow motion. "The mill kid from down the road. Nope. He isn't your friend. You know what he did?"

A smile broke through the line in his lips, but it wasn't comforting. Edgar clutched his hands into fists. Josiah watched over him, protected him like a brother. There was nothing in the world this man could say that would make him think any less of Josiah. He loved him. Josiah was family.

"Yeah? Well he didn't walk out on me like you did! You left us, Papa! Left us! All alone. It's your fault the others make fun of me all the time. I smell like shit because of you. I shovel shit because of you. But you know what? YOU are a piece of shit!"

His father grabbed a hold of Edgar's black shirt collar with both hands and pulled his head close, knocking off his top hat. Edgar tried to turn away from the stench of rot in his breath but he couldn't.

"He *killed* your mom and sisters. He killed them. Burned them alive. Your friend. He's a monster!" He released Edgar, triumphant.

Edgar was stunned beyond words, surpassing comprehension, and his legs wobbled mechanically.

"No," he whispered and let his knees give out from underneath him. "No..." He slunk down into the soil. "Josiah would never do that. Josiah loves us. He said he was going to protect us."

Edgar's father squatted in front of him so they were at the same level. "I'm sorry, buddy. I'm so sorry to tell you the truth. But we never lie, do we?"

Edgar looked at his father with wide eyes. "You're right, Papa. We do say that." He reached over and hugged his father tight, clinging on to hope that it really was him hiding behind the monotone, cruel words. His father gripped him back, and Edgar allowed years' worth of tears to stream down his face, off of his jaw, and into the soil.

His father's words were muffled as his face pressed against the top of Edgar's head.
"He wanted you all to himself, Eddie. He knew you were that special of a person. You were different. You were meant to be strong and powerful, and he wanted to control you. Put an end to the person you were born to become."

Edgar allowed himself the solace of his father's arms while he processed what he had just said. Under any other circumstances, the sting of harsh words made Edgar clam up, to withdraw into himself until he was pebble-small and unnoticeable. Instead he felt his face heat up again. The rage burned deep, pushing down the weight of the metronome in his chest, quickening his life's tempo, causing a wildfire he didn't know he had.

Images flooded his vision showing him every single time Josiah laughed at him, gave him odd looks, told him to tuck in his shirt, or suggested he get a pair of new boots. He made himself experience the moment he realized how powerful this field was. The way he felt when he got here, like he belonged somewhere, that for the first time he might have a chance to be accepted. He only needed to maintain the integrity of the energy that the field was giving out. He would be loved unconditionally and work the land on his own terms.

The more he thought about it, the more he realized how much he loathed himself. *Wimpy, Edgar. Always trying to please everyone. Boo hoo I miss my Papa, Edgar. A Josiah-worshipping ninny!*

Repulsed by his own existence, his tears changed to steam. He reached for the crumpled top hat lying on the ground and disconnected from his father's embrace. Edgar stood to tower over him, placed the hat on his own head, then straightened out his wrinkled suit coat and shirt. In slow calculated motions, he dusted off his black sleeves and pulled at the cuffs.

For the first time, Edgar saw his father's eyes start to well up, and he caught a glimpse of something else there. A smudge of fear perhaps. Or was it loathing? Edgar's father took a ginger approach getting to his feet.

"Good boy, Edgar," he said with hands outstretched as though he were trying to back away from a snarling dog. Edgar winced as if the sheer act of touching his father was heinous and unfathomable. He stood there for a moment, awestruck as the magnitude of his own potential manifested for the first time. He could see straight into his father's soul, and what he saw shocked him.

Inside, he wasn't the strong, smart, genuine, and respectable man he once knew as his father. He saw a paper doll with the word "coward" etched across his arms. The word "betrayer" across his legs. Inside his filmy heart "deceit" was written in pencil, which could be erased. Edgar had it all wrong his entire life. He had always had the upper hand and could do whatever the hell he wanted, but he needed to live through it to truly grasp what it all meant.

He thought of his Uncle Benjamin, the free spirit that his father hated, and wished he had known him. He remembered how he longed to be able to take his hand and pull him out of the cage that made him feel so powerless against himself. He felt deeply of how he himself, felt caged too, and wanted to be free. Edgar understood at this moment that he could be free. For the first time in his entire life, there were no more boundaries.

"Edgar's dead, Papa." He paused as he felt the words leave his mouth like invisible dragons. His father froze, gawking at his son, mouth ajar, hands still up and out as if he were trying to shield himself from the beasts that Edgar had just unleashed.

"And so is your son! Benjamin Slate, at your service!" He swept his arms in a grand gesture, taking off his top hat and bowing low at the waist. Benjamin took one step toward his father, produced seeds from his pocket and threw them in an arc, like sprinkling glitter or blessing him with holy water.

His father froze as his body turned the color of dried mud and his skin appeared just as brittle. Benjamin looked at his father's blinking eyes, the only thing left that was human marking some sort of spirit inside him, and smiled.

***

Everything came together for Benjamin at that moment. He turned his hands around in front of his face, inspecting them with different eyes—he knew that he wasn't really in this field with his father. Rather, he was far below the earth suspended like a caterpillar in its chrysalis. But everything that happened here was very real. It kept the dead soul alive and the live soul dead. Like a black hole on earth where the universe completely flipped in on itself making time malleable. Some might call it an orbiting hell. But to Benjamin, it was an opportunity.

He considered the ground, knowing that his father had been wandering in this place since the day he went missing, succumbing to the pressure. *He must have let them in,* Benjamin thought, now cognizant of the fact that he and his father most likely shared the same gift. *Why did he never tell me?*

Looking back to his father who now stood as a hunched and gnarled crabapple tree, he felt a pang of remorse. Like unlocking some old memory, Benjamin knew what those seeds would do to him, and he had thrown them without hesitation. He was also aware that his father was now stuck between two gravitational pulls. One pull would haul him toward the light, keeping his soul alive while sending it onward. The other kept his soul here, in the place down below. It was up to his father to make the decision as to which place he wanted to go.

Either way his body would die eventually, which Benjamin referred to as "becoming one with nature." If his father resisted the pull, he would be stranded in limbo, indefinitely. But the gravity was too strong, like ropes being tugged by horses in opposite directions.

Benjamin straightened up and regarded his father one last time, allowing the lies he had just spewed about Josiah to soak in. His head began to spin, and he cupped his ears to right himself as he walked away from his father hiding this moment of weakness.

His mind started filling with vivid imagery, thoughts or memories he didn't know, but one thing was certain: They didn't come from him. He closed his eyes to block the scenes playing before him, but they kept coming in waves that twisted his stomach. His father, still in his banker suit, wandering in this field alone, grinding the soil between his fingers with a wondrous smile stretched across his face, the powerful energy of the land overwhelming him. The fog stretching out around him, entering his mouth, filling his body.

Benjamin fell to the ground and crunched himself into a ball like a sowbug. He could feel the fog forcing its way into his father's body as if was an extension of himself that he had no control over. It felt like a supernatural set of eyes and hands that seeped its way into every blood vessel, vein, and cell until it settled on the heart and the deep recesses of the brain.

When it did, Benjamin was flooded with visions and emotions from his father. Somewhere in the involuntary part of the brain, he felt that his father didn't believe his son should have to associate with simple folk such as Josiah. That Edgar should grow up to be a powerful man, but he, himself, wanted more recognition first. He felt his father plotting to cultivate this land, turn it over, bring the railroad through it, which the fog seemed to like. It grasped onto this memory, squeezing it like a fragile egg until it popped, oozing its budding mystery back into his maze of neurons and synapses.

Benjamin could hardly stand the weight of his father's most intimate thoughts. They were too much to bear, and he lay there with lips and eyes so tight they nearly caved in on themselves, hoping it would pass as another obscure vision burst through. It was of a wooden puppet fashioned in his father's likeness, right down to the little round glasses. Spindly branches were controlling his strings, making him dance and point a nubby finger toward Benjamin.

He sat upright as the unwelcome sights and feelings evaporated as quickly as they'd been poured. He took time to process them, counting on each of his fingers the sums. On his pointer finger was his father, still brave, strong, humble, and loyal. The middle was his father's weaknesses, the thoughts he buried inside about Josiah and the people here. His true heart had been revealed.

Benjamin tapped his ring finger and thought about the puppet. He knew that was the most important gift he'd been given. This place, whoever is responsible, had been controlling his father's every word and action. His father is there yes, but they'd been speaking through him. Benjamin petted the ground with his hand, caressing it like a kitten as he considered this. He began to wonder if he had been shown too much. If they knew, far below, that he was aware of what they were doing to this shell of a man that used to be his father. That they pulled out this faux hatred of Josiah to try to get Benjamin to lose all faith and trust in his best friend.

He held onto his pinky finger, bending it slowly towards the back of his hand to see if it would hurt. When it started to fight against his pull and a twinge of pain revolted, his question was answered. It was all very real.

Benjamin tried to stifle his contempt towards his father, feeling more stuck in the limbo between love and hate than anything. He walked over to his father's blinking eyes, "I love you… but how can you be so weak to have let them in like this? Now look at you!"

He decided not tell his father about purgatory, the guilt he was feeling sinking as his anger began to rise. "You have two choices, Papa. Pick wisely."

He turned his back on his father and allowed himself to disintegrate into the fog, back into his womb below the earth. Two thoughts escaped as a blanket of exhaustion started to cover him. "I have to get to Josiah before they do." He exhaled heavily and mumbled the next words. "I have to save my family."

Benjamin slept, transcended into a void of nothing and of everything. Below the frozen earth, through the first sprouts of spring and sun's return, through blazing heat and chill again. Still suspended, still transforming. Through thirteen turns of the wheel. The earth was acclimating his body, leveling him, becoming a single being—an extension of itself in human form.

Until the time came when a surge of heat erupted through his dreamlike state and filled his veins with the power of the returning sun on a day that should be bitter cold. When the summer battled the autumn chill, and the summer won, for a short while.

19 CHELSEA

It's only 8:30 a.m., and I can't keep my feet still. I get a little overzealous when it comes to art class——Autumn makes fun of me sometimes for it. I can't explain it. The smell of clay and paint to me is like some people's incense. It's meditative and reflective... playing with it takes me to a place of complete calm where all my worries don't exist anymore.

Today starts the unit on watercolors, which I have been looking forward to ever since the guidance counselor suggested that I take extra-curricular art to help me with my "emotional issues." I have my mother to thank for that.

It only took one dip of my brush to hook me. As the swirl of paint dripped back into the water, the patterns and colors changed from light to dark, back to light. It's like a whole new universe each time, completely random yet not——because I'm the one controlling it. I don't believe people should be controlled, and the paint reminds me of that, like a spirit set free to do what it will. I'm happy to have a hand in that, to be the one to let it go, to set it free.

When I put the brush to paper, that's when I can set my own spirit free. I love that I don't ever have to create anything specific. Unlike clay, where I worry that my cat won't look like a cat, with watercolors it doesn't matter if my painting selfie doesn't look like me, or if my happy trees aren't so happy. When I paint, I close my eyes and focus, not on my moving hand, but on the memory and emotions I'm trying to convey. My grandfather was the subject of my most recent piece. My mother loved it so much that she hung it over the fireplace, next to his urn. She said that it was uncanny how I captured his love and spirit in there, somewhere soaked in between the fibers.

It's a large canvas with brilliant blues on the bottom, swirling in waves and circles like mini tornados or ocean tide pools. Mixed into the folds are light pinks and purples. In the middle of the piece, yellows and oranges outstretch long arms like the rays of a setting sun. Blacks, browns, and dark blues mix throughout the top layer along with streaks of purple and white and upside-down rainbows, which weren't intentional—they just sort of appeared when I opened my eyes. My heart had done all of the work. If you were to play Grandpa's spirit, project it on a screen, this painting would be in motion.

When I considered the upside-down rainbow sometimes, I decided that maybe it means that people are looking in the wrong direction for the pot of gold. It's not down on the ground somewhere out of reach. It's right above us. People keep their noses to the ground too often without considering others. I guess you could say that many people are self-centered. But in this way, we are forced to look up for the gold. Look into each other's eyes, minds, bodies and spirits, and that's where we can find the gold hidden deep inside everyone.

At least that's what I said when I had to present my painting to the class. Mrs. Hinkley, our art teacher and the lady who runs the extra-curricular class, is big on symbolism and always asks us to find it in our work. Since I don't often open my eyes when I paint, I don't let the idea of symbolism bog me down when I'm trying to create. It's only when I open them that I can really enjoy the process of digging deep into whatever work I've done. It's like my intuitive side tries to open up, and this is just about the only time that I'll let it.

So here I sit rubbing my hand along the brown paper that covers the art table, which makes my teeth tingle in an odd way as if I'm repulsed and attracted to the feeling at the same time. Tania is doodling with a green "sour apple" scented marker across from me, but to me it smells like rotting garbage. I'm antsy waiting for the morning announcements so I can find my assigned easel. I already know I'm going to focus on the field of crabapple trees, on my vision of Raina, on that god-awful pressure in my ears.

After a brief lecture from Mrs. Hinkley about painters like Winslow Homer and Georgia O'Keefe, it's time to find my easel and let the fun begin. I silently thank the schedule gods that I get to have art in the morning. It's the perfect time to paint as I'm not too tired like I am at the end of the day. I can focus all of my attention to creating, and that makes me happy.

The other kids sigh and groan as they stare at their blank pages. My painting neighbor, Molly, asks if I can suggest a topic for her to work. I tell her maybe it should be her favorite animal, and she lights up at the idea, picks up her brush then looks at the colors before her. "You know?" she says, turning to me, tapping the non-brush end to her chin, I think maybe Theo James will do!" We both laugh and I roll my eyes as I know how boy crazy Molly is.

"Animal, huh?" I say.

"Oooooh yeah. Meee. Owww!"

I laugh, kind of wishing what I had in mind was as simple as a celebrity crush… even though people are tough to paint.

"Okay class, you have half an hour to get started on your masterpieces!" Mrs. Hinkley chimes in. "Don't worry about finishing today. We'll have time in the next few classes to work on them. At the end of the unit, we will be displaying these at the museum, so try really hard to do your best work ok? And no dirty stuff, Brett," she says, peering over the lenses of her multicolored glasses. The class laughs at this, and so does she. He's pretty known for depicting parts of the male anatomy on just about everything.

I put all of my paints and brushes in order just the way I like them, brushes to the right, paints to the left, water a bit off center. I set it up the same way every time so I don't have to waste time locating a particular color. As much as I'm reluctant to go back to that horrible hallucination or whatever it was, I have to. I want to hold on to that image and feeling so I can fully understand it, to make something so intangible more tangible in my little painting world. I hope, anyway.

I take a couple of deep breaths and close my eyes. I'm grateful the other kids are also facing their easels because if they saw me painting like this, they would probably think I'm weird.

"Focus, Chelsea," I whisper. *Focus on the experience. The Orchard. Raina. Focus on all the events of the other night.*

And then it happens.

That familiar feeling washes over me. My body becomes warmer, not hot, but comforted, like with hot chocolate on a cold day. The room's noise disappears, the tick of the clock stops, and time itself seems to slow down. It's just me and my painting. I work without worrying about where my fingers should go, lost in the process. Dip, brush, dip, brush, dip, brush, rinse, repeat, until I'm interrupted by a loud chime over the classroom speaker and I snap back into the room with the ticking clocks and squeaking sneakers, and quiet chatter of kids who would much rather be doing something else. I almost fall over, grabbing onto the easel for support.

"Attention students," a voice comes through the intercom. It's Mrs. Balis, our principal. She caught me in the first grade putting my gum on the wall in the line waiting for library class. She moved to the middle school the same year I did. I'm sure she doesn't remember what I did, but I still cringe when I hear her voice.

"Quiet please!" Mrs. Hinkley shouts while banging a wooden stir stick on an empty tub of paint. The chatter that erupted after the announcement dies down, but the fire alarm starts to screech and everyone covers their ears. Following protocol, we march outside, and I notice the faint smell of smoke. I hear cries of "Oh my God!" and "Wow" as flames make their way out of one of the gymnasium windows. It doesn't take long for the fire trucks to arrive, and we all watch with a mixture of curiosity, excitement, and anxiety as they work on extinguishing it.

My head is in a different space as I shuffle back into the classroom, and it takes me a few minutes to notice that Mrs. Balis is speaking again over the intercom, "…at a time when it will be safe to return. For the safety of our students and faculty, the rest of the day's classes have been suspended."

Cheers erupt in the classroom.

She continues, "You will return to school on Monday."

Applause turns to groans.

"Homework packets from your classes will be delivered to your current classrooms where you will stay until you are dismissed. Those of you who don't have an immediate ride home or confirmation of a safe place to go will remain in the cafeteria until you can be dismissed. Please do not worry, this is just a precaution and school will resume as soon as it's been fully inspected. Counselors will be available as well if for those of you who feel you need to discuss the events of today. Jenna Smith and Dusty Albright, please report to your classrooms, immediately."

It takes a minute for the room to burst into chatter again, and Mrs. Hinkley allows it to happen. "If there are questions, please feel free to ask me," she says over their voices. "Talking always helps to ease fears."

I for one, found that last comment about Jenna and Dusty a little unsettling but no one else seems to feel the way I do.

"Umm… Mrs. Hinkley?" I pause. I can't decide if I want to ask about the fire or the missing kids. "What about Dusty and Jenna?" I decide that they're far more important.

"As far as the children on Mrs. Balis's announcement, I'm guessing they are roaming the halls and haven't made it back to their classrooms yet."

I turn from her, succumbing to the fact that I have no choice but to accept that, and I feel my pulse quicken. *What is happening to everyone? And why is it that that not a single freaking grownup can give me any sort of answers?* It's always "I don't know. blah blah blah." *Ugh.* I'm so frustrated right now, and around the room, no one else seems to want to ask any questions. Mrs. Hinkley said she would be at the front of the room and to come to her anytime.

I chat a bit with a few friends, but the conversation just circles in on itself as we come up with empty explanations. Everyone is starting to draw conclusions about the fire in the gym, too, but I don't see how that can be possibly connected to anything. And now I start to hope that the other kids made it back to their classrooms. My mind begins its cycle of worry that they were hurt in the fire… or even worse, what if the dark man took them?

"No, no Chelsea, don't be stupid!" I mumble to my feet, embarrassing myself over assumptions, and make a mental note to stop worrying so much. As we wait for our homework to be delivered, a task that, to me, seems pretty monumental, the chatter begins to die down as everyone trickles back to their paintings or whispers in little circles.

I can't decide if I want to look at what I painted so far before I start again. I always enjoy the element of surprise, but at the same time, I've been so caught off guard by the interruption that I probably won't be able to pick up the momentum again until I know what I have to deal with. "Okey doke, let's see the damage…" I begin to say under my breath but the rest of the words escape me. My eyes dart from the canvas down to my paints, making sure that I had put all the colors in the correct places, surprised that I had hardly used any colors at all.

The painting is all black swirls of hair and waves that form a shape that looks like a top hat. One eye black, the other green. Long strokes of tangerine flames. Figures in grey surrounding the flames. I have trouble determining whether the figures are people or smoke, or smoke that looks like people. Tall lines of tan streak every which way. *Tan? I don't even know what colors make tan?* Red splotches everywhere. Candy apple red. My mind said it before I could even think it. *Devil's fruit.*

I need to take this to Autumn and Jeff. I run over to Mrs. Hinkley and proceed to beg her to let me take the painting home and find myself whining like a professional toddler complete with drawn-out pretty pleases as my hands are clasped in prayer. And then I grab her hand and pull her towards my painting like it's the toy I've been wanting at the store that I can't leave without. Funny how teachers can become like family members.

"Well I'll be!" she says, pulling down her glasses to the bridge of her nose. "Have you been watching many Halloween movies lately? This perfectly matches our season! Just gorgeous!"

"Uhh… thanks. Yeah I uhh… love… *Edward Scissorhands*?" I had no idea what to say.

"Ooooh I don't know if it's the movie I like so much or Johnny Depp." She winks.

"No kidding?" I smile but it's awkward at best, and then a light bulb goes off reminding me that Autumn and I should watch that soon and I erase the thought like an etch-a-sketch.

I try again. "Please? Can't I take it home today?"

"Sorry, dear, it can wait, can't it? First it must dry. I don't want a centimeter of smudge on that painting. And second, I would really love to display this! It's lovely and the theme is right on!"

I sigh like I'm trying to blow a feather into the bottom of a well. "I guess."

"Thanks, Chelsea dear," she says, patting my head like I'm her furry pet and then makes her way to the other paintings.

"Ooh!" I stand up taller as an idea occurs. I grab my phone out of my bag and take a picture of my painting. "Duh, Chelsea," I say as I send the pic to Autumn and Jeff.

There is a knock on the door, and someone comes in with a very large stack of thick packets. Mrs. Hinkley grabs Henry before he sits back down and recruits him to pass them out to everyone. Grunts and sighs erupt as everyone makes their way through quizzes, study guides, and flash cards.

"Everyone!" Mrs. Hinkley pipes in. "Once you all have your packets, you are free to leave."

Out in the hall, I meet Autumn and Jeff in the impossibly long dismissal line and ask them if they've seen my text, but they hadn't turned on their phones yet. A hall monitor glances down at her clipboard and then up to the three of us. "You three," she trumpets, "are going home with Mr. O'Connor."

"Huh, that's new," Jeff responds. I look to Autumn and she shrugs.

We all squeeze into the back seat of the Mini Cooper, and Mr. O'Connor explains, "So I asked your parents if they wanted me to pick you guys up together to give you all time to talk."

The relief was palpable between the three of us as none of us wanted to be alone just yet. It had been too weird of a day with too much to think about.

"I know we are on a bit of a lockdown here as you heard. But I think they are just being way overcautious. Trying to prove our tax dollars are good for something!" he says, trying to cheer us up.

I grab Autumn's hand involuntarily. *Lockdown?* "What lockdown?" I say, looking at the back of his head.

"Oh boy…I thought they would have made an announcement at school. The town put out a temporary curfew for kids under eighteen. In your houses by nine p.m. unless accompanied by an adult. They're going to start patrolling the neighborhoods, too."

"Preposterous!" says Jeff. And normally I'd laugh at his awkward vocabulary, but I'm still caught in the current of Mr. O'Connor's words.

"Quite," says Mr. O'Connor. "But aside from the news of the two children missing, there is a search for a Dusty and Jenna? Do you know them?"

Autumn and I gasp. Jeff responds, "They're in different grades. But there was an announcement looking for them after the fire was put out. What is going on Mr. O'Connor?!" The intensity in Jeff's voice makes me feel like my toes are on the edge of a cliff.

"Not to worry kids, not to worry. I bet when we turn on the news tonight, they'll be safe and sound."

Maybe now's the time I should join Facebook, I think, hoping there'd be news on there, but decide I still don't want to deal with that. It looks too time consuming and I refuse to be one of those people glued to their phones. Instead I just sink back into my seat and try not to think about anything at all.

"Anywhoo..." he says looking in the rearview mirror at us. I swear I sense some nervous tension but maybe that's just coming from myself. "I thought I'd take you to the library... won't that be fun?!"

We sit there in a vacuum. Radio silence as we stare ahead with wide eyes, pretending he didn't just say that.

"I'm just kidding. The Play House is open for a little while. Let's go blow off some steam over there, shall we?"

"Oh Mr. O'Connor, I love you!" I chirp.

"Yes!" Jeff pumps his fist in the air. "I can kick your ass in air hockey again, Mr. O!"

Autumn beams at both of us, her words always so legible even when she doesn't say anything.

"You guys have been through so much lately. I figure there's nothing like some go carts, video games, mini golf, and junk food to lift morale, am I right?"

We agree and allow ourselves to become lost in our thoughts. After a few minutes I figure now would be a good time to show them my painting, so I open my photos and ask what they think. "Wow!" say Autumn. "You know, Chelsea, your paintings just keep getting better and better."

"Thanks," I tell her and mean it sincerely, but that wasn't the point I was trying to get across. "But…do you think it means something?"

"Like what?" Jeff grabs the phone, enlarging the image with his fingers. "It's just a painting, Chells. A fantastic one! But just a Halloween painting, right?" He's all smiles as he studies it. He's just about to hand it back to me when I see his brows furrow above the image reflecting onto his glasses. He brings his head closer to the phone and then removes his thick lenses altogether as if it'll help him see better.

"What?" Autumn and I say together.

"I dunno," Jeff responds, not taking his eyes away. He's now turning the phone upside down, but the picture keeps righting itself. "It looks like it says something." He tries to make the image bigger, but it's already at its peak. "See?" Right on this tree here, but I can't quite make it out." He turns to me. "Chells, do you remember writing anything?"

I frown. "I never know what I'm doing when I paint. It's like I just… disappear."

Autumn takes the phone from Jeff. "Ooh! I see it. Hang on a sec."

We wait while she tries to figure it out. "I got it! Look here. Above the eyes." She turns to me again and says sarcastically regarding the eyes, "You really do have a crazy imagination. But here, it says, 'Choose.'"

"Choose?" I say quizzically. "Why the heck would I write that? Choose. Choose what? To go back in to the orchard or not?" I consider this for a moment. "Well sure, that could definitely have been what was going through my mind, I guess. Makes sense, anyway."

Jeff retorts in his best horror-movie narrator voice while waving his fingers in the air. "Or maybe it's the Dark Man telling you to come with him so you can eat all of his apples until you explode, mwah ha ha ha ha."

I click my tongue at him and sigh, taking my phone from Autumn. "Very funny. Besides that, they're crabapples. You probably *would* explode if you ate too many without cooking them."

"Really? Huh… they never bothered me!"

Autumn looked at Jeff shaking her head. "Why does it not surprise me that you like those nasty, sour little things. Your stomach is iron!"

"Food is my friend," he smirks.

"I guess!" she says sardonically.

As we pull into the parking lot, my brain feels like it's about to ooze from my ears, it's so mushy thinking about the odd events of the day. So far it's gone from typical to terrible, weird to depressing, relieving to amusing. The weather, too. It was a little foggy this morning, but this afternoon it started to rain, and the fog has gotten so thick it's almost hard to see The Play House building. Bizarre, I think, because I can't remember a time it has ever been raining and this foggy at the same time. *Is that even possible?*

As we enter the building, I'm disheartened by the number of police that are hovering around every window and door, inside and out. I give Autumn a wide-eyed look, and Autumn puts a reassuring hand on my back. Jeff doesn't seem to care one bit. Somehow he has already acquired his tokens and is spinning his air hockey paddle around like a gun in an old western, preparing to duel. Even blowing away the imaginary gun smoke.

"Geez, what are you? Superman?" Autumn says sarcastically.

"Air hockey is serious business. Come on Mr. O!" He yells as Autumn's dad pumps dollars into the machine.

"Alright, one second, Jeffrey! Here you go girls!" He gives each of us a large bucket of tokens and sends us on our way, knowing he has nothing to worry about with enough police in here to take down a federal prison.

Autumn goes right for the claw machines. She has always been a huge animal fan and can never resist the urge to win something cute and cuddly. Never mind the number of stray animals she tries to bring home to her parents. It doesn't have to be fuzzy either. They can have many legs or be scaly, she doesn't care. She loves all the critters.

Her parents had to cut her off when she started bringing snakes in the house from their garden when she was seven years old. The first one was fine. It was an exciting event, actually. They bought a little cage and learned on the internet how to care for it. She would feed it worms and mice she found in her yard. Her parents thought it would be a great way to learn how to care for animals and everything. Until she found a nest and started bringing them in the house by the bushel. They were quite literally all over the kitchen floor, and they were so small and moved so fast it took them weeks to get them all out of the house. They found their way into shoes and even under the covers when they were sleeping! To this day her mother still shakes out every shoe and does not make her bed until she lies in it. Just in case.

I hang out with Autumn to see if she actually wins anything because no one ever seems to on these things. On her second try, I laugh as the stuffed snake drops into the bin.

"Oh my God, Autumn! I can't believe you got that! I was just thinking about the time you brought all the snakes into the house!"

"Ha ha, right?!" Autumn is pulling the snake out of the machine. "Think I should put this on my mom's pillow tonight?"

"Oh yeah, she'll love that!" I say, laughing.

An ear-splitting crack and a scream from down at the other end of the arcade changes the scene from fun to chaotic as smoke starts billowing furiously throughout the building. Mr. O'Connor and Jeff are on their heels making a beeline for us. I turn in the direction of the sound and feel the kink in my neck that formed when I shrugged from the shock of the alarm. People are darting everywhere as police try to corral them into the exits, and the smoke follows them in waves.

I focus my attention toward the doorway that leads to the bathroom area right next to where the explosion happened. There's a person standing there, I can't tell if they're hurt or in shock, and I look quickly to see if anyone is around to help. I can tell it's a man by the way he's dressed. Another wave of smoke follows a crying little kid as he is pulled away by an older sibling, and the person in the doorway comes into view.

It's a young man with longish black hair resting uneasily under a top hat. My body grows so cold my hands could probably put out the fire if I touch it, and I hold on to the claw machine for support when he flashes an impossibly wide smile, tilts his hat with spindly fingers and nods his head.

"Out! Now!" Mr. O'Connor yells and grabs Autumn by the arm who takes my hand as he pulls us toward the door. I try to look for him again before I'm yanked outside, to see that face one more time, but he's gone.

We stand by the Mini Cooper catching our breath, trying to see through the chaos and the fog.

"Ok," Mr. O'Connor says between short breaths. "Get in… it's pouring!"

We drive away slowly through the maze of people, police, and now fire trucks. Mr. O. chances getting as close to the back of the building as possible as we are all curious about what happened. There's a gaping hole in the building that we can't look away from.

"Lightning. Right, Mr. O.?" Jeff says still gawking at the hole.

"Sure looks like it!"

"Boy are we lucky! I hope no one got hurt." The worry in Autumn's voice make my hairs stand on end. "Should we stay and help?"

"No honey, there's plenty there to help, and we would probably do more harm than good." He addresses us all. "I'm soooo sorry! I thought I would do something fun for you, and here I go getting you three even more worked up. Are you guys okay?"

One by one we answer, probably more out of shock than anything else. "Fine." "Fine." "Fine."

I'm on the fence as to whether to mention that strange man to them. I open my mouth to say something but close it and slink back into my seat to watch the world go by, instead. I feel like this whole thing is personal somehow and an odd pang wells in my chest. The more I think about that figure, the more I realize I've seen him before.

I close my eyes as we drive and realize that I'm mistaken. He is absolutely a cross between that painting and my stupid dreams, my crazy brain has once again taken over. I shift a bit in my seat as pins and needles start to make their way around my fingers, up my arms, to my shoulders, and down my spine. *Breathe* I tell myself, *just breathe*. My pulse quickens, and it takes all of my energy not to tell Mr. O'Connor to pull the car over so I can run away screaming.

"Phew. I guess I really should have taken you to the library instead, huh?" says Mr. O'Connor.

"Nah. Lightning or none, this was awesome. Thanks, Mr. O.," Jeff answers.

They are talking normally, but they sound distant—muffled, like they're in a tunnel and I'm standing just on the outside. I feel little beads of sweat burst through the folds of the wrinkled skin on my forehead. My head is spinning and swimming at the same time. I'm convinced that I am absolutely starting to go crazy and my body is reacting on its own. *Should I tell them? Should I tell them if I don't get out of this car that I'm going to lose control and go mad?* My hands are shaking so bad, and I start to tap my feet on the floor in a frenzy. I shift again, take a deep breath and look out the window. I'm so relieved that we are turning onto our street.

Mr. O'Connor pulls into his driveway, and I have the car door open before he stops. I mumble a quick thank you and run to my house without saying anything to Autumn and Jeff. I lock myself in my bedroom, curl myself up in a sitting ball on my bed, and rock myself back and forth. We talked about anxiety and panic attacks in health class for Mental Health Day not too long ago. I'm pretty sure this must be what's wrong with me. I'm scared that I'm losing my mind.

I'm not supposed to be seeing things. I don't think I can take all of this craziness anymore. There's no way I'm telling my parents how I feel right now. I tell myself to breathe again and count the breaths as I do. It feels like forever, but eventually, my pulse slows its relentless ticking and I can't feel my heartbeat in my head anymore. I sit up and take out my journal, knowing full well that I shouldn't draw right now, but I have to scrap. I can't help it. I watch my hands fly this time but feel separate from them. Like they're a part of someone else's body.

I see a person start to appear from somewhere hidden inside of the blank page and know without a doubt that it's me. The blue streaks of hair are accentuated as they fall over my forehead past my eye from my deep side part. My hair hangs just past my ears in its way of being notoriously unkempt. My mom calls me her little skater girl. I guess I do kind of look like one of those skateboarders from the 1990s.

I continue watching my hand and see eyes appear on the page behind me, I immediately want to cry because I know they're my grandfather's, but I keep going, letting my emotions channel themselves onto the paper. A train appears in the background behind him, and black dots show themselves everywhere. The last image to appear is an old key with a heart fashioned around it, encasing it.

I know this is all my head can handle, and I drop the pen on the floor. I study the images for a while before I put it all away and check to make sure my door is locked because I barely remember coming into my room. I don't care if my mother hates it, I just want to sleep and get rid of the insanity brewing in my mind and all around me. My phone buzzes a few times, and I turn that off too. I need to completely unplug, and so I do.

20 JOSIAH

"Maddie, how long do you think we've been traveling in this direction?" Josiah asked as he paced between open doors.

"Impossible to tell! One minute the sun is in one place, and the next it's somewhere else. Ain't never seen nothing like it, and to tell you the truth I think it has something to do with you because before you came along, everything was shit fine and dandy!"

Josiah laughed. "You sure have a heck of a mouth for a little thing."

Maddie returned his sentiments with a smile but kept a squint in her eye that told him she may or may not have been serious. "And every time she turns they dump these seed thingies all over the dang place." Maddie picked up a handful of seeds from the floor, sifted them between her fingers, then let them drop. "She been hauling these things all over God's creation, and I haven't got a clue what they're for."

"Let me see those…" Josiah's curiosity was piqued; he'd been too caught up in his own self-loathing to pay attention to the finer details.

He walked to the far corner where the burlap bags were stowed and picked up a single seed, pinching it between his thumb and first finger, rolling it, looking at the strange metallic color, how it glinted in the sun.

He was overcome with a sense of *déjà vu*. "I've seen these somewhere before, Maddie. But I can't place it."

168

"Well your papa works at a mill... do they look anything like those?"

"No... wheat is way different. Dries fast, powders easily..." he mumbled to himself as he tried to pick his own brain. The train continued to clack along, the sun changing its position every couple of hours. They noticed a pattern with the scenery—wheat fields, giving way to miles of green pastures, then a bending river with no discernible end that eventually faded into picturesque hills as tall as mountains, and then the wheat fields returned.

"I'm beginning think we just been circling." Maddie said.

Josiah looked up at her as she gazed over the horizon trying to memorize the scene before them to discern whether or not she was right.

"See! See!" She pointed to a hawk that swooped past one of the hills. "That's the third time I seen that hawk, I swear it. It comes out of a cloud, swoops down like a U then back up. Same hawk! I'd put my hand on a Bible if I had one."

Josiah dropped the seeds, dusted his hands on his pants, then walked over to Maddie to see for himself. After a few minutes he was shocked. "Maddie you're right! What the hell is going on?"

He kept his eyes to the scenery and felt a hand on his shoulder, her grip firmer than he'd expect from her, although he knew that even though she might appear fragile, she was tougher than a railroad tie. Her grip on his shoulder caused a searing pain to rip through his muscle, and he was astonished by the fact that she could hold him steady. With his head twisted to the side, he could just barely inch his eyes upward to see her face. He saw the glint of a sharp object in her other hand. Her voice was dark and deep, covered in mud. "Lock your horses, tuck your children tight, the dark man will come to you at night."

"Maddie, what's wrong with you?" Josiah grunted between agonizing breaths. "Let me go!" He caught her eye, and the beautiful brown was gone, transformed to pure black: vacant. Josiah was frantic, trying to loosen her grip on him. She brought him to the floor and let go. He lay there mostly paralyzed as he looked at her, rubbing out the pain with his other hand.

"I can't trust you. Murderer!" Her voice was hot gravel, and she came down on him hard with the sickle she was holding. Josiah instinctively shielded his face, and the sharp end of the tool went straight through the webbing and muscle between his thumb and index finger. He yelled and rolled over in agony as blood sprayed on the train floor.

She let loose a scream that splintered his ears. He didn't know if she was screaming because she was scared or if there was something inside of her trying to make its way out. He covered his ears with his hands and tried to erase the sound, but he couldn't. He turned his head and watched the hawk, who had been flying so majestically, suddenly drop from the sky, landing like a meteor somewhere unknown. A fire caught in the wheat field, and it began to chase the train. The whole scene melted before his eyes. He shielded his head, unable to stand the sound or vision before him. He was scared, confused, and now… frozen.

He blinked, and everything was gone, silent, save for a breeze that rippled through the leaves like a gentle waterfall. Josiah stretched through his memory, past the clouds in his head, trying to decipher what he was feeling—or not feeling. His limbs were immobile. His body felt heavier than ten sacks of flour. It was exhausting to keep himself upright, although there was nothing else he could do with himself. He wanted to give in, to sleep, to let go. He remembered one time his father fell from the roof when he was trying to repair it and hit his head. Josiah's mama had rushed to him with ice from the box and told him not to sleep even though he was complaining that he was so tired, practically begging her to let him. She did not, until the doctor was able to see him. She said it was too risky.

That stuck with Josiah, and he fought hard to stay awake, wondering if his father had felt the same way. He thought of Maddie, of how those soft brown eyes were as black as the sky during a new moon. Her scream still reverberated through his entire soul, and he couldn't bear the thought that maybe, somewhere inside, she was actually hurting. His heart drowned as he thought of his mother. What would she say to him now? She was convinced he was going to come back, but how could he?

Each time his body tried to fall out of consciousness, he forced himself awake, and a vision appeared before he became alert again. He felt as though he had to choose something. A certain direction to go or a specific path to take, but he refused to make that choice. Finally, he opened his eyes, the only part of his body that he could move. Iron struck his heart as all he saw were mismatched rows upon rows of crabapple trees.

This can't be happening, he thought to himself, not in a panic as all of that had drained out of him. No, he felt something new welling inside: authority and determination. He was tired of making sense of things. Nothing has made sense since Edgar disappeared, and it seemed as though that was his new reality, his entire existence completely on its head. But he was trapped inside this field of trees. He couldn't explain how he got here, and he mourned the fact that he didn't even know whether Maddie was real. *I would have gone to the ends of the earth for that girl,* he thought. *I've failed twice. I've failed Edgar, and I've failed Maddie. Why did she call me a murderer? How can I make this right?*

The pull to choose came to him again, and he fought hard to resist it. He kept his eyes wide open and held his breath as a fleeting thought crossed his mind that he was surprised that he could even hold his breath as he didn't know if he still had a mouth. He was stuck inside this shell of a tree, but at the same time, he felt completely connected to everything. He could feel the other people that were lost, around him. Some were still hanging on just as he was trying to do.

But what made him so special? He felt like a conduit—a conductor for some strange railway of energy that was passing through him. He could sense when some tracks went dark and knew that another poor soul had made their choice. They either went up and out or down below to that place where the children were. They looked happy, laughing and playing with those seed things that Maddie had showed him. He started to fade again and snapped himself back. He knew he had to resist the visions that kept appearing because if he fell too deeply, his own light would go out.

He forced his consciousness to the forefront. If he had a back, it would be straight as a ladder—he was not going to let this energy take him down. He had to save someone, remembering the dreams he had been having whole life. He tried to focus on the little girl. Who was she? He remembered reaching for her, but she kept disappearing. He knew it wasn't Maddie. But who was it? He focused all of his energy on that last image of her in her night dress standing in a field of trees exactly like this one.

Wherever his heart was, it began to pump faster and faster. He felt like instead of his energy sinking into the earth, the ground energy was being brought up into himself, feeding his vision and his own body, giving it strength. A bright light made itself visible as heat rose to the top of his head and beyond. The pressure and the heat became almost too intense, but he managed to channel it as he focused directly on the image of his dream, of getting himself out of this prison, of finding Edgar and that young girl, and maybe even Maddie, but he had a sneaking suspicion that she was somehow lost within this cemetery of trees. He continued to channel the heat and ground energy away from himself, squeezing his eyes against the burn and brightness of the light that had no source.

The moment seemed to suspend itself, and he felt as though he would explode, but a great release of energy from every single part of whatever being he could consider himself at this moment, erupted outward, manifesting itself into something he couldn't understand at first. The release was vast leaving him dizzy and nauseous, but he cast that aside as the revelation of what stood before him now trumped anything he had ever seen before. Someone was in front of him, examining his branches and leaves, trying to peer between the folds in the bark to see his eyes.

Josiah was astonished to see his own eyes looking at him, from the other side. A living breathing extension of his own being. All of it, the longish dirty-blond hair, the hearty build, even the wound on his hand that Maddie gave him! *How is that possible?!* His eyes grew wide and he wanted to grab that hand. But he could only blink rapidly.

His twin reached out and gently traced along the bark for a moment and then nodded. Josiah longed to feel that caress, of some sort of human contact, but he was completely defenseless and numb to the outside world.

Though his body was immobile, trapped somewhere in this unknown purgatory, he clung on to hope. From this day forward, for however long it took, he was going to stay right here, allowing himself to be the conductor of this insane railroad of souls, to guard the life forces that were stuck here with him. He hoped that his presence could somehow make them stronger, and help them to not choose. Or, at the very least, connect everyone somehow so they didn't feel so alone.

This… extension was going to figure it out, to save the girl and get rid of this orchard. Somehow. Josiah could feel him and see him but couldn't live his life. His other half nodded once more and walked away impervious to the fog that lapped at his feet like kittens to milk. Josiah watched him until he disappeared through the dense layer of trees.

Godspeed, Josiah.

21 BENJAMIN

A surge of power rushed through Benjamin's body, kicking it into motion as though he were a machine being turned on, limbs acting like new gears that were groaning and pulling him awake for the very first time. He blinked his eyes open and exposed them to his surroundings, the blue of his childhood melting somewhere in his slumber, turned dark like char and magnetic rock with a hint of fire, a reflection of earth's deepest trenches contained in every cone and rod.

He stretched one spindly leg and then the other, then wrapped his long fingers around the nearest root and pulled harder than he needed, thinking for a split second that he still had to fight. It gave on command, and he dropped to the bottom of the chamber. When he burst through the earth over many seasons past, he wasn't totally able to comprehend where he was, as if a film was covering his eyes, but now he could see every detail and he took his time spinning clockwise to soak it all in. His vision was eagle-sharp, senses keen as he felt every pulse and vibration contained within, above and below his feet.

Tunnels veered off in every direction from the main area that he was standing in. The chamber itself was massive with no discernible beginning or end, and the tunnels appeared through the sides which weren't easy to find unless he allowed his eyes to focus along the walls. Everything was glowing red and pulsing, the very source that kept fire alive. He could only fathom that he was in the center of the earth and this must span the whole of it.

A string of goosebumps rode up his legs and arms and through his spine, a primal instinct that alerted him that a predator or prey was nearby. He continued to scan his surroundings but saw nothing, and it irritated him. He kicked at the dirt and froze, expecting dust to spray from impact but instead a burst of black seeds splayed out like candy pieces. Benjamin squinted and scooped some up, rolling them between his fingers. He inhaled deeply, curious of their scent and noted how they carried the most unusual hint of fresh blossom with a bottom note of embers long burned out.

He blew them from his hands, and they turned into what looked like stardust—a billion particles of glitter, or fairy lights twinkling in the pulsing glow of the room, blinding his vision temporarily. The act of this was exhilarating, like a jump in a cold pond on a hot day. It made him want to do it again. He reached down and grabbed another handful of dust from the floor which turned into seeds instantly in his palms. He blew them again and again watching the glitter fall. He felt like a child on an autumn day with piles of sunset-hued leaves free for his enjoyment and imagination. He laughed as he watched the transformation from seed to stardust but stopped as he heard an echo of laughter that didn't match his own.

He stood straight and realized the chamber was no longer empty, as if a veil had been lifted, and the somber air was replaced with vibrancy. He was floored to find that it absolutely buzzed with activity.

There appeared to be a hierarchy of tall, scaly creatures scattered at different stations. Benjamin was amazed at how they resembled the stick bugs he'd stare at for hours by the pond when he went fishing with Josiah. His heart ached to dredge up the memory. There were building structures fastened by what looked to be old roots or twigs, but appeared solid, which held countless amounts of full burlap sacks.

He tried to wrap his mind around what he was seeing, but it didn't make sense, didn't fit into the world he used to know. Yet at the same time it made perfect sense. He felt as though he had awoken from a long dream just to be propelled into another one.

He watched the creatures, who gathered in groups here and there, farming and tending to... Benjamin's eyes grew wide.

Children! Human children? He thought he must be mistaken and squinted off into the distance. No, he was right. There were children. Tons of them. They looked as though they were at school or learning a trade. The tall creatures nodded over them as they raked and shoveled the floor of the chamber. Some were even playing in the piles just like he imagined himself doing moments ago.

One figure took a few strides toward him and spoke without words or gestures, instead communicating directly into his mind. Benjamin didn't flinch as he was well drained of surprises.

Welcome home! it said. *Welcome home!*

One by one they came to greet him, and Benjamin, still retaining his old sense of humor giggled slightly under his breath. He felt like a Santa to the most demented elves he had ever seen, as though he'd just uncovered the backwards North Pole.

He took note of his own fearlessness as they came closer but kept their distance. One by one they nodded and walked away back to whatever it was that they were doing. One of them motioned to Benjamin and led him to the harvesting area where some of the children were raking piles of seeds which burst into glitter as they reflected the light of the room. He found it fascinating how the light in the chamber ebbed and flowed constantly like the way a fire moves. It acted like its own heat source, its own pulsating energy field.

He smiled as the kids raked the seeds then jumped into them laughing, feeling a kindred spirit in them. Although no longer a child, standing tall and thin like the branch of a tree with black hair cascading over his face, a nest of string accenting his long thing nose and strong jawline, he still felt like one.

A splash of seeds cascaded at his feet. He looked down at his boots and realized that he was standing in a pile of them. *There must be thousands of them,* he thought in awe. *Maybe billions.* Piles were strewn haphazardly here and there. There were barrels full of them lining the chamber walls. He picked up another handful and studied them, trying to think of their significance. They were reflective, shimmering, radiating the glow of the room. He looked to the creature to his right in question and held his hands out as if in offering.

It answered without words. *The very source of our existence. They transform the soul. The fuel for our engine. These,* he pointed around him with elongated twigs where fingers should be, *start the process of excavating, releasing the soul, and encasing the body. These are the beginning of your farm!*

Farm! Benjamin's eyes grew wide like a toddler in a candy store. His farm. His FARM!

He had nearly forgotten as he hadn't had a moment to mourn the dreams he thought he had left behind. He started pacing as his mind alighted with possibilities. He could have it all. Power. Love. His farm... then he stopped abruptly, his bubble bursting before it had time to fill. Benjamin started chewing something in his mind too bitter for him to swallow. He couldn't quite pick out the flavor, but it was unsettling nonetheless.

Why was he so comfortable here? For all intents and purposes, he should be scared out of his mind, but he wasn't. And why did these creatures trust him so much? He chanced a peek from the corner of his eye, worried that they might be "hearing him" but either they couldn't, weren't listening, or they were pretending they couldn't.

He thought of the last time he sat in his favorite place in the barn, envisioning his sisters dancing in his orchard while his mother was in her own happy place, baking and selling her goods—of how the three of them could be finally be content. But they were dead his father said. Dead... He knew that his father was lying. He felt it just as sure as the sun would rise that his father had been overtaken by the energy of this place, maybe by these creatures themselves.

He took a step toward the creature closest to him, the one that stood taller than most, had the most calculated movements, and looked as though he was supervising the whole scene before them. Benjamin chose his words carefully—although he trusted where he was, he felt uneasy about who or what he was dealing with and he wanted to keep his humanity or whatever was left of it, hidden.

"In my vision, I had help. Three people that would make excellent workers and would keep this place hidden. My mother and sisters."

He left Josiah out of this and wasn't sure why. He knew without a doubt that his mother would be miserable for the rest of her life without him or his father there, and he didn't want the girls to grow up like that. They were too attached to their mama, and they would never be happy living in the house like that. Benjamin shuddered when he thought of their misery, especially if something were to happen to her to leave them all alone.

Josiah is a whole other story, he thought, and started to place all of his humanity into the memory of Josiah. He knew Josiah's strength and how he could go on leading a normal life with his father at the mill. Or maybe he'd get out and be the writer he always dreamed of being, traveling the country on the rails, writing everything down that he saw. Josiah had a way of capturing beauty with words. He could describe a spring day on paper in a way that made the paper fall away and replace it with the smell of apple blossoms. He could make you believe that you had an old Aunt Gerta and the tragic loss of her death made you mourn for days—even though she never existed. Josiah was an incredible writer.

The creature before Benjamin appeared almost shocked that he would even consider talking to him about his plans. It bowed the top of his trunk and blinked its eyes. *Why, Mr. Slate. Sir. You can do whatever you want. This place*—he turned in a swift circle—*is yours.*

"Mine," Benjamin said softly. "Mine." He let the word roll around his tongue dipping his toe before he dove in.

"Why did he lie then?" he said before he realized the thought had formed and taken flight.

Lieeeee? The word was long and stretched out with no ending like taffy being pulled to its limit, unable to snap back. *Oh, Sir, he never lied. Josiah did kill them when he made the move to come and get you. He shouldn't have done that.*

Its beady eyes had a way of looking directly into Benjamin's heart that he didn't like. Not that it scared him, but it made him feel more like an insubordinate employee than someone who was supposed to be respected.

"When did Josiah…" he mumbled as he studied the creature. He swallowed the bile that entered his throat, knowing these creatures did something harmful to Josiah. He forced his

thoughts to change gears so they wouldn't pick up on it. *Mama....*
He saw her in his mind along with his sisters and how worried they
must be faring without him there, having no idea what happened to
him.

He understood now that no one could ever come down to
this place the way that he did because they chose him. He didn't
know why exactly, but they did, and he was as much a part of them
as they are him now. He was pretty certain there was no way out.
He had everything he ever wanted and more, even though it wasn't
what he had planned... does anything truly ever go as planned?

The souls collected have a choice at least. They could
choose the light and leave this place, or they could stay and work.
Each soul made this place stronger which in turn gave him more
strength. Just standing there, he could feel the power surging all
throughout his body, and he soaked it up with an unquenchable
thirst.

Even the ones that chose to leave gave him a prize of
another body for his farm. The ones that stayed, both their body
and soul was collected. The ones who resisted—who chose not to
choose—would be stuck, indefinitely. They would continue to be
fed on, as their energy drained into the depths of the chambers
below. Those people, he knew, live in their own hellish purgatory.
Benjamin could feel those too, and there were a few up there right
now. It was slightly draining for him, but he didn't worry.
Eventually they'd give in. They'd choose, and they would die.

As he contemplated this, still looking into the eyes of the
creature, he also came to a new understanding. These creatures
didn't know everything. They couldn't read his mind or have any
clue how hyper aware his senses were. Most importantly, they
didn't realize that he knew that his father chose the light and that
the person he saw in his dream or waking nightmare or whatever it
was, was a farce.

"They aren't dead," he voiced aloud and listened to it
reverberate. He sighed, and it formed a tear in his heart. The pull to
be powerful was agonizing when competing with his humanity.
For now, he had to let power win at whatever cost, for however
long it took.

He released a gust of air from his lungs, feeling like the sad clown from the circus. "Why did my father say that Josiah killed them?"

Because we wanted you to know the truth about Josiah. That he is just as powerful as you are, but he takes it to the wrong place. The dark place. So we put him here, on your farm where we can watch him. It inched closer to Benjamin. *We knew you wouldn't allow it unless you saw the truth. He can destroy this farm, influence all the souls. Now he can still feel them but can do nothing about them.*

The creature then showed him something, letting it play like the moving pictures on a screen he had only just started hearing about in his other life, as the words filled his head.

We've always been here. Since before time.

Benjamin saw the stars exploding. Like nothing existed before this explosion and then it was everything. With the stars so too, were these creatures, but they existed as particles of dust.

We needed the heat to survive so we settled on your bubbling earth, and as it cooled we retreated to the center where it's always hot.

Another image flashed across: of the earth with smoldering fires and water taking their place, of all shades of greens and browns overcoming the globe as the blue retreated. And of the creatures themselves who made their way to the core, where they began planting. Next was an image of a man and a woman eating an apple. This made Benjamin recoil slightly. He wondered if the Adam and Eve story was true then. "The forbidden fruit?"

Not the fruit, Benjamin, it said like a teacher redirecting. *The seeds. It's always been the seeds. And we need you as our conduit to the outside world. We can only go so far on the railroads, slipping bags in through the fingers of the fog. Your spirit is exactly what we needed to bring here, to plant and cultivate our crops, which are now... yours.*

It sounded like it was smiling, but it wasn't—there was no mouth to it as far as he could tell. He continued to stare at the creature as his head started to spin. "I need to be alone."

Yes of course. It nodded and gestured toward one of the tunnels.

Benjamin made his way into a room that had a place for him to lie down. It was fashioned with twigs which made him shudder as he noted the resemblance to the limbs of those creatures. Exhausted, he sunk into the surprising comfort and placed his hands over his eyes. *Josiah is up there in my farm somewhere. And they tell me he's bad... maybe he is. Maybe he isn't. But he's safe for the moment, so I have to let that go for now. Mama, on the other hand. I need her. I can't explain why, but I need her. Oh god...*

His sobbing was uncontrollable. He knew what his next move needed to be, and once he said the word, he would become just as monstrous as these creatures, but he was left with no choice. He would have his farm. His carnival. If he had to collect souls to get it, then he would. But the most important thing for him at this moment would be to have his family together again, despite what it would take to get them there.

He settled into his twig bed to connect with the energy above and was immediately hit with a rush of a dozen horses galloping across the great plains. The timing was impeccable for him to break through, with the struggle between summer and fall at its peak. A time when he could work on materializing everything he'd been manifesting since he was just a simple kid with a dream.

"Mama," he whispered, in a trance-like state, his eyes becoming a mirror to the color of the very depths of space. "Mama, I need you to do something for me. Trust me, it's the best thing for our family..."

His only choice now was to wait. His eyes turned back to brilliant green. What was left of his humanity dripped down his cheek in the form of a single black tear.

22 CHELSEA

"Mom, turn that off, I can't stand to watch this stuff anymore!" The words came out more forceful than I had intended, but the thought of another crappy news report about someone missing or a fire breaking out somewhere makes me want to crawl out of my own skin. It feels like everything has exploded since the school and the Play House fires; all you see or hear about lately are fires and missing children.

She does as I asked, and I decide to go upstairs without saying another word to my parents. The tension in the house has been off the charts lately, for obvious reasons. This is the first Thanksgiving without Grandpa, and we buried Grandma this weekend. I try not to think about it, but the same scene continues to replay in my dreams lately, and in my art. Autumn, Jeff and I approach her grave to say our goodbyes. I balance a wrapped piece of heart-shaped maple candy on top of her stone. Jeff then reads her name out loud. "Dorothy Maddison Heiland." And we stand there, soaking in the finality of it all.

Mom has been trying to keep herself busy with book club meetings ever since, and Dad's been working overtime, so I'm home alone a lot these days. They tell me to set the alarm and keep my app handy and that we can't live in fear despite all that's been happening. I tell them I feel like the apocalypse is starting, and they tell me to stop watching *The Walking Dead*.

I feel like all of my relationships with people are going down the toilet and there's nothing I can do about it. I mean, things are okay with Autumn and me. She left a little early to visit relatives in Massachusetts for the break. She doesn't usually go there, but I think her father felt that she could use a respite from the craziness around here.

I almost went with her, but my parents wanted to keep me close. I rolled my eyes so hard I thought they would stay up in my brain when they said that. They're hardly home as it is. But then I felt bad. I know it's not easy for them either.

Jeff's still around, but I haven't been talking with him much lately, and he seems just fine with that. He's used to me going through phases of being stuck in my own head, and as perceptive as he is, knows it's better to let me work through things on my own until I'm ready to talk.

The truth is, I'm still kind of mad at him for just walking away from all this crap that he started. If I had never known about my backyard weirdness, then maybe I'd have less anxiety about the news. Well maybe not less, but I wouldn't be so confused and frightened or ridiculously determined to find out what's going on. At the very least, to prove that I'm not absolutely mental.

It's become a habit to lock my bedroom door now. My parents have gotten much more lenient with me since all of this started, and I'm really not feeling that any surprise parental visits would do me any good. I turn on my lights and look out into the neighborhood before I close my curtains, wondering if any of the other kids are plotting right now, figuring out how they're going to sneak out of their houses without their parents knowing or the police catching them during one of their nightly patrols of the neighborhood.

Something curious happened at school today that sent chills of both excitement and fright to my entire school. When I opened my lunchbox, wedged right there between the carrots and PB&J, was a red and white candy wrapper, the waxy kind that covers a piece of taffy. Scrawled on one side were the words, **Shhh... don't tell your parents!**

The other had a small picture of a carousel and this:

Midnight Carnival in the Crabapple Orchard. Free rides, candy, and fun!

I glanced to the other kids at my table and saw that they were all staring at their own invitations. Even the ones who bought lunch found them in their pockets! Fast whispers and wide-eyed looks replaced the normal chatter. I looked over my shoulder and spotted a suspicious lunch monitor facing my table's direction, so I jabbed the kid in the ribs next to me with my elbow and quickly shoved the paper in my pocket. The other kids followed my lead, but the chatter continued the rest of the day.

No one knew what to do about it. I thought they were crazy for even considering it. I tried to recite that dark man poem to a few of them, but they just shrugged me off. The general consensus was that the parents and staff were in on this little prank, guessing they all arranged something to make us feel better. There were theories that they chose the time and place to throw off whoever is responsible for the kidnappings. And the "don't tell your parents part" was to just make it more fun. Not to me though, I personally thought it to be disturbing.

I whispered to Jeff about it, wanting his opinion. He stared at the paper for a while and raised it to the light overhead as if looking to see if there was a hidden message on it or something that we weren't otherwise able to see. He then held my gaze while walking over to the garbage and threw it in there. When he sat back down at the table, he watched me twirl the invitation around in my fingers for a minute before snatching it from me and escorting it to join his at the trash can party with half-eaten sandwiches.

"Hey!" I gave him my best sour face.

"Hey, yourself. I thought we were over this crap, Chells."

"We are. I just…" I looked out the cafeteria with furrowed brows, remembering that I was supposed to be done with all "this crap" as Jeff put it.

He had somehow managed to walk over to my side of the table to obstruct my view of the sunshine and kids at recess kicking around all the dead leaves on the ground. "Not without Autumn anyway," he said, smirking. I laughed and pushed him gently in the chest, agreeing, and that was the end of it.

I think of the invitation now and how all the adults managed to dupe the entire middle school population. I have half a mind to text Autumn to see if she got one but decide it's too silly to even try. For starters, she's out of town. And I also don't want to bother or make her worried for no reason. I mull it over for a while and finally decide that I should just let it be. There is absolutely no way that I'm going out there tonight.

"It's time…" a voice whispers through my open window as if carried by the breeze that's making my curtains dance. My heart leaps into my throat, and I have to catch my breath. Then I realize it's probably Jeff, so I open the window and peek my head out expecting to see his goofy smile. It's too dark, so I climb out of my window to get a better look and don't see him. I slither down to the porch railing and yell at him in my loudest quiet voice to quit playing games. I circle the front of my house and can't find him, so I look to his house a few doors down. All their lights are off.

Feeling stupid, I head back to my house, but a voice stops me midstride, carried again as if it's riding on the wind.

"Chelsea… it's time to go."

My pulse starts pushing the sweat out of my body. I didn't make it up that time.

"Now…" it says again, and instead of fright I'm astonished. I know that voice, all gravel and molasses… "Oh my god!" I say out loud. "That's Grandpa's voice! But how…" I stop talking to myself and start following the pattern of the soft breeze. I want to know the direction that it came from, and the moment I turn from the front of my house to the side of it, I am filled with dread.

My heart is pumping faster than I can think, a locomotive at top speed. I close my eyes and clench my hands to my chest. Do I really want go in there right now? Is Grandpa sending me a sign? I know I should turn around, but I keep walking as if my body is on autopilot. It has to be nearly midnight by now—that was the eleven o'clock news that I made my mother turn off. I take a quick glance at my house and see their bedroom light turn off, and I listen for a moment to make sure they haven't noticed that I left. I heave out a deep breath and continue walking, solidifying my resolve that I am absolutely mental.

Crossing the border of the property, I cringe and wait for the horrible pressure I've come to abhor. Two steps in, and a shocking revelation occurs. I don't feel a thing. Nothing is different at all, as if my entire experience of this place has just been another late-night horror movie rerun. I relax a little as I hear footsteps and giggles ahead and quicken my pace to find out who they belong to, nearly forgetting everything that I have been worried about over the past year.

As I approach a small clearing, it's obvious that I must be the last in a long line of kids that have found their way into the forest. I'm still searching for the owner of the irresistible voice that snuck its way through my open bedroom window. I so desperately want it to be Grandpa's voice, but I begin to have my doubts as another voice makes an appearance.

"Come, children! Come at night! The carnival brings sweet delight!"

The words, warm as caramel, reverberate through the swarms of crooked crabapple trees, and we are the tiny horses galloping toward it, seeking our reward. Even though the tenor has changed, the sugar in his voice keeps my feet moving deeper into the forest, until the last of the streetlights have faded like the dreams we were taken from before this journey. I'm a little suspicious—the voice is still far away, and it's hard to tell if it's the same one that I heard in my bedroom, but I've made up my mind to see this through.

Something squishes under my bare right foot. "Ugh, gross," I mutter as I look down and see a pit of mud with my foot directly in the middle. "The only freakin' puddle in the orchard, probably. Figures."

I scrape the mud from my foot using the base of the nearest tree and try not to make eye contact with "it" as I do so. I can't call these trees "them." Or even "trees," but I can't look away, either. They're mesmerizing; they draw me in. It's like I *have* to stare at them.

A shudder slips through my body even though it isn't that cold out tonight. I catch a glimpse of the side of a girl's face ahead of me. I don't recognize her and wonder which way the kids have entered the forests from how many directions, if they are all following the same voice or if they heard voices of their own like I did. She giggles as she trots faster, probably to catch up with a friend. It sounds like they're playing hide and seek in the darkness.

I wish I could share their enthusiasm, but I know I shouldn't have come here. I should have stayed in my room with the blankets secured tightly over my head. But that voice... when I heard it, I knew I had to go. Grandpa needed me to.

Now I'm starting to question the whole thing. This place is creepy enough during the day, and here I am with mud on my feet and kids I don't even... *Kids! Where are they?* It occurs to me that I'm very alone. I hear faint carousel music and laughter ahead of me somewhere, caught up in the branches. A sense of relief washes over me. At least I'm not too far from the others.

I spin slowly in a circle and find nothing but branches, twisting this way and that, and not a single opening to let me join the kids ahead. I've been so focused on the mud, my foot, Grandpa, and the carnival, that I'm completely lost. It's like they're taunting me, these stupid trees. I begin to feel panicky and claustrophobic. The bravery I felt when this whole thing started is dripping away with the beads of sweat down my back.

I should just go home. I mean, I didn't know most of the kids I saw tonight, anyway, so it's not like my friends will wonder where I've run off to. Not to mention that new voice I've been hearing that's been whispering about the carnival doesn't sound so much like Grandpa anymore... but it certainly is inviting. *Hey! Maybe Grandpa was just telling me to go? Maybe that guy's voice I keep hearing is a friend of Grandpa's. Maybe Grandpa has a message for him? Or maybe this guy has a message for me?*

"I don't know what to do, Grandpa, what do I do?" I yell, hoping maybe he'll hear me and give me a sign. But I don't get one. Instead, I have the strong urge to turn around and run home as I'm feeling woozy from the tightness of these trees to my body.

The clearing I passed a little bit ago can't be that far away. Yes, that's my best bet; home. I never wanted to be there more badly than I do at this moment. I finally see an opening in the little maze and decide to make a run for it. With my best foot forward, I take off, but my face connects with something hard and strong. Stars of pain flood my vision, and I'm pushed backwards until my butt lands with inexplicable force into the mud that my foot had already been stuck in.

I sit here in absolute darkness with my face in my hands, resting my dizzy head in the tent my nightshirt has made between my knees. Tears well in my eyes and burn my cheeks before I can help myself. I don't know if I'm crying because I miss Grandpa so much or because of my stupidity of coming to this horrible forest in the middle of the night. I allow one more tear to drop before I wipe my face with the back of my dirty hand, gain my composure, and stand up to walk home.

It doesn't take more than a second to realize that it was NOT the base of a tree that made me fall as I find that I'm face-level with a pair of thin legs covered by dusty trousers. I take an involuntary step back as my eyes work their way up his tall body. A black shirt is encased inside of an old suit coat, like this person had lost his way from a funeral one hundred years ago. A top hat covers stringy black hair that hangs on his shoulders, knotted together like a bird's nest that met a forest fire. A strange fleeting thought makes me wonder if he takes off his hat, will his hair come with it?

As if in silent answer, he bows low at the waist, removes the top hat with spindly fingers, and makes a sweeping gesture with it, the other arm resting across his waist. A cloud of dirt trails alongside his moving arm, making me feel like he had just climbed out of the earth itself, a root from one of these trees. As he looks up at me, still bowed low, there is a glint in his black eyes that appear otherwise to be vacant. My stomach lurches—something isn't right about him.

"Benjamin Slate, at your service," he says through teeth that look remarkably too white for his sooty complexion, and a voice I recognize as not his. "Grandpa?" I take another step back, completely baffled. In my heart of hearts, I wish I could run from this man far, far away. But instead I stay frozen, my mouth ajar, too scared to run, too bewildered to make my legs work.

He winks and takes something out of his hat. It catches the moon in a way that makes it sparkle. *Is it glitter?* And then I remember those seed things that were all around Raina. I bellow the only thing I can think of right now, that my parents guaranteed would save me from trouble, "Fabio has great hair!"

I immediately regret it because I realize that I don't have my phone and Mr. Slate is giving me the most awkward look. If I wasn't completely horrified, I might actually find this funny. Before I can feel or make any other gesture besides standing here staring at him like an idiot, he blows a handful at me. It covers my body from head to muddy toe.

I find now that I literally cannot move; I'm completely frozen where I stand. There is a strange sensation at the bottom of my feet, like they have holes and a vacuum is trying to suck something out of them. *My heart should be pounding, shouldn't it? I have never been so scared, but my heart; why can't I feel it? Why can't I...* Something weird is going on with my legs; there is a tugging and pulling sensation followed by pulsing, like a heartbeat that isn't my own, or something deeper, ancient, like the earth is taking my veins and swallowing them into her soil.

In deepest horror I know that I'm right. That is exactly what must be happening. I make a last-ditch effort to scream but can only form a small "O" with my lips. With painstaking effort, I ever so slowly try to bend over, try to move my arms, but they are stuck. It takes tremendous effort to inch them from my body. My goal is to grab my feet and see if I can manually make them move. But I can't. My one arm is solid in front of me. The other down at my side, which moved way less than I thought it did. I feel like the Tin Man before he found oil.

My eyes are sluggish, and I try to focus on anything except my arm that's in front of me. I know it's a part of my body, but I can't feel it. I can't feel anything. I'm completely detached from reality but completely here at the same time. My emotions are here, but I'm totally lost. I can think, but I can't retain the information. I know, but I don't know.

As I watch my arm harden, turn brown and peel just so slightly, I am faced with the knowledge that I, myself, am becoming one of these loathsome trees. *HOW is that possible? What kind of man can do this? WOULD do this?*

I'm overwhelmed with a new emotion. I'm surprised that it is not panic, not fright, but acceptance. I feel a sense of peace as I realize that maybe I'm dying. Perhaps I'll be with Grandpa soon. I accept that thought and know without a doubt that I am ready.

Mr. Slate stands straight, a skinny tower above me. He pats me somewhere where my head should be and smiles enthusiastically. "Welcome to my farm!"

A final chill rushes over my body when I realize that I will not die. I will be stuck like this for I don't know how long. I can still move my eyes, but nothing else. I am one of his trees; infinitely.

***

A single snowflake drifts past my line of vision. I made it through the long, arduous night, the snow reminding me that I should be home right now helping my mother stuff the turkey with the parade playing on the TV in the background. I guess last night was the end of our Indian summer and now it's back to a blustery reality. Except I'm not cold. I don't feel anything at all.

I used to like to read vampire novels, I think because the idea of living forever was so appealing. I would spend long hours daydreaming about what I would do with eternity. Maybe I would hole myself up in that beautiful house I saw in Maine, the one on the cliff that I fell in love with so many summers ago, and watch the waves crash against the rocks. I could paint the scene a million times and know each time it would be different because every wave that crashes against the rock is a different wave. The water doesn't just crash back and forth aimlessly. One wave rolls in with a magnitude of force and explodes against the shore. Some of it stays behind to drip on the rocks, in the hair of someone close enough to witness it, or to soak into the earth. Then it goes back out to sea, leaving a piece of it behind. And then another wave comes in doing the same thing. Maybe it has more force or maybe it has less than the other one. Two things are certain, however. It leaves a piece of itself behind and then it mingles with the others.

Maybe souls do the same thing? We turn into energy, we mingle with other energies but leave a piece of ourselves behind. Our bodies turn to dust but the memories of us linger with our loved ones, each memory unique because their perceptions are unique and their experiences of us are unique.

But I will never have the chance to experience any of that. My eternity is one of stone and confusion. I have been getting moments of clarity, but my consciousness comes in and out, it feels like I'm in a daydream within a dream within a nightmare, suspended in a state that I can't even science away. The clarity comes in waves. Like the ocean. When my clarity crashes into my consciousness, I find myself wishing that Jeff were here. That maybe he could explain this or find me a way out of this mess. *Oh why didn't I talk to him more recently? Damn me for being so stubborn and pigheaded!*

I almost begin to panic about all of the what if's and his whereabouts, but it melts away as I fall into that void. The void doesn't present itself to me in a sleepy or dreamy way, but rather, I find myself full of vision and confusion and on top of that, two scenarios present themselves to me. In one scenario there are tons of kids playing in a massive glowing room, shoveling seeds, planting trees, pulling roots. Ironically, they seem to be having such a great time. The appeal is almost overwhelming. I want to travel into that place—anything would be better than here! But I have this strong feeling that if I let go and sink myself into that vision, I will never come back, and I try hard to pull myself into the here and now.

As soon as I'm back, I fade again and am presented with yet another vision. I'm in another place bright as the sun, but it doesn't hurt my eyes, and I'm with what I can only describe as beings of pure light. I feel like I'm floating and totally free, surrounded by love and acceptance. This place has more pull than the other or even back in my own body, so it's that much more difficult to resist. But somehow I pull myself back. It's exhausting and frustrating. I've only done this for one night, and I don't know even know how much longer I can take it.

Autumn always talked about how stubborn I am, telling me it's in my nature as a Taurus. She tries to convince me that there's no reason to be stubborn and that sometimes it's best to just let go and give in to whatever situation presents itself because you never know what new opportunity will come from it. I always thought she was picking on me, but I know she was right.

I'm not going to listen to her this time, though. I pull away back into my body, dreading that fact that every time I do, there is a tragic sense of loss. Like I really belong in that place full of light and love and floating and freedom. But I know that I can't be there, at least not yet. There's something that I need to do first, but whatever it is, I just don't know.

I guess sometimes it pays off to be hard headed. I wonder how many others are stuck in this same situation or do they automatically go to those places they are presented with. Do they just go and accept their fate? Do they even know it's a fate they have to accept?

I can feel my consciousness starting to linger for shorter and shorter amounts of time. I suddenly remind myself of my grandmother and wonder if she was somehow presented with the same choices. *Think,* I tell myself. *Think! How can I avoid the drift?* I'm not even sure what to think about because I honestly don't believe there is anything that I can do.

"Oh don't stubborn yourself to death," I hear Autumn's voice in my head. *Right, right right. Come on brain. You are still in here somewhere.* My mind lapses to Grandpa Jo and of a conversation we had when I was little. We were walking together down a trail at Mendon Ponds Park with sunflowers seeds in our extended palms, waiting for the little chickadees to fly down and eat them. It was best to do this when the ground was covered with snow, as the birds are hungrier then, and this day didn't disappoint.

It had just snowed that morning, and there was a good twelve inches on the ground. Heavy snow too, as I remembers thinking how neat it was that I could walk right on top of it without sinking in. Just the *crunch, crunch* sound of our boots as we walked surrounded by the smell of winter and the chickadees singing.

"Red-tailed hawk!" Grandpa gestured toward the sky, pointing out a bird coasting over the trees with his giant wings outstretched.

"I wish I could fly, Grandpa," I said.

"Oh you can, my dear."

"No I can't." I laughed. "I'm just a girl."

"Well I can fly," Grandpa said. "And if I can, you can!"

"You?! How can you fly? Grandma says if you eat any more of those candies, then you won't even be able to pull on your pants."

Grandpa laughed so loud it echoed. "Well true, you are certainly right about that. But this kind of flying" he paused "is a bit... different."

He was thoughtful as he stared off into the distance for a moment. "Here bunny, let's sit here for a minute." He pointed to a tattered wooden bench which had already been shoveled off. "My old bones need a break," he said as he sunk in.

We were facing a break in the trees where nothing but white lay beyond and then another expanse of trees. I was happy snuggled up against him, and he put his arm around me to keep us warm.

"Listen," he said. "Do you ever get the feeling where you just somehow know things and you can't explain how you know them but you just do?"

I thought about this for a few minutes, and yes it was true. "Well sure, Grandpa, but doesn't everyone?"

"It peeks through for people from time to time. But you and I, we're different than most. We can control it. Look at these seeds," he said. And he put a few in my hand. "These live inside of us." My eyes grew wide as I imagined flowers growing in my stomach.

He was amused knowing what just went through my head. "Okay well not THESE actual seeds but seeds that God planted in us. Or the Universe, as your friend Autumn says. Whatever you want to call it, there is a higher power out there that we are all connected to. Like roots to a tree. Or grass to the earth. Some people live a lifetime without ever feeling that connection. Like this maple. He gestures toward an impressive maple tree just to our left. See how it's just standing there all by itself? I suspect it's not producing its own seeds anymore."

"Why?"

"I dunno, maybe it's stubborn," he joked.

I smiled even though I didn't know what he meant.

"Well some people are like that. They choose to be only themselves and not drop their seeds, not try to connect with other people. They just live and die without having spread any of their love and joy onto others. And then there's others who try to connect or do good things, that try to spread joy and drop their seeds everywhere. Creating more trees. Or in the human sense, more energy, more love, more happiness. People thrive on good energy. Bad energy makes them wilt. And there's still other people that can play with this energy and make things happen.

"Like us?"

"That's right, Chelsea. Like us. Let me tell you, honey, if you can let go of yourself for a moment and I mean really let go of all of your senses, except for the one right here," he pokes a finger lightly to the middle of my puffy winter coat, "your heart, your feeling, your intuition… you can fly!"

"I CAN?!" I said enthralled. I looked up at the hawk circling overhead and envisioned myself flying along with him up

193

in the sky and through the clouds, feeling the wind on my face. I imagined myself trying to find my house and seeing the rooftop from high in the air.

"Yes... but not quite the way you are thinking."

"Oh." The disappointment was palpable.

"But it's still exhilarating!" he was quick to point out. "Your body stays here, but your spirit, it goes elsewhere. You can go anywhere you want. Anywhere at all. But you have to really let go of everything. You have to believe that you are pure light. That you are not a human in the regular sense but you are energy. Plain, simple, beautiful, energy. I've been waiting to talk about this to you for a long time. I knew it ever since the day you knew about your father's car accident when you were a baby. I knew that I had finally come to the end of a long search."

"Oh yeah... Mom told me about that. I don't remember it though."

"I know you don't... you were so little, after all. When you started screaming for him from right out of such a deep sleep. When you told your mother to get the phone but it wasn't ringing. And then it rang and it was him... I knew you were like me then. I just wanted to wait until you were old enough to understand."

"Grandpa?" I interrupted him.

"Yes?" He raised his eyebrows.

"I don't really understand."

He laughed in a way that made his eyes sparkle. "That's okay. Maybe you are a little young yet, but I wanted to plant the seed in you so you can think about it and work with it when you are older. In fact, I will need you to, Chelsea. But we don't need to talk about that just yet."

"Seed. Funny, Grandpa."

After some thought I told him I had a question. "Why would God or the universe or whoever make people like you... and me... I guess? What is the point of being able to know things ahead of time to be able to... invisible fly? And if I can invisible fly, can I touch things or am I just like a ghost that can see and not do anything?"

He paused for a moment, looking as though he was trying to chew something and wasn't sure if he would spit it out or swallow it. "I've only been able to touch something once, but never since. You never know unless you keep working with it. I have a feeling that you, my love," he tapped my nose gently, "are more connected than I will ever be. Your seeds are strong, your root system is solid—"

"Grandpa... you're losing me again."

"Okay," he said. "Ok. And to answer your other question. I believe that we were born this way because we were meant to help people, the earth, and the universe. We are like gate keepers. Or the conductors of a train. We know things so we help people to understand this life and what lays beyond. We can fly because we are closer to heaven than most. There is more to this earth than this one dimension. And we can cross through it with pure hearts. I'm not totally sure why. It's just what we can do."

"Huh. So I am special!" My little spirit had been lifted at this revelation.

"Well honey, you've always been special. But now you know that you were destined for greater things than a lot of folks."

"I guess so," I said. This should have made me happy and proud to be whoever I am, but I was my father's daughter, after all. Skeptical and a little fearful of the unknown. I wasn't feeling convinced that this was the path that I wanted for myself. Even if Grandpa needed me to for whatever reason. I wasn't sure if I really wanted to pretend fly. Not without wings. I wasn't sure if I wanted to know things that other people don't. What if it was a bad thing and I got in trouble for using it? What if Grandpa was senile?! *Nooo*... I thought to myself. That's crazy. Grandpa was as sharp as a pin.

My logical side always said not to go there, but I left myself open just in case the need ever arose. Like when Grandpa was dying...

And here I am again, faced with another horrible dilemma. Anxiety rips through me as I realize I have drifted but this time only within myself and the conversation with Grandpa. But from the looks of it, I have been gone a long time. There is no more snow, and the leaves in front of me look like a thousand sunsets.

Has it really been an entire season? Is it fall again? My god, what is this crazy place?! I have to get out of here. Is it possible? Should I choose? If I had a heart it would be a woodpecker boring a hole into the rough texture of my skin. I can't do this anymore, I can't!

And then it hits me. I wonder if I can… fly. Or pretend fly. Or whatever it is.

I'm starting to become dizzy, and I know that means I'll be drifting soon. I'm determined not to lose my way this time, so I try and fight the urge by focusing only on Grandpa. I don't know why I picked him in the second before I was about to dissolve and be sucked into the void of choices, but here he is in my mind, and I'm going to stick with him.

I see his eyes, healthy and glowing through his glasses. I take painstaking efforts to recall every detail again about the conversation we had and the gift that we shared. It's almost too painful to resist the pull, like hanging on with all of my strength at the end of the world's strongest vacuum. But I become the life raft in the lake after the boat sank.

"I can make things happen," I tell his memory. "I understand now, Grandpa."

I imagine myself underwater looking at the light dancing above me, remembering how calm I was and how I knew that somehow, I'd be ok. I feel the pull start to dissipate, but I don't want to let go of the image, so I cling on to the feeling of serenity with every ounce of my being, not wanting the pull to sneak up and take me away. But maybe, I begin to question, maybe it's better to dissolve than to torture myself in this way.

Maybe I'll go crazy, maybe I can't really fly! I feel myself begin to let go, the pull tightening its dark hands around my body, forcing me down with it, and then think *NO! Grandpa! I have to do this for him. To prove to him and myself that I really am as strong as he said I was.*

I bring my focus back to the water, of being trapped under the lake. I see the sunbeams passing under the waves and how, in that moment, I wanted to be a mermaid and play with the waves forever. I keep my eyes open as I do this, not seeing the thick fog in front of me, but the images scrolling across my mind. I only focus on the feeling of freedom and complete contentment. I maintain that feeling while trying to keep my being present by searching through fog and bringing the tree beyond it into view.

There is moss growing in strange patterns that I follow with my eyes; from the top to the bottom it hangs only on one side, reminding me of something. I keep staring at it, trying to wrack my brain on how this could even be familiar to me. I think of our school trip to Corbett's Glenn and how Mrs. O'Hara went on about the vegetation and animals that frequent the area, but nothing that she pointed out rings a bell for me.

A few beams of light make their way through the fog, bringing in an ironic sense of majesty, and I half expect to see a fairy or two flying around. Something catches my eye as I try to adjust my vision in the direction it's coming from. It looks to me like a piece of glass on the ground. *Glass... how odd.*

I think about that one time Jeff left his glasses outside after we camped in his backyard. Autumn stepped on them by accident, and he couldn't see for weeks until he could get a new pair. *Jeff...* A pang goes straight through my heart. I miss my friends desperately, and I wish again that I hadn't been such a shit to him. Jeff... I think of him while gazing at the tree in front of me. The moss keeps pulling at my attention, and I can't even fathom why.

I allow my eyes to trace its pattern over and over again, and it starts to looks like waves from the ocean. Thin layers swoop over and over each other, one of which must be caught on a branch or something because it's rebelling and swooping the other way. I wish I could go over there and fix them so they're all proper, like the tree would be able to see better. I start to laugh at myself for thinking the tree could be a person, but then I stop myself and feel a little sick, realizing that it very well could be. This gesture also reminds me of Jeff, the way he would nonchalantly brush his hair out of his face. His face... Jeff's face.

That's Jeff. OMG that's Jeff! I don't know how I know it, but I do. I'd bet my entire life on it. I'm so excited that I almost forget myself and try to run to him, I want nothing more but to hug him and apologize! But I'm encased in a stony purgatory, and there is no amount of excitement or adrenaline that can break me from these wretched chains. *Did you choose, Jeff? Did you choose?!* I want to shout to him but I can't. I can't do anything but stare at him from this prison.

I close my eyes and try to bring myself back to center, to "stay in the zone" as Grandpa would say. I open them again and soft focus so that I'm looking at Jeff and sort of letting his structure turn fuzzy in my field of vision. I think again to the maternal feeling of being in the water, how it cradled me like a baby. An epiphany strikes through my focus. How much do I love the water? How much do I love the idea of being a mermaid? How much do I love Grandpa, Autumn, Jeff, and my family?

My god. I love it all so much. So that's what I focus on. I try to visualize the place in my body where I feel love. It's not in my head… I don't think about love. And it's not totally in my heart. I recognize it as being deep in my chest or somewhere inside, it doesn't matter where exactly, I just have to bring my focus to it. I close my eyes completely and drown out all other thoughts, feelings, and sounds, to be in that place of love. As I do this, a new sensation happens.

The place where my roots bolt through the ground springs to life. It's as if I've been kneeling too long and my feet fell asleep. Pins and needles give way to another sensation like a fishing line being reeled into my body.

I try to contain my excitement as it's absolutely necessary that I don't lose focus. I draw myself back to the place of love, of finding my part in the universe and that invisible energy Grandpa was talking about. Like the GPS signal on my phone, I try to find the exact coordinates in this energy that connects me to everything.

The place that everyone is connected to. Everyone… Everyone! I need to be the conductor, like one that drives a train. Except this railroad is made of all the souls in this orchard, and even beyond that, expanding the whole of the universe. Just like Grandpa said. That's it, I can do this.

Faster and faster, things are being reeled back into my body, bringing with it a new sensation that I haven't felt in a year or more, I don't even know how long; there is no concept of time here, and for all I know it could be an eternity. I feel like I can move my limbs, but I don't have limbs. It's such a contradictory feeling that my body doesn't seem to understand how to process it.

A snapping sound in the distance puts everything on hold. I close my eyes. Instinct tells me to hold my breath, but of course, I can't. I can only squeeze my eyelids and hope he doesn't notice what's going on. I can always tell when he comes, like the whole energy of the world changes, becomes darker, fuzzier, making it impossible to focus on anything else except for him. I've seen him inspect every tree around me like we are his pets. In a daze or a nightmare, I swear I thought I saw a kid turn once, something I must have blocked out. Try as I might to remember I can only see his face, contorted, almost like it was melting, half of the *Comedy of Errors*. Oh God, how long have I been here?

That man, Mr. Slate, is a sick twisted psycho. His boots rustle through the brush as he gets closer. *If I had feet, I'd kick his ankles.* I hear myself giggle inside my head and am slightly delighted that I haven't totally lost my sense of humor.

Tut, tut, tut... The ray of sunshine becomes overshadowed with a dark cloud. He is standing over me smiling with a hundred teeth and waving a twiggy finger at me.

"My aren't you a naughty girl? Still haven't made your choice yet... Choose, little girl. Choose before I choose for you." He stands tall, still smiling, content in his sadistic power and control over the helpless. I want to spit in his face. I watch as he turns around to inspect the others.

For a split second my mind goes back to that place of light and pure joy and freedom, and then my vision fuzzes over. I pull myself together before the thought can form any further. My anger starts to form bubbles inside of me as I look at his dreadful back. He moves away, and Jeff's tree comes into focus. Two eyes are staring back at me. *Jeff's eyes. They're open. He didn't choose!* If he didn't choose, there is no way that I will. Not caring how close or far Mr. Slate is at this moment, I make another choice. I let go of fear and anger, knowing that I have nothing left to lose.

Love. The energy. I'm ready to ride the wave. I find that place much easier this time, like I've already opened the door and it has been waiting to receive me. My body starts to reel back in on itself. I can feel the earth pulsing through me and all the souls around me. I have found the light, the exact spot where I connect to everyone on the earth and they connect to me. I'm the conductor for the railroad of souls, and I refuse to let anyone else succumb to this abomination. I have found love and the reason why I was sent here.

And so has Mr. Slate. Standing there under a particularly large branch, his smile drains from his face—a mask uncovering the truth. He looks pained and angry as his eyes dart to the ground below his feet like he can't get a grip on what's happening. He picks his feet up, one after the other in calculated and careful movements, as though he'd stepped in a huge pile of horse shit.

"Oh, Mr. Slate!?"

A small voice from somewhere beyond my periphery startles him, and for a brief moment, he seems to forget who he is, turning around like an inquisitive child.

I can hardly contain myself when the owner of the voice comes into view. It belongs to Autumn, and she's waiting for him with a rather large beam of old wood slung over her shoulder like an oversized baseball bat. In the moment just before the wood connects with the side of his face, I catch a glimpse of an emotion that is completely unexpected. It isn't anger or fear or even shock. It isn't his disturbing, toothy grin. It looks like a gentle smile from an angelic little boy. Perhaps with a touch of defeat. But it's fleeting as I watch his body drop in a heap to the ground and blood slowly spill out around his face.

"At your service!" Autumn yells, throwing it to the ground like she just hit a home run, but she doesn't have time to celebrate as the ground quickens and knocks her down.

I can feel the light growing warmer inside of my body. My heart is beating again, I can feel the blood swishing its way back through my ears. I know that I'm protected. I know that I'm safe, even though I can't tell what's coming next.

The light I've been projecting becomes visible through my body, giving off its own brilliant iridescence to the outside, Autumn shields her eyes in the crook of her arm.

I feel my cage split; the prison is being destroyed, and I step out, falling to the ground like a baby horse on a new pair of legs. I crawl over to Autumn and collapse in her arms. I hear cracking and breaking as the earth shakes in violent waves. We hang on to each other, fearful, hoping that we can protect each other with our embrace as there is nowhere else to go.

Our ears are ambushed with an avalanche of heavy crackling and a rush of noise and wind that reminds me of a steam train. We continue to cling to one another as the shaking starts to subside, and our ears ring from the intensity.

A new sensation makes itself known. Autumn and I are being shielded by a pair of arms.

"Jeff!" Autumn realizes at the same time that I do. I couldn't be any happier than I am at this moment. The reunion, however, is cut short, as we begin to take in the surroundings. There are handfuls of people lying on the ground in shock.

Above this, thousands of lights flicker up toward the sky. Looking close, the lights appear to resemble children, with a spattering of adults, making their way towards what I can only imagine heaven to be, or the next dimension. All around us, another light appears encasing us not from up in the sky but from everywhere, as if the orchard created its own light that is pulsing with the same energy I felt within my body.

"Autumn! Do you feel it? This is... everything!" I feel like a little girl putting up a Christmas tree full of hope and wonder. Jeff looks at both of us with tears streaming down his face, this time with no excuses.

"Do you feel it?!" I prod.

"I do." He seems both bewildered and amused.

We stay in our circle watching as the people, the pure energy they had become when they chose, quite literally, cross over. "They are putting themselves to rest. Finally free," I whisper as I watch a woman and two little girls with long red braids hanging below their shoulders make their way toward the light.

I can just make out the dresses they are wearing, appearing old and patterned not unlike one of the porcelain dolls I have tucked away in my closet, replicas from another century. The three of them fascinate me for some reason, I almost want to say goodbye, but they are too far gone, their bodies transforming when they walk through the light. I continue to watch them go until their light completely vanishes. I wonder what happens as they go, but from this vantage point I can tell without a doubt that they are going somewhere good and peaceful.

I look up to the sky which is glowing the color of sunflowers in July, and can just make out a hint of blue beyond that. I silently thank my grandfather. I don't believe that he's up there, but I don't know where else to look. After all that I've experienced, he seems to be everywhere, all around me, listening.

Not too far in the distance, I watch a small girl start to cross over, but she stops and turns around. At first I think she doesn't want to go, and it worries me, but then I spot the beauty mark on her face and my jaw drops. She waves and blows me a kiss then turns around to join the others. Tears stream down my face, and I put my hands to my heart. Raina. I mouth her name, but no noise comes out. Through the sting of salt that blurs my vision, I make out another figure in the distance, partially in shadow, with just the number 72 visible before he disappears.

This is all too overwhelming for me, and before I lose control, Jeff taps me gently a few times on my shoulder, and I grab his hand without looking. It feels rough, like he'd been building houses his entire life. I turn to inspect his fingers, ready to joke about how he's in a desperate need for a manicure, and he begins to hum a song so familiar it covers my soul like a blanket.

I freeze, too scared to see who is attached to these fingers, and if I'm right, I don't want him to vanish.

He puts another hand on my shoulder and turns me around. I meet his eyes and scream, "Grandpa!" I wrap my arms around him and hug him so tight I don't ever want to let go.

"You did it, sweetie, you did it!" he tells me. "You lifted the veil!"

"Veil," I say comprehending, finally. "So that's what this is." I look over his shoulder at all the lights that are still crossing over. I think of my dream journal and everything that Grandpa had told me, when it hits me and I let go of our embrace. "Grandpa, my dream! The man… was that you?"

"Yes darling. The veil won't let me get all the way through, I'm not allowed to pass through it. Only once in a while and usually at a time when you are vulnerable. When you are ill or sleeping. Or feeling a deep emotion like grief. People often lose their guard during that time, and their loved ones can get through for a brief period and give a sign that they're ok."

He pauses to look around and smiles. "You've really outdone yourself here, Chelsea."

"I just remembered what you told me. About love and the railroad of souls… so I'm like the conductor, right?

"No, sweetie. You are the entire railroad. Tracks and all."

This causes the well that has formed in my eyes to run over. For some reason what he just said makes total sense and puts into perspective the way I've been feeling my entire life, but I couldn't put a finger on until now.

"I knew you were special."

He gives me another hug, and I hear a voice in the background say, "I just can't stand this anymore!" Suddenly Jeff's thin arms are squeezing us both. Autumn weasels her way in, too. Tears of happiness warm the ground below us as Grandpa Jo pulls away slowly, saying that he has to go.

"Oh no you don't! I can't let you leave, Grandpa, I can't. Not again." My happy tears turn hot, and my ears turn red and angry. "I've been through too much! I don't want to lose you again!

"I have to, sweetie. I know it's hard. But I have to. My work on earth is done. I have plenty to do where I am now. Plenty to do." He smiles. "But remember the veil, remember I'm here. Let's make a date… in your dreams, okay?"

I can only nod as words are trapped in my mouth somewhere and wipe my wet face with the back of my hands, hoping that it'll be easier than ever to get ahold of him now. In my head and in my heart, I pray this isn't all a nightmare and I'm not still stuck in that tree.

"I love you, Grandpa." My entire body and soul aches.

"I love you too, sweetie."

He gives me a final hug, and we watch Grandpa Jo as he slips past us and crosses over through the veil. As he continues, he becomes pure, golden light. We see him drift up and out with the other souls. The light is beginning to wane as the veil starts to dissolve and fold back into itself.

People in all sorts of dress are milling about now, looking confused and relieved. But mostly confused. Autumn, Jeff, and I look around at them all, our faces contorted and scrunched, noting that the majority of them are children.

"Refugees of the trees," I whisper.

"How are we ever going to explain this one?" Autumn asks. I tell her I don't know. I'm just as clueless, but a question does come to me.

"Autumn!" I turn to her. "How did you find us here? How did you know?"

"Yeah!" Jeff says. "Nice handiwork, by the way."

Autumn looks a little distressed telling us that she found a strange invitation in her pocket when she was at her aunt's house in Cape Cod. And that night she had a dream about Jeff and I becoming lost and her being the only one that could find us.

"You have those dreams too?" I say, astonished.

"Yeah, always did. Especially about that guy." She says pointing a thumb behind her where Benjamin still lies.

"Well why didn't you ever say anything?"

"I dunno? I guess there's just some things I'd rather keep to myself. Plus, I was too afraid I'd freak you out."

I open my mouth to protest, and Jeff butts in before the temperature becomes too warm.

"Really, Chells... you've been through a lot."

"You're right." I tell him.

"Thanks, Autumn." I grab her hands. "So what about that big ol' slab of wood?"

"Oh that." She casts a sideways glance at it, takes a deep breath and says, "Chelsea. Ever since I got that stupid letter and had that dream, I've been in and out of this forest every night and I mean every night. But tonight was different. It's November you know... and it was a super warm day. And I heard noises... odd noises. I saw the little girls running around with braids in their hair and I followed them. Which was crazy believe me, but I was a woman on a mission... and then I saw Mr. Slate and well... you know." One half of her mouth upturned into a smirk.

"The weird thing is that when you and Jeff disappeared it all stopped."

"What do you mean?" Jeff asked.

She looks at him, then to me. "The fires. The disappearing kids. The weird feeling in this orchard. It all stopped, and people tried to pick up the pieces of the missing ones." She looks away and a tear slides down her cheek. She swallows and addresses us again. "Oh my god you guys it was so hard being here without you! Jeff, your parents went to be with family in Buffalo for like six months because they couldn't cope! And Chells, your father and mother have been a freaking mess. I'm not even kidding. Your dad, I think, blamed himself somehow, and he went and dug out the wood that was sticking out of the ground. He said he should have done it years ago and only did it because it reminded him of you. Because you liked to make etchings of it or something?" She waited for me to answer, but I didn't so she continued. "Do you know what was carved on there?"

"No… what?!" I was hanging on to every word as though if she stopped talking, I would literally fall over.

She walks a few feet and drags the solid, half charred piece of wood toward us. Turning it over she points to the crude letters written on the side. Looking close, I'm able to read it.

Edward Benjamin Slate and Josiah Charles Heiland. October 21st 1895. Brothers.

I start to hyperventilate as the news articles that we found at her dad's office have just come completely alive and the fact that my grandfather's exact name is scrawled out in front of me.

"Wow, that's insane!" Jeff is dumbfounded.

"How is this even possible? My grandfather was born in… Well I don't even know when he was born. But if according to this, he was like… what? 15 in 1895? He'd have been one hundred something at least when he died. And there's no way he was that old! This has got to be a coincidence? Right?"

"Probably," says Autumn. "But it doesn't make it any less spooky!"

I nod, my eyes still on the wood.

"And wait a minute, Auto," Jeff says now snapping out of his daze. "Did you say my parents left for six months? What day is it?"

"It's not a day, Jeffrey. A year. It's 2017. And mind you, it was the worst freaking year of my entire life."

"What?!" Jeff and I look at each other. He grabs his chest like he's having a heart attack and mumbles something inaudible.

I try to change the subject to work through the numbness I'm now feeling. "Jeff, how did you end up here anyway? You threw the letter out and told me not to go."

Using his girlfriend voice with a flick of his wrist he responds, "Oh honey, because I know you too well and besides, I can never miss a party!" His playfulness turns somber as he says, "Only I got to you too late."

I take his hand in a sincere gesture of gratitude.

By now it has grown completely dark, and we hadn't noticed the veil had gone while we were talking. The lines of sunset are just barely squinting through soft clouds in the distance, and the moon is gracing us early with its full glory.

"Chelsea!" Autumn says pointing at me. "Your shadow!" I look and understand her excitement right away. It was normal, completely the way it should be.

"Yes! And I feel normal. Like I'm in a regular old orch...ard..." I turn my gaze to the orchard and realize for the first time that there isn't a single tree. It's just an empty field. Barren. Dusty. It shouldn't be a surprise considering all that's happened. But it takes me aback nonetheless.

"You guys, look!" I point to a young man bending over Benjamin cradling his head like a baby. Benjamin himself looks transformed. No longer the lanky monster... more like a kid in oversized dress up clothes.

"Who is that?" asks Autumn. Jeff shrugs but we are all equally intrigued.

"It could be anyone, really? I mean, look at all the people here. But who could care *that* much about Mr. Slate?" I don't have a poker face, so I know the look of disgust is visible in the moonlight.

Autumn and Jeff hang back as I approach the two men like a cat, both cautious and curious. The young man has a stocky build and dirty blond hair that hangs just above his shoulders. There is a journal with a tattered corner hanging out of his back pocket. He is still holding on to Mr. Slate's head when I say, "Excuse me." I croak it out at first so I clear my throat and try again.

He turns to me and locks his eyes with mine. My knees grow weak, and I feel like I need to sit down. So I do. Right there in the dust. He looks exactly like Grandpa Jo. I could swear it's his twin brother from fifty years ago. He too is looking at me as though there is some sort of recognition.

"I know you somehow," he says, squinting. His voice is rough, but soothing, like river stones. I find that my breath escapes me, but I manage to ask his name.

"Josiah," he says. His eyes sparkle, and I'm floored, frozen again to this spot. "H...h...how do you know him?" I point towards Mr. Slate and catch the profile of his baby face thinking he can't be much older than I am. I'm too exhausted to even mull this one over.

"Edgar and I go back a long way."

I feel that Autumn and Jeff are by my side before I hear them and take each of their hands as they help me back up to my feet. I chance a couple of paces toward Josiah and reach my hand to him. He gives it a firm squeeze, and I notice a raw wound in the crook between his thumb and first finger. Chills run straight through to my bones.

"This is Autumn and Jeff," I tell him. "And I'm Chelsea... I have a feeling that we go way back, too?" I didn't mean for that to come out in a question but right now questions are forming so fast that I don't have room for anything else.

Josiah looks puzzled with a half smirk, examining us like he's trying to remember something, but knowing what I do now, I'm pretty damn sure he would have no clue. Or would he?

A person gasps and stops just short of him. Josiah turns in her direction and puts Mr. Slate's head down in a swift, gentle motion. He stands up immediately and says in a way that makes me feel like he hasn't seen her in a very long time.

"Maddie?!" He's dumbfounded.

She seems older than the three of us but not quite the same age as Josiah. It's hard to tell in the dark exactly.

"Yessir!" she says in a thick, southern type of drawl, then runs and hugs him with such force, she practically lifts him off of the ground. I would be wrong to say that it wasn't shocking considering that she seems like such a petite little thing.

Autumn, Jeff, and I just stand here gawking because frankly we don't know what else to do. I am too caught up in the moment to think. My brain is pretty much done with speculation at this point anyway.

They release each other, and his voice drops to a tone of such sincerity that my heart melts right there in my chest. "I wanted to help you, Maddie. To protect you. To do what I couldn't do for Edgar."

She smiles, then traces the wound on his hand gently with her finger. Her voice quivers. "I'm sorry about this. I didn't mean to hurt you. You're too pretty!" She laughs. He smiles. And I catch Autumn in my periphery, putting an open palm over her heart.

"But how, Maddie? How is this even possible? I didn't know if I was real. Or if you were real." He looks past her to the barren field. "Or if any of this is real."

"Feel this, Josiah." She says as she put his hand up to her heart. "This. Is real."

Jeff whispers from the corner of his mouth, "This is way better than any of your guys' stupid TV shows!"

I give Jeff some serious side eye, and Autumn jabs him with her elbow.

Maddie continues. "It's hard to tell exactly the point when we stopped being us, and the dreams took over. But the train. I tried to keep you from going back to your friend, but you were too stubborn! As soon as she slowed down you just hopped off, like a horse's ass!"

"I didn't jump! You attacked me. And then everything kind of just… melted…" Josiah's voice trails off.

"Think, Josiah." She tilts her head in a stern sort of way which makes me wish I could see her eyes right now.

Josiah holds her gaze for what feels like an eternity, and then he snaps out of it, shaking his head, putting his hands through his hair. "I did go back. After you stabbed me. I went back for Edgar!"

"I do apologize, Josiah. I really thought you were making a mistake. You were babbling, talkin' nonsense. And I meant to break your crazy spell by slamming that sickle down next to you, not through you!"

Josiah doesn't seem to care about it. He appears confounded, probably remembering something about that night. "So they just kept replaying the scene over and over again. So I couldn't remember. To keep me from Edgar, to keep me off of that train…but…" He turns to me as though he just solved the hardest math puzzle ever. "You!"

I jump. I wasn't expecting him to sound so angry and accusing, but I stand up straighter instead of cowering, waiting to hear what he has to say. Much to my delight, he softens. "If I had kept going, you never would have been here, would you? Or you and you." He points to Autumn and Jeff who are shocked they have anything to do with this. "The three of you. It was all meant to be."

"It was." Maddie says as she approaches Josiah, slipping a slender hand into his. For the first time, I see her face. I gasp and my legs turn to jelly. Autumn and Jeff grab me to keep me in place.

"Chelsea, right?" she says, and I nod without blinking.

Her accent loses its drawl. "I caught glimpses of you. Here and there. Between teacups and maple candies. But then I'd come back to my cell here in the trees."

"Dorothy Maddison Heiland!" Autumn interrupts as everything registers for her.

"Well at this point, not yet. But I can only hope he'll find me again." She tilts her head toward Josiah who positively beams down at her.

It appears as though he already has.

THE END

ABOUT THE AUTHOR

Jen Brunett is the General Manager of the live concert venue and tasting room at Iron Smoke Distillery. She served as staff, contributing writer, and associate editor for POST Rochester Magazine and the South Wedge Quarterly here in Western New York and have national and international writing credits from magazines such as The Mother UK (now JUNO) and Reiki News. She's also independently published a non-fiction book in 2014. Jen was a conceptual marketing writer for a company that worked for some biggins' of the entertainment industry.

She's been writing fiction in the form of short stories and poetry my entire life, and RAILROAD OF SOULS is her first attempt at a full novel.

Made in USA - Crawfordsville, IN
76826_9781734946703
09.25.2020 1544